THREADBARE
Volume 1:

Stuff and Nonsense

by Andrew Seiple

Cover by Amelia Parris

Edited by Beth Lyons

WARNING: Contains Profanity and Violence

ISBN: 0692047581
ISBN-13: 978-0692047583

DEDICATION

With thanks to Royal Road Legends.com, for their fun community

CONTENTS

ACKNOWLEDGEMENTS

With thanks to Amelia Parris, who went above and beyond to complete this cover in record time

PROLOGUE

Once upon a time, there was a teddy bear.

An old man, bent with tragedy but still daring to dream, made him into a thing that could think and feel.

And if the teddy bear could have said"Status," he would have seen the following words.

Name: ????

Age: 1 minute

Jobs:

Greater Toy Golem Level 1

Attributes		**Pools**	**Defenses**
Strength: 4	Constitution: 16	Hit Points: 50	Armor: 10
Intelligence: 2	Wisdom: 11	Sanity: 14	Mental Fortitude: 0
Dexterity: 6	Agility: 3	Stamina: 19	Endurance: 20
Charisma: 2	Willpower: 10	Moxie: 12	Cool: 20
Perception: 5	Luck: 5	Fortune: 10	Fate: 1

Greater Toy Golem Skills

Adorable – Level 1

Gift of Sapience – Level NA

Golem Body – Level 1

Magic Resistance –Level 1

But alas, the little teddy bear who was now a golem could not speak or even read or write. Not at the beginning. The old man thought that made him a failure. And so the old man made a mistake that would cost him and his loved ones dearly...

CHAPTER 1: AWAKENING

"Golem Animus!"

Nothing became something, awareness flooded in, and suddenly, everything was.

Button eyes wiggled, as they looked around at a cluttered room. A furry neck moved as a cloth-and-fur head twisted, using its newfound ability to look at things. It didn't enjoy it, not precisely. If you asked it, and somehow gave it the ability to reply, then it could have told you that it didn't know what joy was. It didn't know much of anything.

It didn't know that the hard thing it was sitting on was a wooden shelf. It failed to comprehend that the brown thingies lashed around its limbs that ran down through the holes in the wood were ropes binding it in place. It had absolutely no concept of books, which were the things that filled the shelves across the way. It couldn't tell you that the oddly-shaped thing three slots down from it was a wooden hobby horse, or that the thing two slots down was a stuffed ragdoll, or that the black-and-white shape next to it was a taxidermied skunk.

Heck, it didn't even know it was a toy teddy bear, a very old one as they went.

The other toys looked to it for answers, and it looked back, without the mental capacity to question or the vocal capacity to answer.

"There we go. Four should be a good test batch."

The teddy bear swiveled its head forward again, to regard the speaker.

Any human who wasn't currently wearing diapers and had a few years of experience under their belt could have told you that this was an older man. Worn, silver-haired, and haggard, he moved with a slight limp as he paced back in forth in front of the toy shelf. A tailor would have identified the many-pocketed apron and sturdy, patched clothes that he was wearing as artisan's gear, specifically the garb of a fellow tailor. Scissors of varying shapes, spools of thread, measuring tape, and swatches of leather and fur poked out of the neatly-kept pockets. The man rubbed his neatly-trimmed silver goatee, and considered the now-moving toys with a critical eye.

He pulled a notebook from his pocket, and scribbled in it. The toys craned what necks they had to follow the sounds of the quill.

"Standard reactions for toy golems. Visual tracking, responsive to sound, limited movement... here, none of that." He reached out as the loop started to slip from the teddy bear's arm. It was wiggling, and without hands, the ropes were more of a formality. "Feisty one. Superior animation?" He cleared his throat. **"Command golem! Be Still!"**

The words echoed inside what passed for the teddy bear's mind. It became still. It could not conceive of any alternative, nor could it want to, even if it had the ability to want in the first place. It could no more go against that command than it could breathe fire or turn itself into marmalade jam.

But at the time it had received the command, it happened to be pointing at a window. Something moved beyond... a tree branch, heavy with fruit, beset by birds.

The teddy bear was not the only watcher.

On the windowsill, rapt and staring at the birds with the lust for excitement and an ancestral urge for predation bred into its very soul, was a fat, yellow-eyed, black cat. Its eyes darted back and forth in the reflection of the dusty glass, following the bird movements with a passion and quickness far belying its rotund frame.

"Eye for Detail," the man murmured. The teddy bear tried to look at him, but couldn't. *Be Still* resonated within the core of its very being. It was a golem, and a golem could not go against the words that filled it.

"Yes... Hm. Interesting... two superior qualities, good. Same craftsman? Have to ask Mordecai next time." More scratching. More notes.

Followed by a sigh. "No point in putting this off. Test seven, four subjects, two exceptional... here we go. Yorgum watch over me." The man moved past the teddy bear's vision, tucked away his notebook, and stretched out his hand toward the toys down the shelf. **"Greater Golem Upgrade!"**

The room pulsed with golden light, and there came a sound like mighty gears turning. The dust motes hanging in the sunlight seemed to pause, pulled together in geometric shapes before dissipating again. The teddy bear watched the cat glance back at the movement... then yawn, because the cat had seen it all before.

The flashy part went on for a bit, then died away to nothing. The man nodded, and mopped sweat from his brow, before turning a bit and repeating himself, with the same arm motions. **"Greater Golem Upgrade!"**

Again came the lights, and the flashing, and this time the man's eyes went wide, as his worn face stretched into a smile. "Skill up? Good, good." He moved out of the teddy bear's view and wood scraped on wood, then something creaked. "Getting too old for this." Liquid splashed against metal. The cat whipped its head around and made a sort of 'blart' noise.

"No, Pulsivar. This isn't milk, and Celia would kill me if I fed you seventy-proof rum."

The cat yarped again, until it was certain the man would continue to ignore it.

And after some time, the teddy bear found it could turn its head again. It looked at the man, and the toy didn't have the words to say that he was sitting in a chair, scribbling notes, and muttering to himself. "Skill's up to a nice even eighteen, now. Hopeful there, might finally be able to make it work. If I can get at least one functional subject out of this batch, I can move on to the next stage."

Seeing nothing that made sense, the teddy bear looked back down the shelf, and saw the dead stuffed skunk looking back at it. But the other two toys, the hobby horse and the doll, were frozen, save for random tremors that rocked them every few seconds.

"Well! On with it, then," the man rose to his feet again, and the teddy bear watched him walk over, and stretch out his arm once more. But this time he could see the man's fingers moving on the skunk, tracing glowing symbols on its ratty hide that spread to cover the grisly little toy. **"Greater Golem Upgrade!"**

The teddy bear watched, as the light flashed again, and the dusty sunlight formed symbols to mirror those glowing on the skunk. It watched them sink into the taxidermy as golden light poured forth from its every orifice.

And the skunk fell still.

Then the man's hand was on the teddy bear's face, and words thundered forth, filling its being, filling it, blending in and becoming it—

"Greater Golem Upgrade!"

YOU HAVE ACHIEVED A RANK UP
YOUR SPECIES JOB IS NOW GREATER TOY GOLEM
ALL ATTRIBUTES +2

YOU HAVE GAINED THE INTELLIGENCE ATTRIBUTE
INTELLIGENCE +2
NEW SPECIES JOB UNLOCKED – BEAR
DO YOU WISH TO ACCEPT THE BEAR JOB AT THIS
TIME? Y/N?

—and suddenly the world made a lot more sense.

The teddy bear realized that it could think. But right now all it was thinking of, could be summarized by its very limited, intelligence two mind, was *what the heck are these squiggly things right in front of my face?*

It didn't recognize the words as words. It couldn't read. They were just some sort of looming thing in front of it, that overlaid and blocked a good portion of its vision. And without the ability to answer the prompt, the words simply hung there, incomprehensible.

"There we go." The man mopped his brow again, leaning against the shelf. "Woof. Takes it out of you. More sanity drawn at this level. Greater results? No matter." The man stepped back, and spoke again. **"Eye for Detail!"** The teddy bear watched as the man's eyes flashed gold for a second, then returned to normal. "Yes, all Greater Golems. Mental attributes successfully gained for all of them." He frowned. "Odd that the bear's intelligence is so low. Good wisdom though, oddly good. Form following function? Investigate later." He flipped open his notebook and scrawled again.

Not that the teddy bear noticed, it was busy looking around the room with new eyes. New thoughts filled its head. It now had the ability to question, to wonder what things were, and why they were that way. And it found itself growing rather annoyed at the way the glowy squiggles kept getting in the way of its looking at things.

Snap, went the notebook. The man cracked his knuckles, eyes drooping, even more tired than he had been at the start of this whole event. "No point in putting this off. Sink or swim time." He took a deep breath, and spoke clearly. **"Form Party.** Moment of truth... let this work!" The man rubbed his hands together, and looked to the hobby horse. **"Invite golem!"**

Golden light flared between them. The hobby horse looked back at him. It twitched slightly.

"No. Nononono... not another wasted run. Come on, it has to work. **Invite Golem!"**

The hobby horse just stared at him, with its painted eyes. And the man's face sunk into his hands. "Damn. Just... damn." He looked down the row, lips pressed into a thin line. "Ah well. Three more chances with this batch. If not this one, then sooner or later I'll crack it."

He turned back to the hobby horse. The bear turned, angling its head until it could see what he was doing relatively well, around the gaps in the glowy words.

"Waste not want not," the man said. **"Disenchant!"**

The hobby horse evaporated into dust with a flickering yellow crystal dropping down to land in the pile. Just like that, the toy was gone.

The man swayed, then leaned against the wall, breathing hard. "Enough for one more, I think. Mmf. Might as well get this over as fast as possible. **Invite Golem!**" he barked at the ragdoll, and again the golden light flared...

And the teddy bear realized that if the man kept doing that, he'd eventually get to the teddy bear.

INT +1

To the bear, the words shifted for a second to display a much shorter, smaller bunch of squiggles, then faded away to return to the old familiar ones that had filled its vision for the last few minutes.

But inside its fuzzy skull, ideas started trickling in more freely. It was still relatively stupid, but now it was stupid at about one point five times the thinking speed it had before.

"You too, huh? Pity. And you're double the intelligence, so it's not that," the man mused, as the ragdoll didn't react to his invitation. "Goodbye, my dear. **Disenchant!**" Again, the toy turned to dust and crystal.

Though the teddy bear was new to sentience, and new to this whole concept of, well, things and existence in general, a notion formed in its newly-enlightened mind.

And the first thought to cross its mind that wasn't a question, was a pretty simple one;

I don't want to be dust.

The old man stared forlornly at the remnants of the ragdoll, shaking his head. "Such a waste. **Status.**"

He glanced up, nodded. **"Close screen."** With those words he moved over to a pile of glassware on a nearby shelf. Collecting a pair of empty vials, he headed back and plucked the crystals out of the dust and put them into his apron pockets. The dust went into the vials. Though the vials were pretty big, he only put one pile of dust into each vial. "Stupid godsdamned nonsensical storage requirements," he muttered, the lines on his brow creasing.

The teddy bear understood none of this. Neither the words, or the actions were comprehensible to its young eyes, especially with the job prompt in its way. Intelligence three really didn't give it a lot to work with, there, and those words filled most of its vision in a really distracting manner. But Wisdom eleven was a bit better than the average golem, and the common sense the attribute bestowed was telling it that the break in the man's routine meant the teddy bear wasn't at risk of being dusted just yet. So it waited and watched.

The man tucked the vials away, and looked back to the skunk and the bear. "Sit tight. I'll get to you shortly." He reached out and patted them each on the head. "If it's any consolation your essence will save me time and trouble with batch eight." Then he moved over to the door, opened it, and walked out into the yard.

Now that was interesting! The skunk and the bear leaned forward as far as they could, to try and see the new place that the open door had revealed. But it shut before they could observe too much. Lots of green things, more brown things underneath them, and spiky green things poking out of the ground. Gray round thingies made a path leading to the door, and the man was walking up them to a really big brown bulky thing in the distance.

"Mrp!" The cat announced with frustration as the door shut in its face, seconds before it could get out. Its pudgy legs had cost it a bid for freedom, and it consoled its bruised pride by settling back down on its haunches and grooming itself.

The skunk and the teddy bear looked down at it from their post on the shelf. Then looked at each other.

That grooming thing looked kind of fun. The skunk twisted, trying to copy the cat, but the strings holding it down didn't really give it the slack it needed to raise its paws to its mouth, and the one around its tail prevented it from pushing its neck down to them.

The bear, on the other hand, had been more hastily tied. And with its arms full of squishy stuffing, and no troublesome hands to get in the way, it managed to pop its paw-pads out of the string loops and touch them to its mouth. Which accomplished precisely nothing, because its mouth was a few sewn lines of thread. Rubbing its ears with its paws didn't do anything either.

Well, they did do one thing. The bear didn't exactly have much fine motor control yet, so it was pushing pretty hard. This jiggled it in place... and made the loose strings on the knots holding its legs wiggle under the shelf.

The cat immediately stopped washing, and peered at the motion. Slowly, it crept forward, acting as nonchalantly as it dared.

Then, when the string least suspected, it struck! A mighty leap, right onto the lower shelf—

—which, as it turned out, was just a plank of wood suspended atop three metal prongs nailed into the wall.

The cat's twenty-five pound body hit the shelf at an angle, slid as the cat flailed wildly, and whipped right off the prongs, taking about fifty pounds of books, various tailoring tools, piles of fabric, yarn, and spools of thread with it.

In a supreme act of agility, the sort that it hadn't managed in at least four years, the cat twisted in midair. His claws fully extending, legs flailing, one paw catching the dangling strings securing the teddy bear.

The lower shelf crashed to the ground, sending damn near everything flying in heaps across the workshop. And for a bizarre, timeless moment, Pulsivar the cat hung suspended, eyes wide open, as a sort of existential dread crept over the feline.

Because at intelligence eight, he knew pretty damn well what was gonna happen here.

And it did.

His weight pulled the strings down, causing the vastly underweighted top shelf to flip up on its prongs, then come crashing down to the tiled floor below.

Pulsivar gained a level in feline agility that day, and managed to avoid being crushed under the plank.

With a crash and a crunch, the shelf hit the ground, slamming into the two toy golems, before bouncing, rebounding, and ending up on its side. With a burst of something that wasn't pain, but was definitely odd and unpleasant, the teddy bear watched a red number '4' float past its vision.

The workshop fell silent again, save for the sound of feline slurping and frantic grooming. Pulsivar's excuse was that nobody had seen it, nobody could prove nothing, and it didn't matter anyway because the room was more interesting this way.

The teddy bear, now at a very awkward angle, pushed and shoved at the floor. And for some reason, there was a lot less resistance than last time. With one final heave it managed to clear out from under the shelf, turning back as it got loose to see the knots holding its legs in place entirely undone by Pulsivar's little display of chaos.

LUCK +1

Not that it understood string, but it realized it could move now. And looking around at the mess, something told it that it might want to not be here when the old man found the state of affairs in the workshop.

But if it couldn't be here, what did that leave?

There was a much bigger place through that moving part in the wall, it recalled that. Yes, it should probably go that way. That sounded good.

INT +1

So the little bear wobbled to its feet—

—and promptly fell over.

So it tried again, and fell over again. Finally, after about the eighth or ninth try, it managed to stay upright.

AGL +1

Well, for all of two seconds, anyway. Fifty-two tries later it had gained two more points of agility and the ability to stand upright and move around without going head over keister.

Then the teddy bear turned to the door, and tried to amble that way.

But before it could get there, a racket nearby caught the teddy bear's attention.

The skunk had evidently had a worse time of it. The poor thing was still caught by some of its ties, but its paws and part of its body were twisted out of joint. Though the teddy bear didn't know it, the skunk had a sort of internal skeleton to it, a few sticks of wood and some wires binding them together. The force of the plank falling hadn't been enough to break the sticks, but it had torn free a few wires. The effect was similar to what broken bones would be on a living creature.

And though the impact had at least gotten its upper body paws free, the string looped around its tail was still intact, and that kept it from escaping the plank.

The skunk shifted, trying to look at the teddy bear. It had squiggly letters filling its vision too, asking it if it wanted to accept the Skunk job at this time. But like the bear, it had no idea what they meant, and no way of answering the Y/N prompt one way or another. Finally the skunk managed to get the teddy bear focused in the gaps between its words. Its glass eyes sparkled with mute appeal.

And now came a moment that would have sent the old man into a dance of whooping joy. Lesser golems were unintelligent golems, incapable of sentience, empathy, or even the smallest awareness that anything existed that wasn't them. And even if they had those things, lesser golems didn't have the slightest speck of free will. They couldn't act of their own accord, only react to their master's commands.

But the bear, after a few seconds of hesitation, moved in to help the skunk. It didn't know what it was, had no clue what the skunk could be, but it was just smart enough to realize that the skunk was in a bad situation and wanted out.

It also had been in a bad situation, and it had felt good to get out. Maybe the skunk would feel good too?

The teddy bear reached out, and closed its arms around the skunk's bent paws.

Well, it tried to, anyway. When it pulled back, its arms slipped off of the skunk's slick fur. The bear went back on his tail with a bump.

Undeterred, it got back up and tried again. And again. And again. But its stuffing was just too soft, and every time it tried to squeeze harder, the stuffing compressed. It couldn't get a real grip.

Not until the ninth try.

DEX +1

Your Golem Body Skill is now level 2!

Abruptly, the teddy bear found itself changing. The stuffing in its arms and paws thickened where it was trying to grab the skunk's paw. Even though it didn't have fingers, the pads on the end of its hands hardened and got more flexible.

And for the first time since it started this charitable endeavor, the teddy bear had a grip. So it did what it had been planning to do at the start of this mess, and pulled.

Strength four wasn't much in the grand scheme of things. But the skunk was light, and the teddy bear was a bit more solid than he looked, thanks to his Golem Body skill. So he was able to tug the skunk forward, up against the strings securing it to the fallen plank.

Which worked right until the tight loop of the string constricted around the skunk's body right at where the stick supporting its tail joined the stick supporting its back.

CRUNCH! The teddy bear and the skunk froze in shock, as a bright red number '6' floated up into the air and dissolved.

The teddy bear was perplexed.

The skunk was panicking. It had felt that, and knew on an instinctive level that particular sensation was bad.

So when the teddy bear started pulling again, and the string ground against the broken join, the skunk lashed out blindly, assuming that something was attacking it. Blinded by its class screen and the persistent prompt, it flailed with its limp claws and open jaws against the teddy bear. But with what was essentially its spine coming apart, and its own abysmal strength score, it didn't manage to inflict any real damage. From nearby, the cat growled low in its throat as it watched the "fight," tail lashing as red zeroes and ones floated into the air willy-nilly. Though the skunk's claws and teeth were sharp enough to tear at the teddy bear whenever it did manage a good hit, the teddy bear was endowed with an armor rating due to its golem nature that vastly reduced the damage.

The teddy bear, blinded by his own screen, had no idea the golem it was trying to free was resisting. All it knew was that something was attacking it. It came to the conclusion that whatever had trapped the skunk was trying to stop it getting free. The teddy bear found that idea unacceptable! The skunk was clearly trapped and it needed to be free! So to save it, the bear endured the unpleasant ripping, and pulled with all its might!

CRIK-SNAP!

The skunk went limp, as its animus fled. Golems could not die, but they could certainly break, and this one's animus had departed its shell.

And for his part, the teddy bear's joy at freeing the skunk was tempered by the realization that it had freed only half a skunk. It put down the skunk's upper half, and stared at it. Maybe it was just resting?

Then new words crawled across its view, briefly interrupting the optional job prompt;

STR +1

You are now a Level 2 Toy Golem!

All attributes +2

Suddenly, its head swam. Everything made more sense. Its thoughts swirled around it now, almost too much to manage. Some threshold had been passed, some bar invisible neatly limboed under, and concepts that were completely out of its reach now were a lot simpler now.

It looked down at the tail and lower half of the skunk, with sawdust spilling everywhere and wires and sticks poking out, where the strings had constricted and held it in place. And then it looked down at the upper half in its arms, sawdust leaking down to spill over the teddy bear's legs.

The little toy knew sorrow. It had done a bad thing, even if it couldn't figure out what exactly it had done. Slowly, carefully, the teddy bear put the upper half of the skunk next to its lower half, and tried to nudge them back together.

You are not a tanner. Seek out a trainer to obtain this job.

The letters flashed by—

—and the teddy bear still couldn't read them. Six intelligence was better than the two it had started with, but it was still nowhere near what it needed to understand human speech, let alone read written words.

But since it didn't feel any better, and the skunk didn't start moving again, the little bear knew it had failed. Its ears drooped. Then they perked up again, as a rumbling growl echoed through the room, and ended in a hiss.

You are affected by GROWL! You take moxie damage!

The teddy bear watched as a green '6' floated up into the air, then turned, looking around until the gaps around the letters on that job prompt obstructing its vision revealed the coal-black, fuzzy form of Pulsivar. The cat was puffed up to twice his normal size, slit-pupiled eyes fixed upon the teddy bear's sawdust-covered form.

Pulsivar wasn't entirely sure of the particulars of this situation or whose fault it was, (definitely not his though,) but he was pretty godsdamned sure of two things;

One was that he was stuck in this workshop until his hoomin came back, so he couldn't escape.

Two was that he'd just seen that teddy bear straight up murder a fucker.

And to the cat, being in close proximity to such a threat was a call to action. His butt wiggled, his mouth stretched to show all of his needle-like teeth, and he hissed like a demon straight out of hell as he prepared to leap upon the biggest threat in the room...

The teddy bear turned golem's level two brain was still woefully underprepared for, well, everything. But at intelligence six, it had finally evolved to the point where it could tell when it was in danger.

And right now, every instinct was screaming at it to run away.

The bear turned tail and fled, just as Pulsivar pounced! But the bear was a few seconds too late, and the heavy cat's paws collided with the golem, knocking it sprawling across the floor, and into a set of bookshelves across the way. The triple-stacked shelves wobbled, and Pulsivar skittered across the tile, and tried to follow up his pounce with a proper mauling.

Books rained down from above, falling from their piles, and the bear watched with its button eyes as the largest of them wobbled...

...slipped over the edge...

...and fell right toward him.

AGL +1

They missed him by a hair, as he twisted to the side.

Pulsivar scrambled desperately to avoid the rain of books, whirled as his claws slipped on the slick floor, and tumbled in a heap into the bear, knocking him over and against the wall. A forlorn red '1' floated up from the teddy bear as he was smushed between the cat's butt and the hard wood. Pulsivar escaped any real damage, due to the fluffy bear's padding.

The cat's growl rang in the bear's ears again, nibbling at his moxie. A green '4' floated up, and suddenly his thoughts were a lot more scattered. For the second time in his existence, he knew fear.

So he grabbed for the nearest thing, which turned out to be Pulsivar's tail.

And caught it.

DEX +1

The cat yowled in rage, and churned its back legs, trying to push away from the wall, trying to get its tail free from whatever had it. But the frightened teddy bear clung on like grim death, as the cat went lurching and skidding across the floor, slamming itself and the plush toy into the legs of the table, knocking over chairs, sending glass bottles and dirty dishes crashing to the ground in a rain of cacophonous destruction!

STR +1

But the golem hung on.

Your actions have unlocked the generic skill: Ride!
Your Ride Skill is now level 1!

Finally Pulsivar, using most of his remaining stamina, did a damned half-somersault and managed to get himself on his back, and the golem onto his belly. Laying in with his claws in a scratching, spitting fury, the big black cat ripped and tore with wanton abandon. Red numbers flew!

Twenty-one hit points later, the teddy bear's grip finally slackened, as he was hurled away to skid across the floor, through the glass and pottery shards, before slamming into the already-battered table leg—

—and breaking it loose from the table entirely.

The leg hit a wall, rebounded, and shattered an urn next to the window. Ashes puffed out.

The table, down to two legs, promptly fell edge-first toward the prone teddy bear, who rolled as best he could—

—but not far enough. A big fat number ten drifted up into the air, as the table slammed into his midsection, trapping him under it. It would have crushed all the stuffing out of him, if his body hadn't been toughened by the ritual that had made him what he was.

Your Golem Body Skill is now level 3!

The teddy bear lay there for a second, taking stock.

Pulsivar, thoroughly spooked by all the loud noises and breaking objects, relocated to a corner to lick his wounds. He stared at the teddy bear for a long moment, then slurped his paw and smoothed his fur back into place, activating his "Grooming" skill and healing the few scratches he'd sustained during his horrifying ordeal.

Then a scritching caught his ear.

The teddy bear was still moving.

Long rents in its fur, stitches cut, half of its stuffing on the outside, one ear gone, the bear was slowly rocking, trying to wobble the table edge free.

Pulsivar stared. He tried to groom himself again, but his paw was shaking, ever so slightly, and he botched the skill.

Finally the bear gave a mighty heave and a twist, and the round table rolled free.

STR +1

And with the magic ebbing from him, with damage crippling him and every atom of him aching, the bear. Stood. Up.

CON +1

Pulsivar growled again, but he was rapidly running out of moxie.

And the bear didn't seem phased by it. The bear was beyond fear.

WILL +1

The words obscuring its sight were impossible to manage now, but the teddy bear was pretty damned sure that big growling thing in the corner was his enemy.

He was also sure that he was thoroughly dead, if his enemy came for him one more time.

The teddy bear looked around for something to help him out, and saw a possibility.

PER +1

It half-slumped, half-marched its way over to the fallen table leg.

Pulsivar, spooked now, but knowing that it was either him or the bear, puffed himself up and stalked closer, step by step, waiting for the moment of weakness, psyching himself up for one last pounce.

The teddy bear grabbed the table leg, wrapped its arms around it, and lifted. Stitches popping, one button eye half-off, legs flailing to keep upright on the tile, the bear managed to get the makeshift club upright

STR +1

And then he brought it down toward the growling mass of cat.

At least, that was the plan.

What actually happened, when the teddy bear tried to swing the table leg, was that his plush feet slid on the smooth tile floor, he fell backward, and the table leg shattered the window.

And that was enough for Pulsivar, thank you very much! His nerves were shot, his foe was supposed to be dead, and it had been a thoroughly crappy day. Nope, nope, no thank you, and now there was a way out, wasn't there?

Two mighty bounds took Pulsivar up to the shelves near the window, and a third took the scaredy-cat out the window.

"Pulsivar! Bad kitty!" A strange voice shouted from outside. Anything more intelligent than the teddy bear could have told you that it was a female voice, a young one.

The teddy bear, on its last hit point, sat up.

Outside, the cat yowled in despair. "Oh good grief! What on earth possessed you... cat..." the old man's words tumbled to a stop as he opened the door, and beheld the destruction of his workshop. He entered slowly, eyes passing right over the bear... until they fell on the broken urn, and the ashes dusted around it. "Amelia," the old man whispered, gathering up the fragments of the urn with shaking hands. "Oh. Oh no."

"Daddy? Is everything okay?" The strange voice asked from the doorway.

"Ah." The man took a breath, then tucked the fragments into an apron pocket. "Yes. Everything's fine, dear." But he kept his face turned away from her, and mopped the tears from his eyes so she wouldn't see.

"Oh you bad kitty. Look what you did!"

A red-headed girl, hair frizzy and tied back in a fiery poof, stepped into the room. She held the limp form of Pulsivar up to survey it, arms straining to heft the twenty-five pound cat by the scruff of his flabby neck. The cat stared mournfully at the mess that someone had made. Certainly not him. Couldn't have been.

The teddy bear clambered to his feet.

And the girl squealed in joy. Immediately, she dropped Pulsivar who fled for dear life, ran over, and scooped the battered golem up in her hands. "Oh! Oh Daddy, thank you!"

Your Adorable Skill is now level 2!

"I... what?"

"For the toy golem! Oh you finally made me one and Pulsivar ripped it up! What a bad kitty! I can fix the golem, it's okay right Dad?"

Her father cleared his throat, and scrubbed his face harder. "Er, give me a second..."

Excited, the girl started shouting one of her few spells.

"Mend!"
You heal 15 points!
"Mend!"
You heal 10 points!
"Mend!"
You heal 13 points!
"Mend!"
You are fully healed!

The teddy bear still couldn't read worth a damn, but something had picked him up, and all of a sudden he felt much better. He turned his head around until he could make out a freckled, grinning face sitting under a massive pile of red hair.

"I can have him now, right? I mean you were probably saving him for a surprise or whatever, but I'm just glad we got here in time before Pulsivar wrecked him completely."

"What?" The old man finally found his composure and turned, goggling at the sight of the teddy bear golem in his daughter's arms. "Ah... technically he's..."

"Finally, a golem of my own!" She held him out at arm's length and smiled.

The old man sighed. "Are you sure you want that one? He's... threadbare."

"Threadbear? That's an awesome name!"

"No, no, T-h-r-e-a-d-b-a-r-e"

"Okay, that's a dumb name. You didn't name him did you? Because whoever misspelled his name like that was pretty stupid."

"That's not exactly what I—"

"Well, okay. I can work with it. So your name's Threadbare, huh? Sweet!" Celia hugged the little bear close.

And the bear, healed, feeling much better, safe from the horrible black growlmonster, hugged her back. It felt... right.

CHA +1

"All right. Well, take him back to the house then, dear, just keep an eye on him. Let me know if he starts acting funny." The old man shrugged. Every golem he'd tried a greater animation on had been useless. The ritual was flawed somehow, or there was some important thing he was missing, and he had no damned idea what it could be. But none of the golems had been dangerous, just clumsy and stupid. They hadn't even been able to join his party, so he couldn't apply his creator-specific buffs to them, to get them to the point where they were useful. He hadn't ever run into this problem with lesser golems, so he had no frame of reference as to why it would be an issue with greaters, who should be superior by default.

So what harm could it possibly cause if his daughter played with the bear for a while? Less than that obstinate cat, he thought, looking around at the wreckage of his workshop.

Then he thought of the shattered urn, and a lump rose in his throat. "Go on and play dear," he choked. "I'll clean up here."

Celia ran out the door, hugging Threadbare to her shoulder.

But from the shadow of the large pine tree across the yard, Pulsivar the cat watched with yellow eyes gleaming.

Some things could be tolerated. Some could not.

Pulsivar would have his vengeance upon that infernal toy.

CHAPTER 2: PARTIES AND PERILS

Deep in the woods, on top of a lonely hill, was a two-story house. It was pretty good-sized, something a wealthy merchant might live inside. Inside the house was a room that looked like it had exploded a few times. Clothes and toys and books lay about and around in messy heaps, but none had the slightest trace of dust on them. A window full of nose marks and breath streaks let in the noonday light, while a low, poofy pink bed sat against the opposite wall with its sheets and blankets scrambled and twisted. The wall across from the door held a fireplace, currently unlit and sealed with a metal grille attached to a lever.

None of these things made much sense at all to the bear, since it had only managed to attain an animalistic level of intelligence, but it peered at them with intense curiosity nonetheless. Well, as much as it could with those annoying squiggles in the way.

If he'd been capable of reading, they would have let him know that he had a choice to make.

NEW SPECIES JOB UNLOCKED – BEAR

DO YOU WISH TO ACCEPT THE BEAR JOB AT THIS TIME? Y/N?

But he couldn't read, so they stayed there, obstructing about half of his vision. He didn't have a very good perception to begin with, and this didn't help.

"So, this is my room!" His new benefactor told him, using words he didn't comprehend. But he turned around in her arms and looked at her anyway. A small red-headed girl in a green dress, with woolen stockings over her feet. Her hair was tied back into a big poof, and her manically-grinning face was splattered with freckles.

The teddy bear was pretty certain that he owed her his life. She'd saved him from the cat, after all! At least something like that had happened anyway, the whole thing was very confusing to his thirty-minute-old mind.

The girl, Celia, waded through the room without a care for the mess. She absent-mindedly scooted piles of books away with her feet as she passed through the debris, across to a smaller door in one corner. "Okay, okay okay okay. So what do you want to play first?"

The bear stared up at her. It patted her mouth with one hand. Maybe that was what she wanted? Worth a shot, he guessed.

"Chess? Checkers? Cards?" She rummaged through games, and he stared at them blankly. "Hm. Well, let's go simpler, then. It's for babies, but... I guess you're *like* a baby. I'm eleven so I'm supposed to be too old for them..." She eyed him, then smirked. "Ah, you won't tell. Okay, tea party it is! You can meet everyone else, too! Wait here a minute." She tossed him over her shoulder.

Everything spun, and then WHUMP, the teddy bear landed on the bed. He sat up, shaking his head—

—and found himself in a pile of stuffed animals. Frozen, stiff, they stared at him with mute eyes.

The teddy bear trembled as he poked at them with his paw pads.

They didn't move.

They looked just like the skunk had after he'd killed it, with the same unnatural stillness.

And the teddy bear's young mind jumped to exactly the wrong conclusion.

I am among the dead. She means to kill me!

"Here we go!" Celia opened up the closet door, ignoring the tumbling mass of clothes and toys that surged out, and rummaged through them until she pulled out a small wooden table, and a set of well-gnawed wooden cups and saucers. "Let's see... yeah, there should work." She booted a broken wagon out of the way, shoved a pile of blocks to the side, and put the table on the floor, stacking the cups and saucers on top of it. From the piles she pulled out four little chairs, and spaced them evenly around. "Okay. Come on down and... huh?"

The bear wasn't on the bed any more.

The bear in fact had fled out the open door and was waddling for dear life. He didn't want to lose whatever life he had, and become one of the girl's pile of dead things!

He made it as far as a railing-lined balcony, with a double-stair descending to the front room below, and froze in indecision. He'd seen the stairs on the way up, and she'd done something to climb them, but he had no idea what that something entailed. He hadn't had a clear field of vision, or a good angle to see what she was doing. Something with her feet, maybe?

Well, how hard could it be?

He chose the left stairs, approached them, and decided to try to keep on walking.

Nine good thumps later, when the world stopped spinning, he lifted his head and looked around at the front room. A large fireplace filled one wall, with pots full of herbs drying on the mantle. Overstuffed but worn leather chairs provided seats around it, and a table off to one side was set with candlesticks and cloth doilies. Solid oaken chairs with feet on the bottom lined it, two per side. One wall was lined with tapestries and crocheted hangers, showing cats, flowers, and other simple objects. A closed door led out to the yard, a few high glass windows let in light, and two doors went deeper into the house.

And then there was the statue.

Made of blackened iron patched with lighter materials, it stood looming on its pedestal in the corner. Large, rounded pauldrons covered its forearms, leaving only blocky, jointed metal fingers poking out. It had a sort of breastplate for a chest, with gears poking through cut gaps, starting with a big one in the center of the sternum and growing smaller and smaller as they moved in diagonal lines toward the statue's joints. Though the torso was big, the head was proportionately tiny... a helm with two gems for eyes barely visible under its visor. And its waist was narrow, with two sturdy, wide-footed legs supporting the ten-foot-tall armored statue.

It moved, as Threadbare watched, turned its visor to face him with a grinding of metal on metal.

"Intruder!" The armor golem boomed.

Unfortunately, for all its size, it was a lesser golem. Which meant that it had no mind, only the orders it had been given.

And one of those was to destroy all intruders who weren't in the company of someone on the very short list of family members.

Threadbare knew precisely none of these things. He stood up, staring at the creature in awe.

One leg of the massive golem flexed as it shifted its weight, and cables hummed taut as it stepped down from the pedestal. The other leg followed, and out of its niche, the golem spread its arms wide, brassy voice ringing from under its helm.

"Flee or face my wrath intruder!"

Not its words, just the words its creator had given it. It spoke words it didn't understand to a creature who couldn't comprehend the warning.

However, Threadbare sure as hell knew danger when he saw it. He turned and fled.

WIS +1

He waddled away at top speed as the hostile golem chased him around the room, arms lashing out with clumsy swipes. And Threadbare noticed one important difference, between his current predicament and the last one. Unlike the cat, the armor golem was actively avoiding wrecking the place.

PER +1

That was about all that was saving him, though. Threadbare was stuck on one side of the table, darting right every time the golem tried to come around the left, and darting left every time the golem switched and tried to come around the right. If the golem had come through the table, the teddy bear would have been toast. But the lesser golem had no flexibility to its mind, and it had to follow all its orders. Including the one its master had given it to prevent it destroying the house.

"Emmet!" Celia yelled, from the top of the stair. The golem paused for a moment, then resumed trying to get to the bear.

"Destroy the intruder! Protect the family!" The armor golem, Emmet, boomed back.

"Stop! Recognize Threadbare as family!"

"Destroy the intruder! Protect the family!"

"Guh… I'm not his creator… wait, the emergency scrolls!" Celia ran downstairs, giving them a wide berth, and darted into another room. Threadbare and Emmett continued their deadly dance while she was out.

AGL +1

Both of them had enormous amounts of endurance, proportional to the weight they were hauling around, so they weren't burning any stamina for their actions, at least. Such was the benefit of being a golem! They could have continued this until the house aged and fell to pieces around them, without stopping.

But Celia returned, with a pile of papers in her hands, each glowing with golden sigils. "Okay, okay…" she cleared her throat. **"Command Golem! Recognize Threadbare as family!"**

The runes on the topmost scroll flashed! And faded to black, crumbling to the floor like dust.

Nothing seemed to happen. Celia scowled. "Failed? Bah." She threw the now-blank scroll over her shoulder. **"Command Golem! Recognize Threadbare as family!"**

The scroll flared, and golden letters materialized around Emmett, cycling in spiraling patterns… that shattered.

"You resisted it? Oh come on!" Celia howled, stamping her foot. She pulled out another scroll, glared at him, and bellowed. **"Command Golem! Recognize Threadbare as family!"**

The scroll blazed, the letters circled...

...and this time, Emmet stopped.

Without sparing the little teddy bear another look, the armor golem stomped back to its niche, climbed up on the pedestal, and resumed its silent vigil.

Threadbare, unable to believe that his ordeal might be over, peered around the chair legs, clinging to them and shaking like a leaf. This was all very stressful.

"Oh you poor thing! Come here..." Celia scooped him up, and he went limp. Maybe she meant to kill him, maybe she didn't, but Threadbare knew he couldn't fight her. She'd lifted up the monstrous form of Pulsivar like the cat was nothing, and the giant metal nightmare in the corner was totally in her thrall. What chance did one teddy bear have against something that could do things like that?

"Okay. Let's try this again. No running away next time!" Celia shifted the scroll pile, wedging it under one arm as she carried the toy golem back upstairs. "I don't think Daddy will mind if I borrow these. Otherwise you might cause trouble again! What were you thinking, anyway?"

The teddy bear hugged her for all he was worth.

Your Adorable Skill is now Level 3!

"Aw, I can't stay mad at you. You learned your lesson, right? Come on, let's have a tea party."

This time she shut the door behind her as she entered her room. Just in case.

Threadbare went limp as she put him in one of the little chairs around the table. He quivered with terror as three lifeless forms; a dolly, a giraffe, and a dragon, were placed in the other chairs.

"And now for the crowning touch!" Celia giggled, and Threadbare jumped slightly as he felt something settle onto his head.

You have equipped a toy top hat!

Weird sensations flooded his mind, and he shook his head. Suddenly his body was moving more in synch with his thoughts and feelings. He looked up at the girl and raised his hands, trying to indicate confusion. It was a motion that would have been unthinkable for him, before he'd donned the top hat.

CHA +1

"Oh! Don't be confused, this is how it goes. Just wear it. It's a tea party. Everyone has to have fancy hats." Celia put a princess crown on her own head, then equipped the giraffe with another top hat, and the dolly and dragon with a wedding veil and a cardsharp's visor, respectively. "Okay, now, okay. Hold still just for a moment, all right?"

Then she faced the dolly, poked it with a finger, and said **"Animus!'**

Golden light flared, and the dolly sat up in the chair.

And Threadbare slumped in relief. They weren't dead. They were just resting after all. He mopped his brow with one arm, in exaggerated relief. Then he wondered why he'd done that.

The girl chanted her spell twice more, and the dragon and the giraffe twitched and became something more than toys.

"Yeah! Okay, so here's the tea…" The girl put down the empty cups and saucers, and spread them out to each participant. "Now we need the party. **Form Party! Invite Beanarella! Invite Loopy! Invite Dracosnack! Invite Threadbare!"**

And a new set of squiggles popped up in front of Threadbare.

YOU HAVE BEEN INVITED TO CELIA'S PARTY
DO YOU WISH TO ACCEPT? Y/N?

"Come on Threadbare, join the party!"

Its vision became more obstructed, as the words overlapped, Threadbare shook its head and waved its arms wildly, trying to shoo the stupid squiggles away. One of the cups went flying, and Celia sighed. "Just say yes! It asked you to join the party, say yes!"

But the teddy bear couldn't understand her. Threadbare flailed harder, bobbing its head so hard that the top hat threatened to slip off.

"Oh! Wait, duh. You can't talk. Well, there's a spell for this. Hold on." In fact, that wasn't quite true. Vocalization wasn't required to accept a party invite. But Celia didn't know that.

She plucked the bundle of scrolls off the bed, and pulled the next one off the pile. **"Command Golem! Say yes!"**

Yellow runes flared on the scroll, yellow letters surrounded it… then what was left of his sight was filled by big white letters, that faded.

You have resisted the command golem spell!
Your Resist Magic Skill is now level 2!

"Seriously?" Celia shrieked. "I don't suck that bad. I'm a level five animator, for foop's sake. Okay, okay, fine. I have more scrolls, bear! And I'm not afraid to use'em!" She pulled out one more with a flourish, bent at the waist, flexing down until she was looking Threadbare right in the eyes, and snapped the next scroll open. **"Command Golem. Say Yes!"**

The light flared…

And yes became the full extent of Threadbare's thoughts. Yes filled it from head to tail, shining through its eyes like golden enlightenment. Yes! Yes to everything!

You have joined Celia's party!
Words faded, and part of its sight returned.
You have gained the Bear job!
Then all of it sight returned, as the first set of squiggles finally vanished. To be replaced with new words, which faded after a second.
You are now a level 1 Bear!
Strength +5
Constitution +5
Wisdom +5
Armor +3
Endurance +3
Mental Fortitude +3
Unlocked Animalistic interface
You have Unlocked the Claw Swipes Skill!
Your gain Claw Swipes level 1
You have unlocked the Forage Skill!
You gain Forage at level 1
You have unlocked the Scents and Sensibility Skill!
You gain Scents and Sensibility at level 1
You have unlocked the Toughness Skill!
You gain Toughness at level 1

Its fundamental nature changed, Threadbare felt the fluff under its hide reshape, get bulkier somehow. A new world of sensations flooded into the little golem as it gained a sense that it never had before, and suddenly the room was full of odors, clashing and competing and overwhelming as they seeped into its now-functional nose.

But Threadbare couldn't say yes, because he didn't have a working mouth, and so the command golem spell faded. Celia didn't notice though, just assumed the bear had whispered it too quietly for her to hear. Anyway its name was now in her party menu, so that was all well and good.

"There we go! Welcome to the party!" Celia said, pouring imaginary tea. "Would you like something with your tea, Mr. Threadbare? Cream or sugar perhaps?" She offered him a small tray full of empty condiment jars.

And though the toy golem couldn't say why, all of a sudden that honey jar she was offering looked really, really good. Its eyes slid down from the window, to stare obsessively at the little wooden jar with a bee on its side.

Which was why neither of them saw the twisted, evil little face peering in from the other side of the window.

"Oh, she'll want to know about this," the little creature whispered to itself.

And with a sound of leathery wings, it was gone.

Not that either of the pair noticed. Celia taught the little bear the proper method of being a guest at a tea party, even though most of her words went over Threadbare's head.

And the proper way to be a guest at a little girl's tea party, is to listen to her when she talks about her fears.

"I think Daddy was sad back there. In the workshop, I mean."

Threadbare studied Celia's face, bringing the teacup up to his muzzle every now and then. He didn't know exactly why he was doing it, but the toys Celia had woken up were doing it, and she seemed happier with that.

Of course the rest of them were doing it in unison, but she didn't mind if he was a little out of synch.

Celia lay back, her princess crown slipped half off her head, cushioning her back against a spray of pillows borrowed from the bed. "I mean, not about the workshop, not really. There's nothing in there a few mend spells won't fix, right? Okay, a lot of mend spells, but you know what I mean, right?"

Threadbear considered his options. She was looking at him again, turning her eyes toward him with that little wrinkle around her forehead. That probably meant he should nod. So he nodded.

CHA +1

"Yeah! So I don't know why he's sad. He doesn't— he doesn't tell me. A lot of things. And normally when I get a present from him it always makes him happy to see me enjoy it. It's why I act really excited even when it's a lousy present. But he wasn't happy this time. Uh, not that I mean you're a lousy present. Honestly you're pretty great."

Threadbare nodded. Celia snorted to see it. "Geeze, I give you one top hat and you think you're all that, huh?"

Threadbare kept on nodding. It seemed to be working.

"We'll see. I'll put you through some tests later, buster!" Her grin turned manic.

Her tone and her visual cues were something he hadn't run across before so he stopped nodding. Across the table the toys raised their teacups and took a solemn sip. He followed suit.

Celia sat up, and crossed her legs, resting her head on her hands and resting her elbows on her knees. "I really am glad you're here. I mean, I can make toy friends, but they only last for a little while. Not even a full hour yet, not until I'm level six, that's what daddy says. And then they de-animate. And I have to put them in my party to get them to do stuff without telling them to do each and every little thing. You? You're

24

smart. You're the smartest teddy bear ever!" She swept him up and hugged him, before he could react.

Threadbare froze. Was hugging a thing in this situation? He wasn't sure how the top hat and tea cup factored into things. He reached up and bumped the teacup against her lips.

"Hahaha! That's so cute!"

Your Adorable Skill is now Level 4!

The little girl put him back down in his chair. "Why no, mister bear, I shan't have any more tea. But thankyew, thankyew, my dear chap."

Threadbare reached over for the empty honey jar again, and upended it over his teacup. It had made her laugh the last time he did it, and felt right somehow, so maybe doing it again would help him understand her reactions a little better.

But instead of laughing more, she sighed, and her eyes got wetter. "It's lonely out here. I'm really lonely. I'm glad you're here, okay?"

There was that look again. Threadbare nodded.

CHA +1

Celia hugged her knees. "I mean, it's just Daddy and me out here, and Emmet I guess but he has to stand still most of the time so he doesn't break stuff, and there's Mister Mordecai but he only stops by to visit once a week, and Daddy's been sad and angry lately and I don't know why and he doesn't want to tell me and he doesn't tell me a lot of things and I don't have anyone to.. talk... to..." Tears poured down as the little girl spoke, and she drew a heaving sob, before she shoved her face down into the nest of her arms, and wailed.

Oh, oh this was bad. The little golem had never seen tears before, never heard noises like this before. It ran through its options, checked its newfound hat-enhanced social instincts, and decided to go with what it knew best.

In a flash Threadbare was out of the chair, waddling over to her, and locking his arms around her in the tightest hug it could manage. And Celia seized him up, held him to her face, and cried freely into his fluffy belly.

CHA +1

The tears smelled... strange.

PER +1

Your Scents and Sensibility Skill is now Level 2!

It was like her and yet not like her regular smell at the same time. Perhaps different people had different smells when they felt bad? He didn't know the answer to that question, and it made him curious to find out.

INT +1

Finally the little girl cried herself out. "Thank you," she said, holding him at arm's length. "I have a friend now." She sighed, as she saw the state of his fur. Mending had put him together, but he'd gotten pretty dirty during his scuffle in the workshop, and her tears and snot hadn't helped matters. "Okay. Tea party's over. Time to clean up."

The animated toys quickly picked up the table and teacups, and put them back in the closet. Their hats were handed in with solemnity, and Celia plucked the top hat from Threadbare's head. "It was fun though, you did great Threadbare! **Disband Party!**"

Your party has been disbanded!

Threadbare reeled, as his charisma suddenly lost its boost. He patted his head, where the hat had been, but nothing happened.

"No, tea party hats are for tea parties," Celia explained. "Everybody knows that. Now it's laundry time, and you, Mister Bare, are getting a bath!" She scooped him up, paused, and scooped up the pile of scrolls on the bed as well. "Better put these back before Daddy notices. Uh, not that he'd mind. Probably. Maybe."

They trekked downstairs, and this time, Threadbare shifted watched her feet carefully as she traipsed downward. He was amazed to find out that hey, you could bend your legs when you walked! That was a pretty novel idea!

INT +1

That would make things so much easier. He looked forward to trying it out.

Celia strolled through the leftmost door at the bottom of the stairs, into a crowded room full of shelves, books, and papers. It was about as messy as her room upstairs, but there seemed to be some order to it. She opened up a dark wooden rolltop desk, hauled out a book, and opened it to show the pages inside had a big hole cut into them. Threadbare found himself deposited on the floor while she folded up the scrolls, and tucked them back into place in the fake book.

Threadbare watched for a bit, then tried practicing that bendy-leg walking thing.

Five tumbles and two knocked over piles of books later, he thought he might have figured it out.

AGL +1

"C'mon silly old bear," Celia grabbed his arm, and ran out into the front room, skidding on the floor, then taking a sharp u-turn through the next doorway. "Let's get you clean!"

The next room turned out to be the kitchen, not that the bear understood the notion, or knew what any of the objects scattered around might be. Bowls, pans, and strands of garlic wound around hooks set in the walls just under high cupboards, and a hand pump sat in a corner, with a large basin underneath. A pair of windows let in cheery light, and two closed doors indicated more rooms further in.

The garlic really caught Threadbare's attention. The smell was overwhelming, and he covered his nose. A pressure started to build, behind his muzzle.

"Kff!" Air whooshed through his nose, and Celia dropped him, surprised.

"What's wrong?"

"Kff! Kff!"

That went on for a bit, with Celia getting more and more worried. "You're sneezing, why are you sneezing? Are you sick? Oh no!"

This wasn't doing him any good, and the little bear was thoroughly annoyed at it. He wanted it to STOP.

Animalistic Interface Activated!

Instinctual activation and deactivation of BEAR job skills is now enabled.

He didn't know what the words meant, but the smell was gone, and all the other smells were gone, too. But most importantly, the sneezing was over with, and both he and Celia were very relieved at that.

Celia sighed. "You had me worried there for a moment, Threadbare. Here, sit here." She dropped him in the brass basin under the pump, and started hauling on the handle. There was a strange gurgling noise, and Threadbare stared up into the faucet, trying to get a look at whatever was making that noise.

Then, all of a sudden, stuff like tears came flying out, hitting him smack dab in the face, and knocking him over. He flailed, found the water rising around him, and panicked. Scrambling for the edges of the tub, he tried to haul himself out.

You have unlocked the generic skill: Climb!

Your Climb skill is now level 1!

He almost made it too, before Celia grabbed his soggy fur, and tossed him back in. "No no Mister Bear! You need a bath! Back into the water with you!"

After a few more failed attempts, and Celia's repeated insistence, the tiny golem settled down and accepted his fate. He felt bloated, as it seeped through his seams, and made his stuffing swell up inside him. His fur was soggy, and he was thoroughly miserable.

"Hm... water alone won't do it. Wait here." Celia went to one of the doors and opened it, revealing a dark stairway down. She reached up and tapped a crystal hanging from a small chain, and it lit up. "Back in a bit. Don't go anywhere."

She was back in a few minutes with a jar of powder. "Wow the rats are getting bad. Droppings all over the place down there."

Threadbare simply stared at her with accusing button eyes. He was soaked, bloated, and thoroughly unhappy with the situation.

His tormentor giggled, unrepentant. "No, it's fine, watch this." She uncapped the jar and dumped a little powder in. It tingled a bit, and fizzed when it hit the water. Curious, the little bear poked at the bubbles that came out, and watched them pop.

Celia took a brush to him, scrubbing all the dirt and stains away. Then she wrung him out, making him squirm as she twisted his body and squished his stuffing every which way. It wasn't exactly bad, just uncomfy. But he did feel better at the end of it all.

Brushing out his fur was best of all. He settled back into her lap as she sat on the floor and combed him, enjoying the tugs against his hide with every sweep.

"There we go! Just gotta hang you up to dry." Celia bounded up, tucked the comb into her frizzy hair, and pulled a line from one of the cupboards, stringing it between the nearest hooks so that it stretched across the room. "Oh, gotta let some breeze in so you don't get musty!" The little girl popped open the nearest window, and drained the tub, letting the soapy water gurgle away into the pipes. "Just hang out for a little while, okay? Okay." She fastened the teddy bear to the lines with clothespins on his arms, putting a bowl under him to catch any stray drips.

Thus half-crucified, the little golem watched her run out the door back to the front room, open up the front door, and slam it behind her. "Hey Daddy, do you need any help? Are you done? When's dinner?"

Then she was out of earshot, and the golem turned as best he could, surveying his surroundings, trying to make some sense of this new environment now that he wasn't being soaked in water for no good reason.

And then he froze.

Peering in through the open window, scorn written into every whisker, was a feline face. A familiar one.

Pulsivar the cat strolled in over the windowsill, and sat his haunches down on the counter, staring up at the little golem.

Threadbare stared back.

Then the golem began jerking frantically, trying to get itself free of the washing line.

Pulsivar's eyes got bigger and bigger, as the thrashing motion enticed him. He crouched low, wiggling his butt, as his tail lashed in anticipation.

"Daddy, do you think Threadbare can help with dinner tonight?" Celia's voice came from just outside the door.

Threadbare's head whipped to the left, and hope rose within his heart —

"What? Oh hold on, I didn't know there was more. Coming!" Celia's footsteps retreated down the path.

—and swiftly fell, as his salvation left him to the mercies of the cat. But the cat had no mercy, and he leaped upon the hanging golem like a fuzzy, fat arrow loosed from a bow with a catgut string.

Unfortunately, Pulsivar hadn't accounted for one very important thing.

The hooks holding Threadbare's washing line up weren't meant to bear twenty-five pounds of pissed-off feline.

The rightmost one ripped out of the wall, the line swung, with Threadbare pinned to it and Pulsivar swinging below him like a fuzzy pendulum—

—and both of them went sailing through the still-open basement door. Celia had forgotten to close the damned thing.

At the end of the arc, Threadbare's eyes twitched in horror as the pin holding him to the clothesline snapped off, and cat and golem went sailing down together, bouncing and rolling down the steep wooden stairs, to land in a heap on the dirt floor. A pair of red numbers, '6' for Pulsivar and '2' for Threadbare, drifted up into the air and vanished.

CON +1
Your Toughness Skill is now level 2!
Max HP increased by 2!

Above them, stirred by the breeze of their passing and nudged by one of the cat's flailing legs, the door swung closed with an ominous CLICK.

The light, at least, was still on. Threadbare and the cat scrambled apart, rising to their feet. In the light reflected from the glowing stone above, button-eyed determination met a malicious feline glare.

Threadbare found himself irritated by the cat's anger. He was stronger now, tougher, and this creature had fled from him before. Alien instincts flooded him, and he hauled himself up to his full height, putting his arms out wide. He tried to growl, but the lack of a mouth made it impossible.

Pulsivar hissed, with a sound of boiling water. This time would be different! This time the bear would not escape! His fur puffed up...

And in the shadows where the light didn't reach, red eyes blinked open.

Pulsivar paused, as his nose twitched.

Rats. Lots of them.

A chittering filled the dank air, and Threadbare stopped, looked around as well.

And then there was no time for anything but violence, as the rats charged out to kill the invaders.

CHAPTER 3: BASEMENT BATTLES

Months ago, when winter was in full swing and the vermin of the forest were looking for shelter, a pair of rats had found a crack in the foundation of the house, large enough to squirm into. They'd found themselves in a gloriously dark cellar, lit only by one small window, high up in the wall. They'd also found several loosely-stored sacks and barrels of grain and dried vegetables.

Eventually they grew too fat to leave the cellar, but there was plenty of food, so they bred litters, ate, and slept.

But in time, a change came over the oldest of them. Glowing, squiggly symbols appeared in front of the eyes of the older of the original pair. Letters that if they could have been comprehended by ratty minds, would have shown that he was eligible for a rank up.

He had taken that rank up. The next time the rat happened to think positively about something, willing "yes" to a small question that involved ratty life, he'd accepted the rank up. This was how most wild animals ranked up without a benefit of comprehending the words.

And, as had happened many times before, an otherwise-ordinary animal became a monster.

That had been a week ago.

The monster's children had stirred when the girl entered the cellar, gathered around, wanting to attack her with an aggression that normally they didn't have. But the monster was eating more and more of the food, even eating his children at times, and the rats were desperate. The little girl's sheer size was the only thing that kept her safe.

But Threadbare and Pulsivar? They were just the right size.

And so the monster lurked behind a row of pickle jars, watching through multiple red eyes, as its children swarmed. It would let them take the brunt of the intruders' attacks, and wear them down with numbers. Then it would come out and claim its due from its ratty children, taking the choicest bits from the kill. It was only natural, really.

It was, after all, their king.

Threadbare was aware of none of this, having too low a perception to see the monster hidden behind the pickles, and Pulsivar the cat was too goddamned busy for a clear look around. The rats hurled themselves at the two creatures like a tidal wave of furry flesh, cramming in tightly together and charging, leaping upon the pair.

Pulsivar moved with lightning speed, sweeping out with his claws as they came at him, dancing back and batting them away as they came, but there were too many angles to cover. One larger rat took a bite out of his tail with its chisel teeth. Another one latched onto his ear and the cat howled, spraying blood as he shook his head, sending the rat flying as a red number '5' floated up to the ceiling.

Threadbare, without the benefit of the cat's agility, stumbled back as half a dozen rats harried him, ripping into his furry body... and finding it tougher than anticipated. A virtual storm of red zeroes floated up to the ceiling of the basement, with only one or two forlorn '1's among them. But it was still aggravating, and he really didn't know how to handle the situation. He looked to Pulsivar, and saw the cat's paws flickering like lightning, slapping and slamming the rats as they came.

Well, why not? That looked like it might do something.

INT +1

The little golem flailed his arms in great clumsy sweeps, losing more and more of his hide to ratty nibbles as they easily evaded his attacks.

Up until the point one of them didn't.

"Squeak!"

You have unlocked the generic skill: Brawling!
Your Brawling skill is now level 1!

The injured rat rolled backwards, bounced off a few of its brethren, then surged back into the fight. But Threadbare was busy trying out his newfound skill, and didn't have time to notice. Again and again his arms slapped down on the rats, battering them, wearing them down. Eventually a few of them fled, bruised down to only one or two hit points.

The teddy bear kept going as fast as he could, ignoring the numbers and letters scrolling through his field of vision. The rats fought back, and he felt his body get more and more unresponsive as needle-like teeth tore at him.

He dodged a few of them...

AGL+1
But there were just too many, so he had to resort to battering as best he could.

Your Brawling skill is now level 2!
CON +1
Your Brawling skill is now level 3!
STR +1
Your Brawling skill is now level 4!
STR +1
Your Toughness Skill is now Level 3
Max HP +2

Then, with a lucky strike, he managed to catch a leaping rat full in the mouth with a wild haymaker, sending it up a full four feet, before it fell down to hit the floor.

CRUNCH!
Critical Hit!
LUCK +1
Your Brawling skill is now level 5!
You are now a level 3 Toy Golem!
All Attributes +2!

And suddenly, he felt good. He felt stronger. Still banged up, true, but... now, somehow, he felt more confident about his chances. He had no idea why these things were trying to kill him, but he figured he'd be walking out of here one way or another. He bonked a few more rats, smacking them until they retreated, and glanced back to Pulsivar.

The cat was not having a good day. Unlike the golem, his feline hide was a lot thinner and softer. And while the rats had to work harder to hit him, there were a lot of the little bastards. Also, it didn't help that unlike most of the nests of vermin he had dealt with before, these little bastards weren't going down or fleeing when he thumped them or batted them away. So he switched to more lethal tactics.

At the cost of taking more hits to his unprotected flanks, Pulsivar popped his claws and slashed wildly, getting stuck in and tearing screaming rats into meaty gobbets. He tore two to bits, losing a tip of his tail in the process, stood on his haunches and raked three more with long swipes as two more bit into his back, then rolled, scooping up a large rat with his claws and jaws as he eviscerated it with his hind feet.

The golem would have blinked, if his eyes worked that way. He watched, fascinated, as Pulsivar turned into a screaming, hissing whirlwind of blood and claws and teeth—

—and something within him realized that at least part of that sort of fighting was within his reach.

Movement to his side, a rat coming in with a furious charge—
PER +1
—And Threadbare turned and SWIPED it out of the air.
Claw Swipes Activated!
Your Claw Swipes skill is now level 2
The rat disintegrated. Bloody bits rained down on the somewhat-thinned crowd, and for a second, the lot of them hesitated.

Threadbare, oblivious to the momentary reprieve, studied his paw. Black, hardened claws about an inch long stuck out of it, dripping red, red blood in the dim light of the crystal.

And Pulsivar, seeing the opportunity, used his ace in the hole.

Rats weren't the only ones who could rank up. And long ago, two years at least, Pulsivar the cat had slain enough rabbits and rats and birds to unlock the next part of his evolutionary chain.

Pulsivar was a Tomcat, and he unleashed the full force of his mightiest skill upon the ears of all present, as a screeching, hissing, buzzsaw of a howl echoed through the tight basement and shook the mason jars on the shelves!

This was Caterwaul: The sanity destroyer!

Instantly, the area effect skill ripped through the rats like a hot knife through butter, as scores of blue '17's filled the air of the basement.

Threadbare felt the pain too, as a blue '3' floated past his vision... but it wasn't that bad, just mildly disconcerting.

You have successfully resisted Caterwaul! Sanity damage halved!
WILL +1
The rats fell to the ground, stunned cat-atonic, their sanity gone.

And in the silence, Threadbare turned to look at Pulsivar. And the cat sat on its haunches, panting, looking back.

Threadbare looked at his claws, then at the cat.

The cat crouched low, and prepared to resolve the unfinished business it had with this infernal thing.

Then, from behind the row of pickle jars, came the strangest sound that either of the two enemies had ever heard.

A royal fanfare, trumpets and all, followed by officious-sounding squeaking. Though without words, it somehow had the weight of dignity behind it. It spoke of valor and duty, to rat, king, and pantry...

...but most importantly of all, it added a sanity buff to its fallen subjects.

And around them, the fallen rats rose, one by one. The ones slashed to death were unmoving still, but the effects of Pulsivar's caterwaul were thoroughly undone.

The two enemies looked to their renewed foes. They looked back to each other.

Threadbare knew he couldn't survive this alone. And while the cat wasn't exactly a friend, the rats sure as hell were enemies to them both.

INT +1

So he gave the cat a small nod, and turned his back on Pulsivar, taking the biggest risk of his short life, and hoping that the cat understood the message.

Fortunately for both of them Pulsivar had spent long hours grinding his perception.

Threadbare relaxed slightly, as he felt a furry flank slide against his back.

CHA +1

The message had been understood. They might just walk out of here after all.

The rats, down to two-thirds of their starting number, charged in; the real battle began.

At first it was slogwork, with the cat and the golem ripping them up and taking bites in return. More words flashed by, as the seconds turned into a minute;

CON +1
Your Brawling skill is now level 6!
STR +1
Critical Hit!
LUCK +1
Your Claw Swipes skill is now level 3!
Your Claw Swipes skill is now level 4!
Your Brawling skill is now level 7!
Your Claw Swipes skill is now level 5!
Your Claw Swipes skill is maxxed, raise your Bear job!

But as time went on, the bear began to feel an alien sensation.

It was getting tired.

Unbeknownst to the teddy bear, the Claw Swipes skill ate up a little of its stamina with every hit. And while it was brutally effective, it wasn't designed for prolonged fights. Bears were more of an "overwhelming force" fighter, as melee combatants went. Trying to fight like Pulsivar wasn't doing him any favors, especially since he didn't have a mouth to bite with.

Pulsivar, fortunately, was coming to the same conclusion. While they were covering each other's flanks, he was getting tired too. His own Catscratch, and Rake skills were getting the job done, but his endurance was running very low. Too many hours grinding Nap, not enough grinding Hunt. He contemplated another Caterwaul, but dismissed the notion. He was already low enough on Moxie, another shot of that would surely knock him out.

Then the teddy bear had an epiphany;

Pulsivar was better at killing, but judging by the rips in him versus the less-severe wounds in the teddy bear, Threadbare could absorb damage more easily.

He thought he could maybe use this to their advantage.

INT +1

Threadbare gave Pulsivar a shove, then waded out into the regrouping remnants. Pulling his claws back in without knowing quite how, he went back to thumping at the rats, deliberately letting himself get surrounded, and taking the bites. His already abused hide was rent further, stitches giving way, and desperately he fought, hoping beyond hope that the cat got the message.

Fortunately for him, the cat did.

LUCK +1

The rats were thin on the ground now, depleted enough that they weren't filling the bloody, corpse-strewn ground. They had to peel off into two separate rings, one around the golem and one around the cat. And when the cat got surrounded he simply leaped out of it, smacking with both paws on one of the ones snapping at Threadbare.

CRUNCH!

Before they could realize that death was among them, the cat mowed down the distracted rats like a scythe through grain. Then Threadbare ran past him, intercepting the next string of rats, and making them ring up around him again. And Pulsivar was free to rip and tear without fear of reprisal. He had much more stamina left than the teddy bear, even if his endurance was abysmal. And so, when the last rat fled squeaking, the cat settled back on his haunches once more, glaring with cruel eyes. Threadbare, for his part, sat on the ground and tried to push the few puffs of escaping stuffing back into the holes in his chest.

You are now a level 4 Toy Golem!

All Attributes +2!

The cat looked at the bear once more. The bear looked back. Then the cat started to groom itself.

Threadbare couldn't tell exactly, but he thought maybe that meant that Pulsivar might stop trying to kill it now?

PER +1

CRASH!

Both cat and bear jumped upright, as a row of pickle jars broke.

And something crawled out from the darkness.

At first it looked like another group of rats... bigger, filthier, and even more angry. But they were moving strangely, jerking and stopping, straining against the floor, practically clawing their way along.

Then they got into the light, and Threadbare saw why.

Their tails were twisted together into a pulsating knot, and sitting on top of this knot was a rat twice the size of the others, In its clenched paws was a scepter, a little golden shiny stick with a stylized rat's head on it. And as Threadbare watched, it sat upright on its knot, pointed the scepter at Threadbare, and let out a screeching warcry.

Threadbare turned to look at Pulsivar...

... who promptly leaped up on the nearest shelf, eyes wide and full of nope.

Threadbare stared after him, hope fading. Then there was no time for despair, as the rat king was upon him.

These rats were stronger than the last, well-fed and sleek, with muscles about double that of the subjects Threadbare had tanked without much difficulty. Three bites in, he knew he was in trouble, as red '5's floated up into the air.

CON +1

Your Toughness Skill is now Level 4!

Maximum HP +2

Claw swipes took down one of the big rats, but there were nine in total, and they dragged along their fallen comrade, only slightly slower for the effort.

STR +1

Your Brawling skill is now level 8!

Your Claw Swipes skill is maxxed, raise your Bear job!

Shuddering, with a large gash in his left side, and one arm limp and only hanging on by (literally) a thread, Threadbare stumbled back, out of the light. Sensing weakness, the rat king pushed forward.

Up on the shelf, Pulsivar moved forward to get a better look, nudged a jar of strawberry jam, and thoroughly failed his agility check.

The jam careened downward, narrowly missing the rat king. It squeaked and ducked, chittering, and directing its bearers to the side away from Pulsivar's shelf.

Threadbare watched all this with button eyes.

And he remembered the workshop, and the table, and what it had done to him. And he came up with a plan.

INT +1

The rat king resumed pursuing him, murder in its gleaming red eyes. This blood-stained bear, this filth-smeared slayer, it would pay for what it had done! With a wave of its scepter, the rat king gave in to its instincts and leaned forward, puking green smoke from all nine of its remaining mouths!

The skill was called "Plague Breath"

And it affected the little golem not at all.

Your Golem Body skill is now level 4!

Threadbare leaped out of the cloud, leaped past the king onto the nearest shelves—

AGL +1

—Moved himself between the shelf and the wall, grabbed one of the wooden rods supporting the shelves at its back, planted his feet against the wall, and pulled.

His arm gave way and fell off, and he doubled down with his last arm, curling it in tight, and pulling, feeling his stitches along his side give, feeling his stuffing slip and fall out of him, straining with every inch of his augmented body regardless of the damage done to himself—

STR +1

CON +1

Your Toughness Skill is Level 5!

Max HP +2!

And he toppled the shelf, and all the jars and cans on it, onto the rat king.

The shelf went to pieces, dowel rods flying. Threadbare hit the dirt floor and rolled, streaking his bloody form with mud, his loose arm landing next to him.

He lay there still for a minute, while the rat king screamed. The shelf rustled, stirred, as Threadbare looked at it... then fell still.

Threadbare stood, limping, wrapping his right arm around to his left side to hold himself together, and stumbled over to peer into the shelving.

The biggest rat, the king itself, was straining, trying to get free of the wreckage. Around it, the corpses of its nine dead bearers lay broken and dying among the shattered glass, fallen wood, and heavy cans.

The rat king hissed. It was cornered now, and all its stats gained a nice buff for it. When that little bear came near, the rat king would shred him to death.

Fortunately, the bear saw that, too. Though he didn't know about the buff, he was pretty sure the critter was still highly dangerous to approach.

WIS +1

Threadbare went and picked up a dowel rod. Much easier this time, he noticed. Which was good, because he was down to one hand.

Then he limped back to the rat king and slowly beat it to death, staying well out of its reach the whole time.

INT +1

You have unlocked the generic skill: Clubs and Maces!
Your Clubs and Maces Skill is Level 1!
Your Clubs and Maces Skill is Level 2!
Your Clubs and Maces Skill is Level 3!
Your Clubs and Maces Skill is Level 4!
Critical Hit!
LUCK +1

Somewhere around Clubs and Maces Level 6, the thing finally succumbed to its injuries.

You are now a level 5 Toy Golem!
All Attributes +2!
You unlocked the Innocent Embrace Skill!
Your Innocent Embrace Skill is Level 1!
You are now a level 2 Bear!
CON +3
STR+3
WIS +3
Armor +2
Endurance +2
Mental Fortitude +2

He felt good for all of three seconds. Then, to his horror, a new set of those squiggles showed up in his vision and did not leave!

Congratulations! By committing regicide you have unlocked the Ruler job!
Would you like to become a Ruler at this time? Y/N?

Threadbare was entirely irate at the new sight-blocking squiggles. This was just too much...

...but fortunately, he knew how to make those squiggles go away, now didn't he?

He concentrated on the feeling he'd had at Celia's tea party, concentrated on the feeling that was "Yes!"

You are now a Level 1 Ruler!
CHA +5
WIS +5
LUCK +5
You have Unlocked the Emboldening Speech Skill!
You gain Emboldening Speech at level 1
You have Unlocked the Identify Subject Skill!
Your gain Identify Subject at level 1
You have unlocked the Noblesse Oblige Skill!
You gain Noblesse Oblige at level 1
You have unlocked the Royal Audience Skill!

You gain Royal Audience at level 1
You have unlocked the Simple Decree Skill!
You gain Simple Decree at level 1

None of this meant anything to the bear. But he did feel different. He couldn't say how, so he shrugged with his remaining arm, and turned with a weariness that his body language hadn't had the complexity to show before.

Then a gleam caught his eye.

The golden scepter lay next to the fallen rat king. Threadbare marched over and scooped it up, examining it curiously... and the stylized rat's head on the end of it turned into a teddy bear's face.

His thoughts swam again, and jumbled into order. Well beyond animal intelligence at this point, he was now somewhere around the level of a sharp toddler or a very simple adult.

Twenty-five pounds of cat leaped down onto the dirt floor next to him, and Threadbare turned to study Pulsivar.

Pulsivar, for his part, leaned in and sniffed the bear.

He didn't smell rage, or fear, or hostility. He smelled rat blood and rat dung, sure, that was everywhere...

...but under it all, he smelled soap. The soap that Celia used to launder every piece of clothing and sheet in the place. It was a scent that to Pulsivar meant home, and family. He'd known it all his life, and associated it with shelter, food, and love.

Pulsivar looked at the bear, and wrinkled his nose. Why hadn't anyone told him the little golem was part of his family? His hoomins would get a stern lesson later. Perhaps a hairball in a shoe, or maybe he'd spray the big one's pillow. This whole thing could have been avoided.

He was still miffed at the little guy, but he had earned Pulsivar's respect during the fight. Besides, what he was dealing with here was obviously some sort of malformed kitten, thoroughly clueless and dumb. But cute.

Threadbare watched words go by.

Your Adorable Skill is now level 5!

"Marp," Pulsivar told Threadbare, less an apology and more of an explanation. Best to let bygones be bygones.

Just to show that there were no hard feelings, he leaned in and started grooming Threadbare. Normally this would heal anyone he groomed, but sadly, the little golem was incompatible with standard healing effects.

But the little bear had no idea what the cat was doing. It had seen Pulsivar doing that before, to himself, so to his newly-socially-boosted instincts, it seemed to him that the cat was telling him that he was no longer an enemy. That he accepted Threadbare.

So, the bear leaned forward and gave him a hug as a "thank you". And as he did so, a golden glow enveloped his arms and sunk into the cat.

You have healed Pulsivar 10 points!

Your Innocent Embrace skill is now level 2!

Wow, he felt light-headed. It had cost him five sanity to do that.

Pulsivar stopped, surprised. Then he gave Threadbare a few more licks, and pulled away. None of that touchy-feely stuff, thank you very much.

The bear stared at him for a bit, then started looking around for a way out. Celia was around here somewhere, she'd know what to do. Maybe she could clean up this mess.

He made his way back to the stairs, tucked his new scepter into one of the holes in his body, and did his best to climb the stairs one-armed.

Your Climb Skill is now Level 2!

Your Climb Skill is now Level 3!

AGL +1

After some time and repeated falls, he managed to make his way up to the door. He pushed on it, but it didn't open. He pushed harder, and stopped once more stuffing threatened to bulge out of him. He didn't have that much left, so this clearly wouldn't work.

He clambered down the stairs once more, and looked around the basement. No way out, except...

PER +1

One window, high on the wall. About five feet up.

Threadbare looked to the dowel rod, picked it up, and smashed the window.

INT +1

Immediately, just like before, Pulsivar jumped up on the nearest shelf and fled through the newly-made exit. Much slower, and with a great deal more effort, Threadbare followed, fell a few times, kept trying until he got up there...

Your Climb Skill is now Level 4!

...And managed to squirm through the window.

AGL +1

He lay there for a bit, in the grass, watching the trees overhead. The wind swayed the branches in the sunlight, and he dared to hope that finally, just maybe, this particular ordeal was over.

"I think it came from over here!" Celia's voice came from around the corner of the house. Tired, drained, and hurt, Threadbare clambered to his feet and ran as fast as he could toward her voice.

"Oh my gods! What happened to you?" Celia grabbed him up, then wrinkled her nose. "Ew ew ew you smell horrible! What is this— is this blood?" She went pale. Then she fled, shrieking, toward the front door. "Daddy! Threadbare's dying!"

She hugged him to her so tight that she pushed the scepter well down into his body, without even noticing. The bear just clung to her and hugged her as best he could, with one arm gone. This time no glowy stuff happened, and he didn't know why. Someone could have explained to him that Innocent Embrace only triggered if the target was injured or the caster had enough sanity to use it, but again, he probably wouldn't have understood.

Not yet, anyway. He'd been through a lot, and he was starting to learn, learn and grow.

"Celia, what's... wrong?" The old man burst into the front room as his blood-smeared daughter cried and thrust her toy at him.

"Oh dear heavens! Ah, let me... ugh, this is horrible. Give him here, give him here."

"Can, hic, can I mend him without his arm? Will it stay that way?"

"Mend will work just fine, he's a golem. The severed parts will dissolve from where they're at and reattach as he's mended, so it shouldn't be a problem. No, don't mend him yet, if there's anything inside him the mending will seal it in. We'll have to get the blood and filth off him first." The old man held Threadbare at arm's length, and cleared his throat. **"Clean and Press!"**

Instantly the grime fled Threadbare's body. The old man nodded. "Now you can mend him."

Celia shouted her "Mend" spell until he was whole again. Relieved, she hugged her best friend close. "Oh thank you thank you! And I even skilled up! Yay me..."

"Then it was worthwhile, whatever happened." The old man frowned. "Er, what did happen? That wasn't your blood, so whose was—"

"Wait a minute." The little girl's face turned into a mask of dawning comprehension. "You cleaned him in like an instant. How did you do that?"

The old man coughed, and reddened. "Ah, we'll discuss that later. For now, let's figure out how he got so bloody in the first—"

"You said you were low on sanity, and couldn't do any more magic today! And that was a spell!"

"Well I was, I mean, it's only a level one spell."

"I've been doing the laundry for years, and you could have done it just like that with a level one spell? What the hell, Daddy?"

"Celia!"

"It's like hours a week out of my life and you could have done that at any time? Seriously?"

"It's a very important chore! You can't depend on magic, you have to learn how to do things without—"

"Well why not teach me, then! I'm old enough to be a level five animator, why don't you teach me that level one trick!"

"It's not an animator trick, it's a tailor skill—"

"Then teach me to be a tailor!"

"You're not ready to make such life-altering decisions yet—"

"Not ready? Not ready! That's all I ever hear from you is that I'm not ready!"

"No! There's an upper limit, you can only ever have so many jobs! You can't waste your potential with the trivial stuff—"

"But it wasn't too trivial for you! And you're okay with wasting my potential on doing laundry by hand! Seriously, what the hell?"

The old man stood bolt upright, glaring down at Celia. "I will not be talked to like this in my own house! Go to your room, young lady!"

"Fine!" Celia stormed upstairs, threw herself onto her bed, hugged Threadbare to her, and cried her eyes out.

Inside Threadbare, the scepter itched a bit. He settled into Celia's embrace, and moved by new instincts, stroked her hair. He'd been frightened and upset when Celia and his creator started shouting, but it hadn't come to a fight. Which was good, because he didn't have any shelves around to drop on the old man and he was pretty sure the guy would be harder to take down than the rat king had been.

Outside, the light faded as dusk came on, and night covered the land. The little girl fell into a troubled sleep, and Threadbare settled into the crook of her arms. For now, at least, all was well with the world.

*****

In the dark of the night, in a sprawling hillside village set among several scrawny farms, a batwinged form settled onto the window of the largest house. It slunk in, peering with beady eyes, as it folded its wings against its scaly back.

Sitting up in bed, a blanket clutched to her voluptuous form, a raven-haired woman smiled sweetly at the imp. But the smile didn't reach her eyes, which might as well have been chips of ice.

"Caminthraxus? You have a report to make? About the girl?"

"No, milady. About Caradon."

"Ah... So the old man has figured it out, then?"

"Er, no. The old man has made no real progress with his research."

"Then why do you waste my time?" Her tone didn't change, but the imp knew how close he was to torment, right now, unless he found a way to make her happy.

The tiny demon shuddered, and tried to find his courage. "I, I learned that he keeps a set of scrolls within his house. An emergency stash. Many of them are spells that let the user command golems."

Icy eyes gleamed. And a set of perfect white teeth smiled. "Ah. Yes, that will make things easier. I'll send word on to the master, and we'll see how he wants to use that information. Thank you Caminthraxus, you've done well."

"Just my duty," the lesser demon hissed. Then a motion on the bed drew his gaze to the figure next to the woman, just visible through the sheets. "Are you going to finish that one?"

The woman turned, and considered the man next to her. Drawn skin over shriveled bones, his paper-like eyelids moved up and down, as horrified eyes moved from her to the imp. Muscles thoroughly drained from the night's earlier activities twitched, and the woman easily held him down with one red-nailed hand.

"Mmmm... no, I think I'm done. You can have what's left."

The imp grinned, showing teeth that Pulsivar would have envied, and moved in for the feast.

CHAPTER 4: QUESTS AND QUESTIONS

The tension in the house lasted for a few days. Celia spent most of her time in her room, playing with Threadbare. On the few occasions she left, for food or to use the toilet or whatever, she'd hurry back as quickly as possible.

Occasionally Threadbare heard Celia talking with Daddy downstairs. They didn't shout, but his new-found social skills could hear the tension. The discussions were always short, and Celia usually showed up within a minute afterwards.

Threadbare spent a lot of time playing with Celia. It was good for a few more points of Charisma and Perception, and a few Adorable Skill level ups, not that he knew what was going on there. He just knew that the more time he spent around his little girl, the better he could understand how she was feeling.

But as the days went on, the attribute and skill bumps slowed down. The little bear had no way of knowing that the higher a primary attribute rose, the more time and practice it took to increase.

He did gain a small Int boost, as well. And his newly-grown intelligence was starting to comprehend a few words, here and there. Celia was the girl, he understood. Daddy was his creator, and Celia's too, he guessed. Threadbare was his name. And Pulsivar was the cat, who was roundly cursed when the smell from the basement started emanating into the house proper.

That ended the stalemate between Daddy and Celia. He knocked on her door, humbly asked for her help in cleaning up Pulsivar's mess, and agreed to take over the laundry from that point on. Celia enlisted Threadbare and her squad of stuffed toys for the task, and the lot of them marched downstairs, to look at the mess below. Flies had gotten in through the broken window and found the rot, and the hum of their eager feasting filled the basement. Spilled preserves sent up a sickly-sweet smell that mixed with the rotting rat flesh, and it was all the two humans could do to keep their lunches down.

"Um. I don't suppose your cleaning spell will handle this?" Celia asked.

"If it could I wouldn't need the help. My spell only works on textiles."

"What's a tek style?"

"Cloths, furs, that sort of thing."

"Oh."

"Well. Let's make this a proper quest, then." The old man blinked a few times, staring into the distance.

And to Threadbare's surprise, a whole bunch of squiggles appeared in his vision.

CARADON GEARHART HAS OFFERED A PUBLIC QUEST!
DETAILS: CLEAN THE BASEMENT
REWARD: TWENTY-FIVE EXPERIENCE POINTS
COMPLETION: AUTOMATICALLY FULFILLED WHEN BASEMENT IS CLEAN
DO YOU WANT TO ACCEPT THIS QUEST? Y/N?

Annoyed, Threadbare willed "Yes!" and the squiggles disappeared. Stupid things!

But now the old man had a light glowy shine to him, for some reason. He didn't know that only people who had accepted a quest from Caradon could see that shine.

Celia grinned, as she accepted the quest as well. "Yay! Twenty-five experience! Let's get to it! Okay. Okay okay," Celia said, glancing back to the six stuffed animals she'd brought. "Let me get my party going, then you can clean them."

"Capital idea. I'll handle Threadbare."

"What do you mean? I'll just tell him to—"

The old man shook his head, and pointed at Threadbare. **"Command Golem: Clean this mess."**

Threadbare straightened up. He marched up to the old man, took the bucket of soapy water and scrub brush that the man offered, and got to work.

Celia shrugged. "Okay, I guess. Come on guys, hup to it!" The toys bumbled down around Threadbare, and contributed as best they could.

"So what happened in here anyway?" Celia asked. "I knew we had rats, but… this is a lot of them. I think. It's really gross and I don't want to look too hard at this."

"As best as I can figure out, Pulsivar got trapped in here somehow and panicked, like he did in my workshop. He killed all the rats in a frenzy, tearing my shelving to pieces in the process, then broke the window to escape." The old man rubbed his eyes. "That cat's stronger than I thought. I'll have to keep an eye on him, make sure he doesn't go monstrous."

"He wouldn't!" Celia turned to him, shocked. "He's our kitty and he loves us!"

"He does love us. But there's always a chance, and if his instincts are this violent, I can't take the risk of inattention."

Celia just stared up at him. After a time, the old man's stern face softened, and he rubbed her frizzy red hair. "He'll be fine, though. He probably won't become anything dangerous. That cat's five, if he was going to go bad he'd have done it by now." He glanced back at the cellar, watching the glass chips and broken crockery get piled in one corner by the giraffe and dolly, as Threadbare tossed armloads of dead rodents into one of the few intact wooden crates. "What I wish I knew, was how Pulsivar got trapped down here in the first place. The glass was outside in the flower bed, so he came out that way. And I'm pretty sure he can't get the basement door open by himself." He shook his head, but his eyes slid back to watch Celia, catching the way she bit her lip. "It is a mystery."

Long minutes passed. Threadbare got a couple of points of dexterity from chucking rat corpses and handling cleaning supplies. He paused every now and then to glance back at his family.

Finally, Celia swallowed hard. "I uh, I think I left the door open. The basement door."

"Oh? Did you now?"

"I was washing Threadbare so I got the soap, and I might have left the door open. I guess... Pulsivar could have... gotten in. And maybe the door shut or something. It was shut when I came back in the house, so maybe he accidentally knocked the door shut. I guess."

"Why didn't you say anything?"

"I didn't think anything of it! Threadbare had wiggled loose from the clothesline so I went looking for him, and then he was all bloody, and—" The little girl put two and two together and got three point five. "— Pulsivar must have grabbed him on his way down to the basement! Then the door shut and he panicked, and got the mess all over Threadbare! THAT'S where the blood came from!" Celia looked down, and her eyes went wide. "Oh gods I got it on my face when I hugged him oh gods... MRP!" She covered her mouth with both hands and ran upstairs, retching.

The old man looked after her, and nodded. "I knew you had it in you, girl. I'm proud of you," he whispered. Then he turned around, and frowned as Threadbare tottered toward the stairs. "Here now, has the command worn off already? **Command Golem: Clean this mess!**"

Golden light flashed, and Threadbare went back to his task. But it didn't stop him from worrying for his little girl, so he kept sneaking glances back toward the stairs. The old man took no notice of this, standing on the bottom stair, arms folded behind him, waiting for Celia's return.

Eventually she did, wearing a different smock, looking pale. She shook as she stood at the head of the stairs, too afraid to come down. "I'm sorry. I didn't mean to leave the door open and this whole mess is because of me. I'm really sorry."

"Celia..." The old man winced, as he walked upstairs, and folded her into his embrace. "No, I'm not mad at you Celia, it's okay. You didn't mean for this to happen. It's not your fault. This is on Pulsivar, and even then he was panicked so I can't truly blame him. It's just bad luck, that's all. And, look at it this way; Pulsivar saved us the trouble of having to chase the rats out."

She snorted laughter into his chest, as she hugged her Daddy for all she was worth.

"In fact, I'm proud of you for confessing what you did... what you THOUGHT you'd done. So I've come to a big decision."

"Yeah?"

"I was planning on stepping up your lessons, telling you some of the things I've been holding back. You're mature enough to handle the truth now, I think." A shadow passed across his face, unseen by the little girl or her bear. "Some of it, anyway. Bear with me, you'll get the whole story in time."

"Really?" She looked up at him, snuffling, but her eyes were filled with hope.

"Really." He glanced back down to the basement. "Come on. The toys can't reach everywhere. Get your gloves on, it's time for us to do our part."

At the end of the job, Threadbare felt no different for being twenty-five experience points richer. It took the old man a few tries to get "Clean and Press" to work on him. Threadbare silently and uncomprehendingly watched his Magic Resistance skill kick up a notch. The old man saw nothing but a stubborn toy that couldn't help but resist him.

"Golems," the old man snorted. "I swear, that skill is more trouble than it's worth, sometimes. Normally beneficial magic bypasses it, but since the golems don't care if they're dirty or clean, it doesn't hurt them either way."

"Is that how it works?"

"More or less." The old man tossed Threadbare to her, then beckoned her back upstairs. "Come on. Let's go to the back porch and break out the slate and notes. It's a good day for lessons."

With the promise of answers, Celia eagerly scrounged up the schooling supplies and followed her Daddy through the study, and onto the wooden porch overlooking the downward slope of the hill. The forest lay beyond, thick, towering trees blooming with springtime growth, birdsong heavy and filling the branches. In the distance she could just make out the river that marked the edge of their property, such that it was. As she watched, a brown figure stomped through the trees briefly, and she smiled to see it. The Raggedy Men were a familiar sight.

The old man took no notice of this, as he took the slate from her, and settled back into his chair. Producing a piece of chalk from his apron, he started scrawling on the slate.

"The thing that I must tell you, before anything else, is that the world was not always this way."

"Uh, what?"

"Letters in the air. Little boosts to your fundamental qualities, for doing difficult tasks. Jobs, status screens, even quests... The world didn't work that way, forty years ago."

Celia stared at him, uncomprehending. "How? That doesn't even make any sense!"

"But that's how it was." The old man scrawled words on the slate, and crossed them off one by one.

"But... how did people learn skills without jobs?"

"We didn't have skills. Not as you know them, anyway. We got better at things by years of practice, and trying to learn new things."

"Like unlocking generic skills?" Celia still looked unconvinced. This was a lot to swallow.

"Sort of, only without the words appearing to tell you you'd gotten better at something." The old man snorted. "I was a wizard's apprentice, back then. I'd spent years learning the basics, and my biggest trick was animating a rope. I could do that once per day.... Twice a day if I didn't memorize detect magic, and double-stocked animate rope spells."

"What?"

"Things were very different back then. We had spell slots, and a thing called thaco, and don't ask me to explain those. Anyway, it took years to get good at things. Decades, even, for some complex skills. I suppose it still does, now, if you take it slowly and avoid danger."

Celia shifted, hugging Threadbare tight. "So what about level ups?"

"They weren't called that. I think... I think what happened was that the numbers still appeared, but nobody could see them. You had to guess what you had, if you cared about that at all. Most of us didn't, we were too busy living our lives."

"So what happened to make everything change? How'd we get to level ups and jobs and stuff?"

"Nobody knows."

"Seriously?"

"Seriously. One day, the words started appearing, and everyone found out that they had status screens. And qualified for various jobs."

"Awesome!"

"No, actually." The old man looked at her with solemnity. "It was utter chaos."

"What? Why?"

"Think about it. We'd gone for years without knowing exactly how smart, or how strong, or what our limits were. Then, in a heartbeat, all that knowledge of ourselves was at our fingertips. In fact, we couldn't get away from it! You'd be right in the middle of kissing your girlfriend, and CHA +1 would float up out of nowhere!"

Celia's eyes went wide. "Wait, what?" The lesson had gotten even more interesting. "Tell me more about how kissing levels charisma."

The old man flushed, as he realized his mistake. "Ah. Uh, later. Much later. Anyway, nevermind that. The thing was, once we started figuring things out, and looking around, as the months went by we found out it just wasn't us, here in the Cylvanian Valley. It was Baramor to the west, and Mighty Hallas to the north, and the Cane Confederation to the south, and pretty soon we realized that it was everywhere. Everywhere was like this. Still is, probably."

"Why do you say it's probably like this?"

The old man sighed. "It's not a very nice subject. Which I suppose is why I've avoided talking with you about it. But... cards on the table, as it were." His chalk scratched the slate. "Those early years, we thought the words, the jobs, we thought they were a blessing. Even when monsters grew in numbers and the first dungeons formed, we took it all with a sense of adventure. We even had seven heroes, that swore to protect Cylvania. Seven brave souls, that deserved better than they got." He stared off into the distance, watching the wind over the trees. "Much better."

Celia bit her lip. "I don't understand."

The old man shook his head. "I'm woolgathering. But essentially, it turned to chaos. Jobs only go to level twenty-five, that we found out in the first few years. But the monsters kept getting tougher and tougher. Soon we were losing the smaller settlements. Then we were fighting to keep the larger ones. And it never ended, more monsters came in from outside, drifting in from the bigger countries, where more people were around to kill them more easily. We didn't have enough people to manage them, and for a while it was pretty ugly." The old man took a breath. "But even that, we could have lived with. In the end, as it always is, the biggest threat to our little kingdom came from other men."

"Worse than monsters?"

"Oh yes. Monsters just want simple things, like to eat you, or take your treasure, or to act as their nature tells them to. Men? Men want to rule you. To change you, until you're what they want you to be, rather than what you want to be."

"So what happened?"

"You remember how I told you once, that jobs can't go beyond level twenty-five?"

"Yeah."

"Well that's not exactly true. And in one land, they figured out a way around it faster than anyone else did. So we knew the time had come for drastic action—"

Celia blinked. Then she whipped her head around, and stood, as a figure broke the treeline at the side of the house. "Oh! It's Mister Mordecai! Hi hi hi!" She waved, lessons forgotten, as the brown-coated figure waved back.

"Ah! Is it that time already?" The old man smiled, and put the slate down. "We cleaned the basement just in time, then, I'd hate to have him subjected to that smell. Come on, let's go meet him."

They got inside just as their visitor rapped at the door. Celia ran ahead and answered it, squealing with joy. Threadbare watched from under one arm. He hadn't understood a word of that lesson earlier, but this seemed interesting.

Leaning against the door frame, clad in a hunter's brown leather coat that had seen much wear, collar turned up against the cool winds off the mountain, and a brown, floppy-brimmed hat over his bald head, was a man not much younger than Threadbare's creator. He was whip-thin, with a face rounded by nature rather than good eating, and the only hair on his face was a stubbly brush that parted to reveal missing teeth as he reached down and lifted Celia up by the armpits. "Garrr! What've we got here, then?"

Celia laughed. Threadbare held onto her arm for dear life as she flailed in the newcomer's grip. "Put me down! Hee hee! I'm not a little girl any more! Ha ha ha!"

"Whew! Truth in that, you're getting big little Celia!" Mordecai knelt and deposited her on the floor. "Ere we go. Big hug?"

"Big hug!" Celia embraced him. Threadbare found himself shoved up against the man's neck. Curious, he followed his instincts and sniffed at his hat.

Your Scents and Sensibility skill is now Level 3!
PER +1

Oh, right, that was a thing he could do. The teddy bear compared the scents to those he'd sniffed around the house. Some similarities, but more differences. He rather thought he knew what all this huge two-legged scents had in common, though. And even though he didn't know what humans were, he was starting to figure out that he could smell something and tell if it was human or not.

INT +1

"Mordecai." The old man nodded.

"Caradon." The newcomer gave the old man a sober look, over Celia's shoulder. "Run silent."

"Run deep," Caradon replied, and gave the woods a cursory glance, before shutting the door. "Did you bring the usual supplies?"

"That and news."

"News?" Celia pulled back from him. "What's happened? Is it something with Taylor's Delve?"

"Er… big picture stuff. Borin' stuff. I'll tell yer Daddy later. Want to help me bring the supplies in?"

"Sure!" Celia trekked outside, next to Mister Mordecai, who listened somberly, nodding as she burst out with a week's worth of words, telling him all about Threadbare and how Pulsivar had gone crazy twice, and how she'd seen her first cardinal redbird a few days ago, and how they'd had to clean up the cellar. Mordecai spent a lot of time nodding, and Threadbare was glad to see that the newcomer's technique for listening to Celia matched the one that the teddy bear had figured out. Lots of nodding, and she was happy.

They reached four stuffed packs at the treeline, and Celia went for the smallest one, grunting as she tried to heft it. Threadbare slipped free of her grasp and tried to help her…

…but holy heck, was it heavy. The little girl staggered back toward the house, grunting and sweating. Threadbare was nearly crushed several times, but managed to take the weight off of her now and then.

STR +1

"How do you get these up here?" Celia whined.

"Told ya before, Scout's a good job. Got skills ta help with that."

"I want to learn that."

"You always say that. An' what do I always say back?'

"Not... without... Daddy's... permission..." She made a farting noise with her mouth.

"Ayep."

The rest of the trip was silent. Mordecai went ahead, walking with the three, heavier packs slung over his shoulder like they had no weight at all. Celia and Threadbare finally caught up, to find Mordecai and Caradon talking in low, solemn voices. Threadbare caught a bit of it, just before he and Celia staggered through the door.

PER +1

"...don't think he'll look out this far right away, but you best watch yourself. Had a few people askin' about where all them toys are going —" Caradon cleared his throat, and Mordecai glanced over his shoulder, rubbing the back of his neck as Celia stared at them, curiosity writ large on her face.

"Celia?" Caradon spoke, tousling her hair. "I've got some catching up to do with Mister Mordecai. Why don't you go play outside?"

"Can I go down to the river?"

Caradon looked to Mordecai. Mordecai nodded. "River's clear. Ent much rain. Worst of the snowmelt's down from the mountains. No sign a' monsters."

"All right, but stay to this bank of the river," Caradon told her. "Give us about half an hour."

"Okay! Okay okay. Come on, Threadbare!" She gathered up the little bear, then ran up, and came back down with an armload of stuffed toys. "Bye, Daddy!"

Celia jogged down to the treeline, went a bit further down the hill, to where the pines stood in the loamy soil, and glanced back at the house. "There we go. Out of sight." She knelt down and put Threadbare and the other toys on the soft cushion of pine needles, and leaned in close. "Did you know something, Threadbare?"

Threadbare nodded his head.

"Well you don't know this. If you go down to the river and keep going west, then circle around on the sycamore's bluff, you can get right up to the other side of the house. And you can hear what they're talking about, without them knowing!"

Threadbare nodded.

"That's our quest! We're gonna go figure out what's got Mister Mordecai so worried! I mean, I'm not gonna give you any of my experience for it, but that's our job. Are you with me, Threadbare?"

The little golem nodded once more, and Celia clapped her hands in glee, before turning around and animating the rest of her toys.

And from a low pine tree, its black scales blending into the hollows between the needle-filled branches, an impish face smiled at the opportunity presented. A short, stealthy flight, a quick hop over the river, and a woman's arm rose to meet him, as he settled onto her wrist, and met her icy blue stare.

"Well?"

"The girl's playing outside."

"Finally!" The woman shook her head, staring up at the little house, just visible through the trees. "Can you run distraction without revealing yourself?"

"Maybe. Mordecai's no slouch. I can barely sneak by him when I'm invisible."

"Get as close as you can, and prepare yourself. We'll only have one shot at this, and I don't want to meet the master empty-handed when he arrives..."

Meanwhile, across the river, Celia was gloriously unaware of the strangers plotting their approach.

Celia stared at the blade in her hand, then back to Threadbare. Her face grew solemn. "I'm afraid you don't make the cut, Mister Bare."

Then she giggled, and tossed the little dagger high up in the air. **"Animus Blade!"**

The knife fell toward the ground... but it slowed as it did so, stopping at mid-height to Cecilia. It turned over a few times, then settled into an upright guard stance.

"That's one of the spells I learned when I got to level five," Celia told Threadbare, grinning. "Neat, huh? It acts like there's somebody holding it." She patted the little bear's head.

Threadbare nodded, watching the dagger move. It swung around Celia as she moved back and forth, inspecting her toys. There were five of them, now. The usual tea party guests plus a wooden skeleton string puppet, and a stuffed knight, with knitted wool for chainmail.

"I'm sorry I'm not inviting you into my party Threadbare, I don't have any of daddy's scrolls. But I guess it doesn't matter since golems don't get experience. And my buff doesn't work on you. It works on them, because I animated them, but not you."

Threadbare nodded. He really didn't understand what she was talking about, but it seemed to satisfy her.

"Here we go... **Form Party! Invite Beanarella! Invite Dracosnack! Invite Loopy! Invite Sir Dashing! Invite Morty! Invite Dagger Underscore One!**"

The toys perked up, and fell into lockstep beside her. The dagger shuddered, slashed the air several times, and resumed its orbit around the little girl. Somehow he could tell it had more confidence to it.

Seeing what the toys were doing, Threadbare fell into line behind them. That was what she wanted? Maybe?

Celia giggled. "Okay. For'ard Marsh!"

The little group set off down the well-worn path through the pines, heading down the hill. Soon the trees thinned, and the sound of trickling water filled the forest air. Trickling water, then something more.

Celia stopped as pine cones crunched in the distance, and glanced down to Threadbare. "Hold still, okay? We uh, we might have to run quick if I'm wrong about this."

There, at the base of the treeline where the hill met the riverbank, moved a patchwork figure in loose brown leathers, furs, and clothes. Haphazard cloth covered it from head to toe, and its lumpy head was entirely covered by a brown sack with holes cut in it. Straw poked out of one hole, and from holes in its mismatched gloves, thorny vines twitched and coiled.

"Hello Raggedy Man!" Celia waved. The Raggedy Man gave her a long look, then surveyed the party. Its gaze stopped, when it looked down at Threadbare.

Threadbare looked back. He did what he'd saw Celia do, when someone approached her from the woods, and waved.

"Uh-oh," Celia whispered, as the Raggedy Man tottered three steps closer. It swayed straight-backed, as things under its coat rippled and writhed.

But then, it simply turned and walked back to the treeline, resuming its patrol.

"Daddy made them. The Raggedy Men keep monsters and bad people out," Celia explained as she scooped up Threadbare. "I didn't know if he'd think you were an intruder, like Emmett did. I think it goes by how big things are. I mean, I've seen Raccoons and Raccant's up on the hill, but the deer stay away. So I guess you're small enough it doesn't care." She headed out into the sunlight.

Threadbare goggled, at the rushing river in front of him. So much water! Wait, she wasn't going to wash him again, was she? Threadbare turned in her arms, and gave her a suspicious look, pointing to the river then at himself.

Celia seemed to understand his concern.

CHA +1

"What? No, you don't need a bath. And if you fell in there you might drown! Well I guess you wouldn't do that but you'd get swept away. But come on, we've got a ways to go and if we don't hurry and spy on them they'll be done talking before we get there."

Threadbare nodded. Celia hurried on, following the curve of the river out of sight from the house. As she went, flickers of silver motion caught the little bear's eyes. Something was in the river, something that blended in well against the foam and rocks.

PER +1

Threadbare had no concept of fish, but that's what they were. And something in him stirred, told him that he should probably try to grab some of those. He squirmed in Celia's arms.

"What? You want me to put you down? Okay."

Celia turned away, heading back down the river. The rest of the toys followed.

And Threadbare, with no obligation to follow, toddled over to the river to investigate those silver flashy things.

"Threadbare? What are you—"

It would have probably been fine, if Threadbare hadn't hit the slick mud that the Raggedy Man's path had worn into the banks, and thoroughly blown his agility check.

"Threadbare!"

He slipped on the mud, skidded into the river, and instantly the current grabbed him up, bouncing him off rocks and whipping him downstream!

Red '0's and '1's drifted up as he careened from stone to stone, arms flailing, trying to get some traction. And mostly failing.

He did manage, for a few seconds, to flail against the current.

Your actions have unlocked the generic skill: Swim!

Your Swim skill is now level 1

Celia's cries receded behind him, his body got more and more sluggish as it got waterlogged. The surface receded away from him, as the river started to spill out into the deeper waters at the base of the hill, and the sun vanished as he sank into the muddy depths...

...and a crimson-nailed hand, much bigger than Celia's own hand, darted down into the water and scooped him out.

The world blurred, and Threadbare found himself lifted up, water pouring from his seams, staring at a strange woman's face. Any human who looked upon it would have called it beautiful... not a single blemish on the skin, perfectly symmetrical. Black lipstick covered tiny lips, and large, almond-shaped eyes surveyed the tiny bear from bedraggled foot to soggy head. Straight, long black hair blew in the breeze, as light as feathers.

But those eyes were ice, and they held as much emotion in them as the Raggedy Man's eyesockets had.

"Threadbare, come back! Whoa—"

Threadbare twisted in the woman's hand, and looked over at Celia. She'd skidded to a stop, so quickly that her toy retinue slammed into the back of her feet. With a squeak, she went head over heels backward. "Ouch!"

The woman approached, swinging Threadbare easily. "I think you lost this," she said, in a low, warm voice. It seemed to resonate somehow, and made Threadbare think of good things. It was a comfy voice, and it brought to mind the tea parties with Celia, the hugs, and the purrs of Pulsivar as the cat groomed him.

Curious, he sniffed the woman.

PER +1

Your Scents and Sensibility skill is now level 4!

And he was very surprised to find that she didn't smell like a human at all. She smelled like that weird, spicy scent he sometimes caught around the windows of the house.

"Uh... thank... you? Who are you?" Celia tried to scramble up, tripped over the knight, fell to her knee again. "I, wait, you're a stranger. I'm not supposed to—"

The woman bent and swept back her green cloak, offering a perfectly manicured hand. Celia took it, and with effortless strength she hauled the little girl to her feet, before tucking the teddy bear into Celia's arms.

"It's all right Celia, you can talk to me."

A pressure in Threadbare's skull, just a brief one, as the words whispered of warm days in the sun, and the lovely quiet of night in a warm bed, and—

WILL +1

Your Magic Resistance skill is now level 4!

—and suddenly her tone changed. It sounded different. Kind of... smug? Like Pulsivar's purrs sounded when he was sitting atop the wardrobe and Threadbare tried to join him, but just couldn't climb the side of it. Threadbare, puzzled, burrowed into Celia's arms.

But Celia didn't seem to notice the shift. "How do you know my name?"

The woman smoothed her hands down her green cloak, and the traveling leathers under it that hugged her voluptuous figure. "I don't have time to go into details, but I knew your mother."

"You knew..." Celia frowned. "How?"

"It's too long to go into detail here. Let's just say your Daddy made some choices, and... cut ties with my employer. We think he made the wrong choice, but he doesn't listen."

Celia snorted. "Yeah, he's bad at that."

The woman shot a glance downriver. "I have a lot to tell you. You've got a choice to make, Celia, and it's going to make a lot of difference. But we just don't have time right now. I can't approach openly, because Caradon's going to attack me if I turn up. And if we scare him, he might kidnap you and vanish. Like he did last time."

"Kidnap? Wait, what?"

The woman reached out and smoothed Celia's frizzy hair. "But I've got a solution. We can talk here at the base of the hill, if we can fool those walking scarecrows into ignoring me." She glanced upriver, at the shambling, brown-coated golem still a kilometer distant. "It's almost on us. Here, the quest should sum it up."

And words filled Threadbare's vision, once more.

ANISE LAYD'I HAS OFFERED A PUBLIC QUEST!

DETAILS: BRING HER THE GOLEM CONTROL SCROLLS FROM YOUR HOUSE

 REWARD: 500 EXPERIENCE

COMPLETION: DROP THEM OFF AT THE CHEST HIDDEN IN THE DEAD TREE TWO MILES DOWNRIVER

DO YOU WANT TO ACCEPT THIS QUEST? Y/N?

Annoyed at how they blocked his vision, just when something really interesting was about to happen, Threadbare sighed and thought "Yes!" as hard as he could. The words went away, and he could see again.

But Celia frowned. She took a step back from the woman. And her eyes went wide as an idea struck, and her intelligence, for the first time in a long while, rose by one.

"How did you know about those scrolls?"

"What?"

"Have you been spying on us? Those scrolls are a secret, even to Mister Mordecai."

"Well, it just makes sense. Caradon's an enchanter and a golemist, of course he'd—"

Celia backed off further. "No. No, I won't. He told me never to take them out of the house. And I don't know you. You could be a monster in disguise." The orbiting dagger suddenly snapped around to put itself between her and the strange woman, and the toys formed a line in front of her, paws and hands and mitts raised. Threadbare, realizing the tension, slipped out of Celia's arms and spread his own paws wide, like he'd faced the rats in the cellar.

The woman sighed, and massaged her face with her hand. "Celia. I'm not your enemy. But fine, I understand. I won't ask you to disobey your... Daddy." She glanced up and smiled, showing perfect teeth. "Amelia would have been proud of you." She gave one more look over

Celia's shoulder, frowned as the raggedy man in the distance switched from marching to running, making a bee-line toward the obvious intruder. "It's not perfect, but maybe we can have a talk later. As long as you don't tell Caradon."

"I'm not going to make any promises."

"It's in your own interest, to keep it secret. If he learns of me he'll take you away from everything you know. Everything you ever grew up with." The woman sighed. "I'll be out here again in one week. If you want to talk, find an excuse to come out and play. Goodbye, my dear." And the woman turned and fled across the river, hopping nimbly from rock to rock, despite the high traveling boots she wore.

The raggedy man slowed as it watched her go. Celia stared after her with a mix of emotions, confusion warring with caution, warring with curiosity.

She looked down to Threadbare, and knelt down beside the little teddy bear, put her hand on his shoulder. Threadbare looked back.

"Do you think she was telling the truth? About knowing Mommy?"

Threadbare looked her over carefully. She had that look that seemed to want reassurance. He knew how to handle that, and nodded.

"She didn't seem to mean me harm." Celia sighed. "I'm not giving her the scrolls, but maybe we can talk. And if she tries anything funny you'll help defend me, right?"

Threadbare nodded again. Celia smiled and swept him into a hug, standing up to watch the woman disappear into the forest on the other side of the river, her traveling cloak blending into the underbrush. Behind Celia, the Raggedy Man resumed its patrol, neither taking note of the intruder it had routed or caring. Its orders had been fulfilled. Back to its job.

Celia put Threadbare down, and gestured upriver. "Okay. Let's try this again. Follow me and don't go in the river!" Celia pointed at the river, at Threadbare, and shook her head, sending red frizzy hair whipping everywhere.

Threadbare got the message.

PER +1

Not that he'd go back in that river if he could help it, that thing would surely kill him if he tried.

WIS +1

Celia started back downriver again, hurrying to make up for lost time, glancing back every now and then to make sure that Theadbare was keeping up.

He was, but it was kind of tough going. He'd never had to walk across this sort of varied terrain before, and as the trail broke away from the river and went up another hill, he was having to struggle with fallen branches, steep grades, and loose footing, things that were very troublesome for a small toy.

AGL +1

AGL +1

Your Climb Skill is now level 5!

But he managed, even if he did fall behind a little bit.

And then his nose picked up a familiar, troubling odor.

Your Scents and Sensibility skill is now level 5!

Blood.

Slowing, he turned right, pushing through the underbrush to a small clearing on the hillside.

And the gutted fawn carcass, lying broken in the middle of a small tree, weighing it down. Dried blood dyed the spring flowers under it.

"Threadbare?" Celia whispered, from up the hill. This close to the house, she didn't dare call out, for fear of drawing Mordecai's attention.

Threadbare moved in to examine the carcass, completely failing his perception check as the branches overhead rustled...

CHAPTER 5: WHERE EAGLES BEAR

At the minute, Celia shouldn't have worried about drawing the old scout's notice. Caradon and Mordecai were in the middle of a weighty discussion. The most troubling news was done with, and they were on to more pleasant topic of discussion. Even if this topic was vexing in a way all its own.

"I'm running out of ways to stall her," Caradon confessed, staring at the bottle of rum he'd dug out of the hiding spot in his study. "She's asking more and more questions, and not taking because I say so as an answer any more."

"Figured the day was gonna come. Takes after Amelia, that one does." Mordecai held over a tin cup, accepted the splash of rum with a tip of his hat. "What level is she up to now? Eight? Ten?"

"Five."

Mordecai squinted at him, and leaned forward in his chair. "Why?"

Caradon sat down heavily, with his back to the woods. "What do you mean?"

"Me youngest is nine, and he's stompin' around at level six. Celia's got two years on'im."

Caradon scowled. "Yes, but we're not like you, we can't run around as we want. We're trapped up here, so long as he's alive we can't risk leaving."

"Mm. Maybe so." Mordecai tilted back. "She asked me to teach her to be a scout again."

Caradon rolled his eyes. "Dear gods. No, of course."

"She ent gonna be satisfied wi' just one job, Caradon."

"And if I let her go after every adventuring job she wants, she'll fill up her choices before we know it, without the one we need. Then we'll all be sunk. You know the stakes, Mordecai."

"I do, but..." Mordecai finished his rum. "Scout's good fer passin' unnoticed. Good fer seein' danger, and escapin' it. Veeeerrrrry useful skills, wi' how the kingdom is right now. Verrrrry useful."

"And absolutely no synergy with her animator job."

"So what? It'd help 'er get more well rounded. Gi' her a few wisdom boosts, that's good for sanity too. And hells, if I ever figure out how to unlock ranger, I'll share the trick wi' her. And you knows what a second tier job can do, mister Golemist."

"What it should be able to do," Caradon corrected, swirling his own rum in a glass tumbler, and staring at it moodily. "Research isn't going so well. I should have a way to make golems sentient by now. I don't. Every test fails, they don't come out right. When the time comes, if we don't have our army—"

"About that." Mordecai looked at the empty tin cup, and turned it upside down on the table. "She's gonna have to meet more people. Learn how to get along with'em. Polish her charisma till it shines, if you want this fing to work."

"Gods." Caradon rubbed his eyes. "Too risky. Too risky by half."

"Nah, lessn' you fink. Dye her hair, mud up her face, take 'er into town as me apprentice from a family out in the hills, won't nobody bat an eye."

"Mordecai, I don't want to hear it."

"Then you sure as hell won't wanna hear this. Right now she's eleven. In a year or two she'll get her woman's blood. And if you fink she's restless now, what d'ya fink she'll be like then?"

The silence stretched. Caradon closed his eyes, and sunk back into his chair.

Mordecai broke it. "I'll teach'er woodlore, get'er some practice in a safe space that won't kill her, so she can level up. Start 'er off spendin' time wiff me lads, learning how to be around boys wivvout the downside of puberty muddlin' er head and loins. And then, once I'm sure she can handle it, I'll take'er to the town. She has to learn people, Caradon, if we want to win. She has to learn people."

Caradon studied Mordecai for a long minute. Then he smiled. "And while you're at it, you'll introduce her around to the other leaders as well. Let them get a look at her, to settle their worries. To show them that I'm not the crazy old hermit who's forgotten about our cause, up in the hills alone in his workshop."

Mordecai coughed into his hand, and had the grace to look guilty. "There's been talk, Caradon. This last round of purges at the Capital... things are gettin' tight. People gettin' worried. I know you, I ent worried, but they... people talk."

Caradon rubbed his head. "This would give me more time for my research, without having to worry about her. I hate to admit it, but she is a distraction."

"All kids are. Ever parent needs a li'l time off." Mordecai grinned. "Benefit o' being a scout, ya get plenty, out in the wild spaces."

"Your wife's a damned saint, Mordecai."

"Shaman, actually."

"You know what I mean."

"Is saint even a thing?"

"I don't know. Maybe cleric blended with oracle, but I've no idea how people qualify for that unlock."

"Here's to us that ent saints. Not sorry to not make that cut." Mordecai raised his cup, and frowned. "Ah, empty."

"Bottle's dry," Caradon sighed, rubbing his hand through his wispy gray hair.

"I brought some a' the good stuff this load. Lemme go get it." Mordecai rose and went inside...

...and not ten seconds later, Caradon glanced over as a large bird, easily as big as a human, shrieked with a deafening wail and burst out of the trees with its prey clutched in its claws.

"A Screaming Eagle? Hunting this close to my land?" Caradon frowned, and finished his tumbler. "Have to check the perimeter later, make sure the Raggedy Men are doing their jobs."

From this distance, with his perception, he had no way to see that the Eagle wasn't clutching its usual prey.

Still, it wasn't an uncommon occurrence, so at the minute he thought little of it. After all, the Wintersgate mountains had always been home to eagles.

Long before the world changed, almost forty years ago, they were there, hunting and breeding along the spine of the continent, and roosting among the cliffs and towering trees, far from civilization. Even when civilization crept in and they found themselves hunted for the prestige of their feathers, they were too well-established to truly be threatened.

Then the world shifted, but for the most part, their lot remained the same. They kept clear of the bigger predators, struck down intruding aerial predators and prey with swift, terrible strikes, and remained overall the most common apex aerial predator in the region.

But as the years rolled on and the eagles slowly leveled up, inevitably, some of them started reaching their maximum ranks.

As far as scouts, shamans, and other people who studied nature and beasts knew, the Eagle job had three rank-up options.

The first option was that of a Golden Eagle. Found mainly in areas where seams of gold were common, or treasure was simply lying about near or in its nest, the golden eagles had dazzling light-based attacks, and a hard, armorlike skin. They gave up some maneuverability in flight, but could hit like a falling comet if they got a proper diving strike off. Golden eagles were uncommon but sometimes seen in these hills, often followed by prospectors looking for their nest and the nearby seams or hunters who thought they could take one down and make a killing from their feathers.

The second option was Totem Eagle, usually only found where certain monster tribes or human cultures worshipped eagle spirits or a related pantheon. They could deliver blessings unto the faithful, call down rain, and had raw perception boosts that were unmatched in the monster kingdom. At least for most in their level range, anyway. There weren't any Totem Eagles in the Wintersgate mountains. The cultures that could produce them lived far from here, or had died out in the region long ago.

The third option was Screaming Eagle, and they were pretty much everywhere in the mountains. They were eagles who had focused on their "Piercing Cry" skill and used it at every hunting opportunity.

Like, oh, the one that had come up twenty seconds ago.

This particular screaming eagle had nabbed the fawn from its mother up slope, as they strayed out of the treeline foraging. Its piercing cry had gone unnoticed by the residents of the home nearby, as had the falling deer as it bashed its life out on a high rock above, then bounced to land in a clearing only one hill away from the structure. The eagle didn't care, and had feasted from it. It was a fat creature, and the eagle had returned today to finish eating. Carrion wasn't its first choice, but it hadn't found many other options in the last twenty hours, and it was hungry.

So when the appetizing little furry morsel had toddled straight into the clearing, the eagle did what it always did. Emitted a piercing scream, watched the green seven and "Stun" float up above its head, then dived in and scooped the prey up.

From Threadbare's perception, one second he'd been staring up at an unfamiliar corpse, the next second a sound ripped through his ears and he was reeling, he'd lost a chunk of sanity, and then by the time he could move again, some bizarre creature was carrying him off. Off and up.

He hadn't even known you could GO up. It didn't seem right, somehow. So he turned his face from Celia's pale, panicked visage and looked up at the bird carrying him.

Silver feathers mixed with white, on a form that was shaped roughly like an arrow. Its wings were double-jointed, and beat the air with a whistling shriek. A sharp, serrated beak crowned a feathered head, with no visible neck. A series of smaller-beaks, currently shut, lined its torso.

Blood stained its beak. The same blood smell as the deer, Threadbare realized. Then his button eyes shifted to the wings. Those were the reason it was flying, he realized, as they flapped above his head and he felt the wind shift by with staggering force. The songbirds he saw through the windows had wings too, and this must be how things flew. No wings, no flight, no matter how many times he'd tried to jump off the bed in hopes he could fly like the birds.

Well, at least he could stop doing that, now.

INT +1

Perhaps, like so much of his existence-to-date, this was all just a big misunderstanding? Threadbare hugged the eagle's claws.

The eagle didn't spare him a glance. But its claws moved back, ripping into the bear's hide, sending a red '4' floating into the air, and falling away in the slipstream.

Nope, no misunderstanding. Threadbare drew his arms back, called up his own claws, and whacked the eagle right back! Surprised, the bird's grip loosened, and Threadbare dropped through the trees, hitting every branch on the way down before bouncing off a rock, so hard that one of his button eyes cracked.

But he had no bones to break, or organs to damage, and as he sat up amidst a floating red '11', he eyed the words in front of his face with a bemused stare.

Your Golem Body skill is now level 5!
Your Toughness skill is now level 6!
Max HP +2

He still couldn't read the squiggles, but he was starting to remember the shape of some of them. And these shapes in particular always turned up when his body was getting beaten up. He wished they'd turn up less, but hey, at least this had ended well. Threadbare toddled to his feet, and started looking around for Celia.

Then that scream came from above again, and ten more sanity went poof.

You have been affected by piercing scream!

But this time, it was slightly different.

Your golem body renders you immune to stun!

His head ached terribly, but unlike the last time, he could still move. Could still think. So when the eagle came howling down at him again, all of its beaks open, Threadbare rolled to the side.

AGL +1
Your actions have unlocked the generic skill: Dodge!

Your Dodge skill is now level 1!

The eagle's claws closed on air, and it swept by, flapping its wings furiously as it pulled up.

Threadbare ran over and grabbed the biggest branch he could find, hefting it with a strength out of proportion to his twelve-inch tall body. He waved it around a few times, hoping the eagle got the message.

But sadly, the eagle's intelligence was far worse than his own. The bird pulled up, reversed, and hovered in an action thoroughly unbelievable for its ten-foot wingspan.

Threadbare watched as the creature's chest inflated, beaks clamped tightly shut, and he had one slim moment to wonder why it was doing that—

—and then it SCREAMED.

All of its beaks slammed open in unison, as the vents on the eagle's back drew in deep breaths of air, slamming them through its mighty lungs to unleash solid sound on the offending prey.

The skill was called Raptor's Racket, and this wasn't one that the eagle used for hunting. Which was good news, since it hadn't practiced and leveled up this skill to its maximum, like it had the piercing scream.

The downside was that this skill was designed for defense, and it was, simply, designed to HURT.

Threadbare found himself flying, fetching up against a tree, as the sound thundered around and through him, and a great red '29' floated up into the sky.

CON +1

Your Toughness skill is now level 7!

Max HP +2

Fur shredded, stuffing blew out of the holes and gaps in him, and seconds later when the blast ended, Threadbare fell to the ground, wondering what the heck he'd done to deserve this.

The eagle, tired from its rarely-used skill, flapped to the ground and stalked over, torso-beaks once again shut, studying the twitching form.

Threadbare watched it come, and racked his brain for ideas. This thing was like Pulsivar, it pounced and killed small things. But Pulsivar didn't care about things that weren't moving, so maybe Threadbare could stop moving, and the Eagle would go away?

INT +1

He tried it out.

But the eagle's perception was far, far more advanced than the bear's poor agility, and Threadbare thoroughly failed to be convincing.

With a rapid, shuffling stride the eagle half-flapped, half hopped forward, and lashed out with his head. He did have a neck, it was just buried in the feathers and skin of his shoulders and wings, and it strained as he bit into the bear and tore, gashing Threadbare open and sending him flying down the hillside. Threadbare rolled to a stop, feeling more and more of his body going unresponsive. He wasn't sure how hurt he was, but he knew he didn't have much more to go.

He stood up, looking around. A small hollow, a crumbling log, and pines all around. He could run, could maybe find someplace to shelter. Maybe.

But no. The thing would just hunt him down. This was a good enough place to die.

WILL +1

The eagle burst up from the treetops, glaring around and acquiring him immediately. The bird looped back and prepared another dive as Threadbare hauled up the biggest branch he could find, staggering and feeling his remaining stitches start to go, as the twelve-pound branch weighed down upon him.

STR +1

The bird screamed, and more of his sanity fled, but he drew the branch back and waited, waited for the moment as the bird dove...

...and veered off, as a red-haired form ran up through the trees down slope.

"**MEND!**" Celia shouted, puffing and panting.

You heal 17 points!

Celia's toys pattered downslope, having fallen far behind, and the eagle, thoroughly annoyed, took note of the smaller prey, dismissed it. Too small for the amount of energy and effort it had expended.

The little girl, on the other hand, didn't look like she weighed much more than that fawn from yesterday.

So while she shouted her mending spell, over and over again, the eagle switched targets and screamed, watching the green number drift up...

...but this particular prey resisted the 'stun' effect.

For Celia was an animator, and on top of that her willpower had been honed by years of arguing with her father. She turned, saw it coming, and her animated dagger lashed out. The eagle evaded, hastily, coming within a few feet of the ground as he swerved—

—and met Threadbare's heavy club head-on.

THWACK!

Your Clubs and Maces skill is now level 7!

The pine branch broke, Threadbare staggered back, but the makeshift club and mighty swing had done its job.

The great bird crashed to the ground, a red '13' floating up, surprised and hurting for the first time in a very long while. It struggled to its pinions and claws—

—only to be swarmed by the five animated toys, bashing and thumping with their magically-hardened extremities. Boosted by Celia's magic, '4's and '5's floated up as the creature screeched and turned, backing up until it had both the girl and the toys in its arc. Its beaks snapped open again, the unseen vents on its back below its feathers drew in air...

...and Threadbare dove forward, shoving Celia out of the way as the bird screamed once more, throwing the toys across the clearing and over a small rise, sending Threadbare tumbling, mended rips tearing open again, catching ahold just barely of a low-hanging tree branch, and riding out the storm.

The eagle fell silent, gasping. It felt its blood running down its chest, felt its head pound. Its moxie was drained, its hunger forgotten as the toll the toys had taken registered on its nerves.

Then, motion. Celia sat up, glaring, and pulled two more daggers from the sheaths under her coat, tossing them into the air. **"Animus Blade! Animus Blade!"** They joined their steely brother, orienting toward the eagle as she pointed at him.

On the other side of the clearing, Threadbare dropped from his branch, stood up, and spread his torn arms, meeting the eagle's disbelieving eyes with a black-buttoned glare.

Following an impulse, the bear thumped his chest with an arm, and pointed at the bird. Then down.

This time, the message was received.

CHA +1

Faced with a foe who could take whatever he could dish out, and those weird, dancing blades that really shouldn't be moving like they were, the eagle flapped until he was sky-borne, and whirled to head up slope.

The rising arrow caught him in the rump, tore through the mostly-hollow part of his chest, exited through one shoulder, and ended his life in a microsecond.

From below, Threadbare and Celia watched as a red '182' rose above the falling corpse of the bird.

Then the girl and her bear looked backward, to where the trees rustled. Barely a second's warning, then a brown flash of leather, as Mordecai bounded from branch to branch, landing in a crouch, whipping an arrow from under his coat as it flared back revealing four quivers bandolier-style across his body, and nocking the shaft as he tracked the falling eagle. After it hit the treeline he nodded, straightening up and letting the bow go slack. "Sorry," he offered. "Not tryin' to steal yer kill. S'why I waited till I was sure it'd escaped—"

He broke off, as Celia glomped him. She wailed, crying into his coat, and he sighed, dropping the arrow and hoisting her up, adjusting her arms until he could slide the bow away. He bent down to scoop the arrow up...

...and found Threadbare there, offering it to him with both hands.

Mordecai blinked. Then he nodded down at the little toy.

The teddy bear nodded back.

Mordecai took the arrow and juggled Celia, sliding it back into its quiver. "Sh, sh, sh. That's right. Sh, yer safe." He had to watch his movements, as the three daggers she'd animated orbited around her, taking a slightly wider route to go around Mordecai as well. It was unnerving, to tell the truth, but the old scout ignored it as best he could.

"I was so scared," Celia whispered, but the scout's sharp ears caught it.

"Why?" Mordecai said.

"What?"

"Why? Were you afraid it'd kill yer?"

"No. I mean, I was, but... I was afraid it would kill Threadbare."

"Threadbare. That yer little bear down there?"

Celia shifted in his arms, looked at the teddy bear. "He was so brave."

The bear, somewhat annoyed at being left out of the cuddle puddle, stretched its arms upward.

"Oh, he's still all torn up. Ah..." She sniffed. **"Status."** Then she winced. "Oh. No, no, my sanity's a wreck. I spent way too much today, I can't heal him any more."

"S'all right," Mordecai said. "Cavalry's comin'."

And indeed, heavy iron footsteps echoed through the forest, as Caradon charged up the hill, breathing heavily, with Emmet the armor golem right on his heels. Branches broke against Emmet's form as he lumbered through them, feet grinding heavily into the pine needles and soft soil, sending sprays of detritus to the rear.

"Celia!" Caradon shouted, and she barely had time to blink before Mordecai deposited her into the old man's arms.

"I'll just find them toys you lost, eh?" Mordecai asked. "Be hard for any but a trained scout, eh?" He gave Caradon a knowing look. Then he was gone, slipping into the shadows of the pines.

"Daddy?" Celia asked, her voice very small as she smushed her face against Caradon's chest. "Can you please mend Threadbare?"

The old man looked down at the teddy bear, stretching its arms up for a hug, smeared with pine needles and mud, torn nearly to shreds.

For a second he wanted to punt the damned thing down the hill. He didn't know how, but he was sure the little golem was at fault, somehow.

But only for a second. It was Celia's prized possession, after all.

Besides, even torn to hell and back, it was still bizarrely cute. And while objectively he knew that it was all due to its Adorable skill, the truth of the matter was that he wasn't immune to it, nor did he mind so much.

Threadbare watched as letters rolled by.

Your Adorable Skill is level 7!

Caradon sighed and released Celia. **"Mend Golem,"** he told it, simply. The bear had earned those battle wounds honestly, defending the little girl. It was the least he could do.

You have been healed for 202 points!

Threadbare shuddered, as golden light pulsed through him, bringing him back instantly to full health. It really was overkill, though not as much as the old man thought.

"I'm okay," Celia told her father, scooping up Threadbare. "The Eagle didn't hurt me. Threadbare saved me when it screamed. He pushed me out of the way."

"Must have been a small Screamer then," Caradon said, remembering the teddy bear's pathetic hit points. "Well. That's over with."

"It wasn't all bad. I... I skilled up in mend for the first time in a long time. And got some intelligence and willpower, and agility, and constitution... and, I kind of lost track, I'm sorry. Uh, no, wait, some Animus skill too. Wow, a lot of skill." She studied the air for a second, then shook her head.

"Yes. That was because you were in a real fight, with real consequences," Caradon said, taking her hand. "Are you sure you're all right?"

"Yes." She blinked, as realization struck. "Is that what I'm going to have to do? To get more levels? I'm going to have to keep doing... that... again?"

"Yes," Caradon said, feeling every second of his fifty-eight years weighing down on him. "Yes it is."

Celia turned and vomited on the pine needles. Caradon let her go, then held his hand down once she was done. "I'm sorry. But this is the world we live in. It is what it is, now."

The little girl took it, and hugged Threadbare tight with her free arm. Then she took a deep breath, and looked to her bear, and back to her old man. "If this is what it takes to protect Threadbare, and you, and everyone I don't care. I'll fight a dozen times or a hundred or whatever, so he doesn't have to. I won't let any monsters or anything get him! Or anyone else!"

Deep in the woods, perched on a hollow log with the remnants of the toys sitting beside him, Mordecai took a puff on his pipe and smiled to himself. He'd heard every word of the conversation from a quarter-mile away, and more importantly, he'd heard the spirit in her voice. There was hope after all, he thought.

"Well, let's get back home," Caradon said, draping his arm around her shoulders. "That's quite enough adventure for one day."

"Okay. Yeah, okay." Celia spat to the side. "I need a drink of water."

"Easy to do. Come along, Emmet."

The mighty armor golem fell in behind them, as Threadbare's family picked their way back down toward the home. A few steps in, Caradon cleared his throat. "I've been thinking."

"Yeah?"

"Are you serious about learning to be a scout?"

"Oh heck yeah? Did you see that thing with the arrow? Where he shot the Eagle out of the sky? It was like POW, and then that was the most damage I've ever seen in my life! Well aside from when Emmet punched that raccoon who was hissing at you on the porch that time. I want to learn how to do THAT!"

"Ah, technically that's an archer trick, Mordecai's good with that job too."

"Can I learn that?"

"We'll see how you do with scout. There's a test they go through, and it involves a spending a few days in the wild alone..."

The voices faded into the trees. Behind them, Mordecai chuckled and took his own path back to the house, giving Caradon and his daughter time to themselves.

And in the deep woods, the imp faded into view, crouched among the pine needles and grinning. "So the little girl's leaving the house for the first time ever. Oh, this'll make things much, much easier. Anise is going to laugh her tits off when she hears this one—"

Twenty-five pounds of the gods' perfect killing machine crashed down on the imp.

Before he could react, Pulsivar the cat grabbed the demon's throat and slashed his claws on the target below, rending its shrieking form into shreds.

FINALLY, it had caught that annoying weird bird which taunted it from the windows. It had been worth it, following its sulfurous trail from the house when his hoomin had rushed off into the woods. Now vengeance was Pulsivar's, and no more would the little thing be annoying.

To the cat's annoyance, it faded into smoke and puffed away, before he could even eat it. Even in death, the thing taunted him. Pulsivar groomed himself, pissed on the pine needles where its stench lingered, and waddled off back to the house, keeping a weather eye on the skies.

There were eagles out. One had to be cautious, after all

CHAPTER 6: DOES A BEAR SIT IN THE WOODS

Threadbare never left Celia's sight for the rest of the day, even when she bathed. Which was weird, because he hadn't known that her clothes could come off. (She'd been too shy to change in front of him before and he had never been in Caradon's bedroom, so he had just thought that humans could shapeshift.) But now everything made more sense, and it explained why she and Caradon looked different every day. That was worth an intelligence point.

And later, as he rested in her arms, cared for and loved after a long day of playing and hugging, his reverie was interrupted by a chime. His Toy Golem level had reached six, and once again, he felt a little better in every way.

The next morning, he found that he could follow Celia and Caradon's conversation a bit better. "Yes" and "No" made a lot more sense, he caught the occasional one or two-syllable word, and he practiced nodding and shaking his head at appropriate times. His charisma ticked up a few times when Celia talked with him, but Caradon scarcely took notice... the old man was too busy assembling a quick lesson.

Dusty books came out of the study, as did a notepad, and Caradon showed Celia pictures of trees, plants, and animals, and made her read and copy down words from the books.

And Threadbare stood there stunned, as he realized that hey, those words on the papers matched the squiggles he kept seeing in front of his face.

INT +1

There it was! There it was again! That was the one that meant he could think more easily! The squiggles MEANT something!

INT +1

In fact, those letters were on the page too, just usually not in the order that they were in his vision. Fascinated, he watched Celia write. It had never occurred to him that you could draw pictures of what the words you saw looked like!

INT +1

Gleefully he reached out for a quill—

—and toppled ink across Celia's notes.

"Threadbare! Be more careful." She scooped him up before the spreading puddle could stain him. Caradon sighed, and got water and rags.

"In any case, I think this is enough for now." Caradon glanced at the sun's angle through the windows. "He'll be here soon. So I suppose I should do this formally..." He finished scrubbing, then sat down in his chair.

Once more, words scrolled across Threadbare's vision, then stopped.

CARADON GEARHART HAS OFFERED A PUBLIC QUEST!

DETAILS: GO WITH MISTER MORDECAI TO OBLIVION POINT AND FOLLOW HIS INSTRUCTIONS

REWARD: 1000 EXPERIENCE

COMPLETION: RETURN TO CARADON FOR REWARD

DO YOU WANT TO ACCEPT THIS QUEST? Y/N?

"One thousand experience?" Celia's already pale skin went paler. "Daddy, are you sure?"

"Positive."

"Then yes." Celia beamed. "And thank you."

Threadbare's mind worked overtime. Now that he knew the words meant something, he thought that he might want to know what they said. But he didn't know how to read them, like Celia and Caradon did. Maybe if he copied what they looked like his family could read them?

INT +1

He reached out for the quill again... and Celia pulled him away, again. "No Mister bear, that's quite enough of that, I'm sorry."

Fine, fine. Threadbare sulked a bit, crossing his arms like Celia did when she and her Daddy argued, and Caradon snorted laughter. "You're teaching him bad habits." He teased.

"Normally he's not this fussy."

Grudgingly accepting the fact that he couldn't try his idea right now, Threadbare sighed, and thought "Yes". The squiggles-that-weren't-just-squiggles disappeared.

Half an hour later, a knock came on the door. Celia answered it, and gave Mordecai a happy hug.

Caradon just looked him over, rubbing his goatee. "Run silent," he greeted his old friend.

"Run deep. Ya ready, Celia girl?"

"I am!" Celia gestured at her pack, about half the size of her.

Mordecai winced. "Give that 'ere." He sorted through it without mercy, ignoring her wails as he pulled stuff free and sat it on the dinner table. "No... no... no..." He pulled out Beanarella the doll and looked to Caradon.

"Yes on those."

"Guess you'll need some backup. Yes, then."

Practically dancing on the balls of her feet, Celia reached for the doll. "Okay, just let me animate her—"

"Nah."

"No? Then what's the point of bringing her?"

"I seen how yer animated toys move. Where we're going, they'll just slow you down. If you need 'em break 'em out. Otherwise keep them in tha pack."

"I can carry them."

"You ent gonna carry that one?" Mordecai pointed at Threadbare, who pointed back.

Your Adorable skill is now level 8!

The old scout fought to keep his face straight.

"...yeah I'm gonna carry him." Was Celia's subdued reply.

"Good." Mordecai cinched up the much smaller pack, ignoring the books, writing supplies, snacks, changes of clothes, and rock collections that Celia had lined up for the trip, leaving all those behind on the table. "Here yer go. Come on. Gi' yer Daddy a hug and let's be off."

Threadbare found himself smushed between Celia and Caradon, and then it was out the door and off through the woods.

"So where are we going? The quest says Oblivion Point," Celia said, following Mordecai's even, long strides as he strolled through the pine bluff.

"Tha's where. Ya never heard of it?"

"No. It sounds... dangerous?" There was just a hint of excitement in her tone. Mordecai chuckled.

"Only if ya get really stupid. And I know you ent stupid."

"Oh that's a relief. So Daddy showed me a book today, and I learned how to tell trees apart, and—"

Mordecai stopped, turned on her, knelt down to her level, and put his finger on her lips. "Shhh."

"Buh-what?" She froze, staring at him with hurt eyes.

"Look around, Celia girl." Mordecai's voice went low. "Do you know this place?"

She did. "It's the pines. Just a hill or two over. I think, right? I've lost track."

"Yeah. Tha's why yer here. Scouts don't lose track. Scouts look and remember. Can you do that?"

"I... oh. Oh, sure!"

"Scouts also know to keep quiet when they're in strange lands. So things don't know they're coming. Can you do that?"

Celia opened her mouth, and he shushed her again. Instead, she nodded, and he smiled for the first time since he'd turned around. "Good. Come. If you have to speak, keep it quiet and short."

She followed him, chastened, but with excitement growing in her chest. She was going to be a scout!

So instead of talking, the little girl held Threadbare tight... except when they came to a steeper grade, and she had to put him down to clamber on all fours. The bear followed, doing pretty well as he went.

AGL +1

Your Climb skill is level 6!

They moved through the pines and down into a small valley, filled with rambling streams, wildflowers, and different sorts of trees.

"Oak," Celia whispered to Threadbare as they went. "Sycamore," she named another, as they passed it, leaves just starting to grow from its buds. "Willow," she pointed at a mass of tangled branches over one of the creeks they splashed through. And though the old scout's ears twitched under his hat at her every whisper, he tolerated it. This was good. He'd have less to explain, later on.

Then it was back uphill, up a rocky slope, to where a moss-green boulder jutted out over the path they'd just taken. "C'mere," Mordecai said, scrambling up. "We can talk up 'ere. Time for a break."

Celia nodded. She'd long since stopped whispering, conserving her breath for puffing and panting as she climbed. "I just... got... a con up," she said, dropping to her rump and dangling her legs over the edge of the boulder.

"Good. You'll get more afore the day's through. We're a quarter of the way there."

"What?" Celia's jaw dropped. "I, I need a snack! My stamina's way down! There's no way I'll make it all the way there with what I've got."

"Yes, you will." Mordecai sat down next to her, pointing across the way. "See over the little culvert of woods we just came through?"

"Yeah. It looks so small, but it seemed so big while we were in it."

"Now stand up and look over it."

Celia did, and blinked. "Is... is that our house over there?"

"Yeah. Only two miles off."

"It looks so small. And I just got a perception up."

Threadbare caught most of that, and he turned in her arms, trying to see.

He DID see the house!

PER +1

But he turned too quickly, and wiggled right free of Celia's grasp! He tumbled toward the slope below as Celia shrieked—

—And Mordecai's hand shot out like lightning, snagged him, and deposited him back on the boulder.

LUCK +1

"Careful there. Don't wanna lose yer toys."

"Oh! He's so naughty sometimes!" Celia backed away from the edge, knelt, and picked up the trembling bear. "Oh, he's frightened. Come here." She hugged him, and Mordecai chuckled.

"Anyway, that's why yer out here. Eleven years old and ya never been two miles from yer house. We're gunna fix that, today. And you're gonna rake in bonuses you ent seen in a long while, unless I miss my guess. You're worried you can't do it, because every time before when you lost stamina you went and ate to get it back. And you didn't bring no food."

"No. You took it out of my pack!"

"So yer gonna rest here and get it back the old-fashioned way."

"But that takes so long…"

"What else are ya gonna do?" Mordecai shrugged. "Scouts have to travel hungry, sometimes. Key there is to pace yerself. You don't not have the option of going where you need to go."

Celia parsed the sentence, then looked at him. "Okay. Fine. Whatever." She flopped down, and played with Threadbare, but eventually, the vista got to her. It really was a nice view, and she found herself staring off in the distance, watching the birds, following the leaping forms of deer from afar, and studying the river as it wound on its way.

Then she blinked. "I just leveled up?"

"Weren't an animator level, was it?"

"No. How'd you know that? It was a human level. I haven't gotten a race level since… wow."

"Humans are built to wander. S'called exploration experience. Like a built in quest wi'out words. The more you explore, the more you see, the higher ya get. Key is followin' yer instincts. Ya do that, then the better a human ya are." Mordecai frowned. "A course, sometimes it's bad if you foller your instincts. Got ta find a balance. Use yer intelligence AND yer wisdom. Like me wife. Level nine half-orc, she is, and couldn't be happier. Mostly cause she's got wisdom ta match her strength."

"I don't have any jobs that get wisdom boosts. Well, human does, I guess."

"A little bit. But Scout gets more." Mordecai stood. "And now since ya leveled up, yer stamina's full again, ya?"

"It is." She rose, and stretched her legs. "I'm ready!"

Three hills over, he took her to the peak, pointed at the tallest oak tree he could find, and made her tell him all about it. He seemed pleased with her assessment. Threadbare was more interested in the busy beehive that churned up in its branches. But Celia held him tight, and it was a bit far away from her, anyway.

One valley later, Mordecai's eyes went wide, and he whipped a hand up. "Monsters," he whispered.

Celia instantly started pulling out her daggers, and he shook his head. "I got this. Come along an' stay quiet."

He led her through some young trees, past stumps and corroded metal bars set into the ground. And there, at the base of a solid stony cliff, lay a series of planks nailed across a cave heading back into the mountain. A few crumbled, rusted metal carts lay scattered nearby. Obviously it was one of the abandoned mine shafts that her Daddy had told her about.

Two strange creatures patrolled back and forth in front of the mine. They had black and gray and white fur, bushy tails, and each one wore a crude wooden mask. The one to the left had one that said "KITY" and a crude caricature of Pulsivar's face. The other one had a mask that looked like no creature Threadbare had ever said before, and had the word "DOGY" scratched into it.

"Wait here. Do NOT move, **Camouflage**," Mordecai said, and then he was gone, blurring into an outline before the blur itself moved away and vanished in the afternoon haze.

Threadbare had understood that sentence, up until the last word. But the rest of it was simple, and it made sense for the situation.

INT +1

So he froze. Celia froze too, but her breath came a little heavier, and one hand crept inside her coat to where she kept her knives.

Minutes crawled by, and then Mordecai crawled up, reappearing. He pointed at Celia, pointed back the way they came, and straightened up, heading back through the underbrush. Celia followed, glad to be away from the monsters.

Once away, they resumed their walk. Finally, Mordecai gestured a halt, at the base of the tallest, steepest hill yet. "We can talk. Those were Raccants."

"Raccants? I think I heard Daddy swearing about those once. They're what raccoons can become, right?"

"One o' the options. They're raccoons what like livin' around humans. They see how easy pets got it and want to be pets, but they can't pull it off. Just ain't got the temperament. So they wears masks and nicks stuff and causes trouble."

"So what are they doing here?"

"There's a steading or two just on th' other side o' the ridge. An' yer father's house ent far. They roam. As to what they're doin' here, they made a dungeon."

"What?" Celia almost shrieked, then clapped her hands over her mouth. "Dungeons are bad!"

"Aye, they can be, if ya let'em go. But this one's small yet. Figure it'll take a few years before it even reaches a level where ya'd find it a challenge. So fer now, it can stay."

"But shouldn't we take care of it? You and me, we could stop it from being a threat."

"Celia." Mordecai knelt to stare into her eyes. "Everyfing has a purpose. Dungeons have a purpose. And raccants ent likely ta kill, not like some o' the other monsters out here. Time goes on, it'll make treasure, too. Be a good trainin' ground, and source of loot."

"But... I mean..."

"Not all monsters is bad. Some just *is*. And bad or good, this'll be a good spot fer ya to level up later." He straightened up, and cast a gaze up the cliff. "Come on. One mile left ta go, and it's the worst part."

Two hours later, as dusk fell, Celia clambered up the last slope, and stared wide-eyed at what lay in front of her.

It was nothing at all.

Literally, nothing at all.

Around her she could see a high mountain plateau, with snow melting and forming a pool, that ran off into a small waterfall she'd passed on the way up. A few straggly pines grew up here, but nothing else.

But on the other side of the mountain?

Nothing. Blackness so deep that light seemed to vanish into it. It filled the horizon, wrapped around with a visible curve, and literally bisected mountains to either side.

"What is that?" She whispered.

"Oblivion Point," Mordecai told her. "Easiest place around here ta see the evidence of our stupidity."

"I never heard of this."

"It's not somefing to be proud of. Not as I count it, anyway." He sat on a rock, next to an old fire ring, long burnt-out and now filled with snowy ashes. "Yer Daddy tell you how we got afraid, when the changes hit? Started losing settlements?"

"Yes. But not much further. We were interrupted." She pulled Threadbare out of the back where she'd stowed him, and sat him down. and walked toward the pit, with the little toy golem following. They pulled up their own rocks, eyes staring into the nothing.

Threadbare had no idea what it could be, but he wasn't about to leave Celia's side, so he figured it could stay over there and he'd stay over here, and that would be fine.

Mordecai spoke again. "So the king at the time, he gets the notion that we need to seal off our kingdom. Cut ourself off from the madness. He goes to the high wizard, th' oldest member o' the Seven."

"The Seven?"

"Tell yer about them later." Mordecai coughed. "Much later. Anyways, Grissle, the high wizard, spends years figurin' out the spell. Then he gives it a try." Mordecai scowled, and hucked a pebble into the void. It disappeared without a trace. "And damn his eyes, it works. Sort of. Nothin' goes out a' Cylvania. Nothin' comes in. But we didn't know that the trouble was already in here, sealed in wi' us."

"How does it work? I mean… does it kill anyone who tries?"

"No. Yes. Nobody knows. Knew a man once, swore up and down that the farther you go in there, the weirder it gets. Said that you go far enough, you start seein' numbers. Nothin' but numbers. And he said that if you do that, you turn and get back as fast as you can, or you start turnin' INTO numbers." Mordecai shook his head.

"Is that man a friend of yours?" Celia asked.

"Don't matter. One day he went in and didn't come back. Which is what happens ta most who go in there." Mordecai shrugged. "The wizard's gone, too. His labs under Castle Cylvania are a dungeon now, the most dangerous one left in this sealed-off little land. If there's any way to fix it, it's lost forever."

Celia shuddered. Then she clapped her hands with glee as Mordecai pulled out several plants he'd foraged, and a pair of rabbits he'd hunted on the way up.

He showed her how to build a fire, striking a steel knife against a flint stone, and how to dress and clean rabbits. Threadbare watched, fascinated, gaining a point of wisdom as he learned that living things could be disassembled too.

Mordecai also showed her how to build a bed of branches and pine needles, sheltering it out of the wind and close enough to the fire that it'd hold a little heat. And as she slept he sat across from the fire, looking at her, then around, keeping watch.

She was tired by then, and never thought to question why he didn't make one for himself.

Threadbare didn't sleep. And as he lay in Celia's arms, he watched Mordecai take out a piece of paper and dig out a stick from the fire. The old scout scratched the stick against the paper, leaving charcoal letters. Then he stuck his knife through it, stuck it into a nearby tree, and hung his waterskin from the knife's handle.

The bear stirred, and Mordecai caught it. "Stay still, Mister Bear. This is her test, savvy?"

Threadbare didn't know what a savvy was, but he understood most of the rest. So he nodded.

CHA +1

Mordecai nodded back, and vanished into the night.

And when Celia woke up in the morning, he was long gone.

Threadbare watched as Celia woke. She didn't panic when she saw Mordecai was gone. And she didn't burst into tears, which is what Threadbare thought she was going to do.

She gulped air a few times, rubbed her face, and retied her frizzy hair into a braid, plucking out pine needles that remained from last night. Threadbare helped with that, managing to get a few out with much effort.

DEX +1

After he was done, Celia sat on the rock, next to the smoldering remnants of the fire, and stared at the knife in the tree.

"I'm afraid," she told Threadbare. "I'm afraid of what that note says."

Threadbare tried to understand. He didn't think the note was saying anything right now. It was pretty quiet up here, except for the wind howling across the slope below.

"If I open it up, and it says I've failed, and I shouldn't bother, then I'll never be a scout. And I really, really want to be a scout. I want to show Mister Mordecai and Daddy that I'm strong enough to do something on my own, with only a little help. Just some help learning, that's all." She swallowed. "But if it tells me I've failed, then I don't know what I'll do."

Threadbare hugged her.

CHA +1

"Oh, I'll still have you, of course. I'll always have you. That won't ever change." She beamed down at him, and ruffled his head. He leaned into it, like he'd seen Pulsivar do now and again.

Your Adorable skill is now Level 9!

Celia shook her head. "You always know how to cheer me up. And..." She bit her lip, as she looked back to the note. "On the other hand," Celia said, staring at the note with hope so raw even the bear picked up on it, "If he says I've passed, then this is everything I ever wanted. I mean, out of this trip, anyway. But it could say either. And I don't know which one it says. And I won't until I go and read that note."

The wind howled, then faded.

"And I'm afraid of it, and I don't want to, because so long as I'm sitting here and the note's unread then it's not telling me what I'm afraid it'll tell me. It's stupid and it's cowardly but that's how I feel right now."

Threadbare curled into her arms. She looked down at him, then back up at the note, and her face scrunched up. "Oh to... to hell with it." She clapped her hand over her mouth, then looked around, and giggled. "To hell with it! No one out here to hear me say that! Let's go read that fu—" training, discipline, and a lifetime of manner lessons warred with the exhilarating freedom of being finally out of earshot of anyone who cared, but a lifetime of good manners proved too hard to break. "—fumping. Yes, that fumping note. Let's go read it."

And before the little girl could lose her nerve, she tugged the knife free of the tree (it took a few tries and a strength increase), let the waterskin fall, pulled the paper away from the blade, and read it with her hands all-a-tremble.

Celia's whoops of joy echoed around the mountaintop. "Yes! Yes! Whooo-hoo, yes! Look, look!" She said, thrusting the paper down to Threadbare.

Threadbare took it.

And instantly more squig— more WORDS appeared.

MORDECAI SKUNKTHUMPER HAS OFFERED YOU A TIMED QUEST!

    DETAILS: GO HOME BEFORE TIME RUNS OUT
    DEADLINE: 42 HOURS 32 MINUTES
    REWARD: YOU WILL UNLOCK THE SCOUT JOB
    COMPLETION: RETURN TO YOUR HOUSE TO QUALIFY
    DO YOU WANT TO ACCEPT THIS QUEST? Y?N?

Threadbare looked at the words, tried to peer around them to the note, couldn't quite do it.

Wait, Mordecai had written last night, using the charcoal stick like a quill, hadn't he? There were sticks a plenty in the coals. Threadbare could easily grab one and copy the words he saw onto this handy piece of parchment...

    INT +1

But the stick burned the parchment as he touched it to the paper.

"Threadbare!" She tugged it from his hands, and shook it out. Then reconsidered. "We probably should burn this. Even though it's a timed quest, the quest is tied to the paper. So if the Raccants come up here and grab it they might come to my house and be scouts, and I don't want either of those things to happen." She shuddered. "Invisible little furry monsters. Horrible notion, huh?"

The little furry toy golem thought "Yes", and nodded his head up and down as soon as the words disappeared.

"We've got two days. We reached this place in one. It should be easy to get back, right?"

Threadbare considered. He understood most of what Celia said. But this place was very new to him, and he had no clue where home was from here. So he shook his head instead.

"Don't worry, I think I can do it. I have a really good memory. Animators get good intelligence boosts each level. But uh..." her stomach rumbled. "First we need breakfast. Did ah, did he leave us any food?" She looked around the camp hopefully. No food presented itself. Even the bones and offal from their baked coney skewers was gone. "Maybe he hid it. As a test. You go that way, I'll go this way." Celia started poking around through the little grove of trees.

Threadbare followed her suggestion, and went hunting around the tiny plateau. There wasn't much up here, really. A few drifts of snow, the copse of trees that Celia had slept in, and that little pond.

That little pond did have those silvery things swimming around in it. Threadbare gave a nervous glance toward the stream that trickled from the pond to the waterfall, but it was pretty tiny.

He looked left. He looked right. And then he gave into his instincts, and waded into the shallow pond.

The salmon were young, recently spawned, and exhausted from hatching. In another day they would have worked up the strength to navigate the lip of the rocks between pond and stream, and made their way down the waterfall. As it was, they had no hope of dodging the fuzzy creature that waded into them, claws flashing out left and right. He wasn't very dextrous but they were pretty tightly packed; it was a target-rich environment.

STR +1
Your Claw Swipes skill is now level 6!
Your Forage skill is now level 2!
Your Forage skill is now level 3!
Critical Hit!
LUCK +1
Your Forage skill is now level 4!
You have unlocked the Grizzly job! Level up to meet rank requirements!
You are now a level 3 Bear!
CON +3

STR +3
WIS +3
Armor +3
Endurance +3
Mental Fortitude +3

Threadbare paused, hip deep in the now-bloody water, as that good feeling rippled through him again. His stamina, drained from claw swipes filled up once more, and he felt a rightness to it, a satisfaction that he couldn't put his finger on.

Then fingers wrapped around him. "Threadbare! What did you... oh." Celia said, looking at the five small fish drifting on the surface of the water. "Oh! Breakfast! Thank you!"

Twenty minutes later, with the stoked fire drying him out and the fish sizzling on makeshift skewers, Celia's eyes opened wide. "I just unlocked the Cook job. What should I do?"

Threadbare looked at her. What was a cook? What was a job? He shrugged.

"Is this all it takes to unlock that job? No wonder Daddy never let me cook." She bit her lip. "There's only so many jobs you can learn, and I know that the adventuring ones and the profession ones are different. I'm a human so I can learn up to three profession jobs without cutting into the adventuring ones. But..." She sighed. "No. No I won't be a cook right now. If I change my mind I can select it from my status screen, I think. Status!" She checked. "Yes, we're good." She hauled the salmon skewers, slightly charred, out of the fire and ate them. "Ugh. Well, it's better than nothing. Thank you Threadbare!" She ruffled his soggy head.

Once he was dry and the salmon were consumed, the sticks and bones were hurled into the Oblivion to dispose of them. Celia and Threadbare started down the mountain, with Threadbare poking out of the top of her pack, watching as she carefully climbed down the steep slope, backing down and moving from handhold to handhold.

It worked pretty well until her foot slipped. She managed to catch herself but the sudden jolt threw Threadbare out of the pack, and rolling madly down the cliff.

She shrieked, as he banged off of one rock after another, and wound up at the treeline, caught up in a tangle of thorny bushes and down a few hit points.

He sat up with more annoyance than anything else, and tried to pull himself free.

And the bush pulled back.

Gropevines were a hazard in this region, even in the highest mountains. They usually subsisted on all sorts of birds, small animals, and even bugs. They were also attributed all sorts of questionable actions and had a lurid reputation that was entirely out of keeping with their motivations and modus operandi. All they wanted to do to people was rip them up with thorns and strangle them, it's not like they were weird about it.

All of this was lost on Threadbare, as the bush opened up to reveal masses of vines, long thorns, and two clusters of white and black berries that looked like eyes. The bear glowered at his attacker, and drew back his hand for a swipe—

—and promptly got a dagger stuck through it as one fell bladefirst into his paw.

The little bear and his viny foe looked at it. Then they both looked up, ignoring the red '3' that floated away from them.

"Oops! Oh no! Uh, sorry, I was aiming for right next to you. Just use that to fight it!" Celia shouted from above. "I'll be down as fast as I can! Hang in there!"

Threadbare pulled the dagger out of his paw, looked at the vines trying to wrap around him, and got to slashing. He'd seen how Celia had used the knife to gut the fish, so that was probably how it worked, right?

INT +1

Well, he tried, anyway. The vines were all thorny and covered in bark, and he was pretty clumsy with the blade. It was more like a sword to him, not that he knew what those were.

Fortunately, his armor was more than enough to ward off the worst of the vine's efforts. A few squeezes and 4 points of damage later, he got a good cut in.

Your actions have unlocked the generic skill: Dagger!
Your Dagger skill is now level 1!

The gropevine sizzled, sounding like the fish had as they fried on the fire, and swept Threadbare's legs out from under him with one quick sweep. Then it piled vine on vine, binding his arms, and trying to keep that blade from nicking it again...

...to no avail, as Threadbare twisted his dagger, snapping through the vines binding him. The little bear didn't look it, but he was about as strong as the average teenage human now, and the gropevine couldn't match his concentrated muscles.

STR +1
Your Dagger skill is now level 2!

Then more noise from above, as Celia reached a safe spot, yanked out her toys, animated and invited them into her party. They rained down from above, and waded into the gropevine, pummeling it relentlessly. The gropevine tried to peel its vines away from Threadbare to deal with the new threats, but Threadbare well-remembered the lesson of the rats and team-fighting with Pulsivar, down in the cellar.

INT +1

Threadbare dropped the dagger and pulled the vines to him, as many as he could get. With him tying up the enemy, his friends were free to beat it up with impunity.

Your Brawling skill is now level 9!

This allowed his toy allies to get past the exterior vines and attack the interior. It sizzled again as they laid into its vulnerable berries, then fell silent and limp, amidst a cloud of red numbers.

"Woohoo!" Celia shouted, from above. "Level Six!"

Threadbare let the vines drop, just as his little girl got to the bottom of the cliff, and ran up behind him. **"Mend!"**

You have been healed for 18 points!

She considered him. "Are you okay?"

Threadbare nodded, and offered her the dagger back.

"Why don't you keep it until we're back home," she said. "You always seem to end up in trouble way more than I do."

Threadbare shrugged, and rested the blade over his shoulder.

"I figured you'd be okay. Gropevines aren't that big a deal unless they're really big." Celia collected her toys. "But we should—"

A drum sounded in the distance. Celia froze, and peered into the trees.

"Threadbare?" She said, eventually, "Does that sound to you like a big raccant banging on a stolen bucket with a stick as it charges and leads seven other raccants this way?" She bent down and gathered up her toys as she spoke, stuffing them into her pack.

Threadbare looked up at her and shrugged.

"Well it should because that's what's coming towards us." She knelt and grabbed up the little bear, and ran for her life.

CHAPTER 7: RANDAHM ENCOUNTAHS

The Raccants chased Celia and Threadbare around the hills for the better part of a day. It had the side-benefit of unlocking Threadbare's generic stealth skill and raising it a few levels, but it was mostly an annoyance. From his safe haven of Celia's arms he waved his knife at any who got too close, and the little wooden-masked varmints steered clear.

At some point during the chase Threadbare unlocked the qualification for Black Bear, and got told he needed more experience. But he barely had time to notice it as he watched the pursuing monsters with fascination.

Celia, on the other hand, was terrified. The irony of it was that she shouldn't have been. Raccants were territorial creatures, but not aggressive. They were trying to scare her off from their claimed turf, that was all. Mind you, if she dropped any interesting trinkets or slowed down enough to the point where they could nick her pack, they would've in a heartbeat. But they wouldn't have hurt her. After all, maybe they could fool her into adopting them someday! Then they'd have easy lives…

But the chase went on far more than it should have, because Celia kept getting hopelessly lost, and turning back into their little valley. She was smart, and her perception wasn't lacking, but fear and exhaustion did a number on her, and she made mistakes.

Threadbare had a different sort of brain, one that… well, it did have fear, but it wasn't the same sort as most organic types knew. It was afraid of something bad happening to Celia, or to Daddy, or Pulsivar, but that was about it, really. He wasn't afraid for himself.

So when he noticed her turning around to pass the same boulder for the third time that day, he knew that they were going the wrong way.

PER +1

He tugged on her sleeve.

"Wh-wh-what?" Celia chattered, simultaneously drenched in sweat and cold from the chill air of the peaks.

Threadbare tugged on her sleeve again, and pointed with the dagger.

"That way? You're, huff, you're certain?"

Behind her a stick banged a bucket again, and she flinched. "That way it, ha, it is!" Exhausted, barely jogging, she set off past the boulder, and down a winding deer path that vanished into a mass of tangled scrub.

She didn't see the lone Raccant Chief heave a sigh of relief behind his BLLDOGY mask, and put away his bucket. Finally she'd gotten the message. He looked back to where he'd left his minions behind, and waddled back to find them. For a second he considered keeping a watch, to make sure she didn't come back. But then he decided against it. She'd gone down into *that* valley. She wouldn't be back.

Five minutes later, peering out at a slope full of dead trees, Celia knew she was well and truly lost. She turned to head back...

...and Threadbare stirred in her arms, shaking his head.

"No?"

Threadbare put the dagger under one arm, and covered his face, then pretended to drum an imaginary bucket.

"You're right. They haven't followed me down here. But they're probably waiting for me up top." Celia swallowed, and looked around. "I don't know where this is. I didn't see this place on the walk up." She swallowed. "And my throat's dry." She reached to her side, then froze. "I totally left Mister Mordecai's water skin up at Oblivion Point, didn't I?"

Threadbare nodded.

"Stupid. Stupid stupid stupid." She palmed her face.

Threadbare patted her arm. He'd forgotten about it too.

"Um. Well, finding water is totally a thing a scout would do. And Daddy's books said to only drink from moving streams and rivers. There's tons of little brooks all through these parts, we crossed enough of them. Just have to keep an eye out." The pair descended into the dead trees. Celia put Threadbare down after a bit, tired enough from even his small weight.

Eventually the slope evened out, but the dead trees didn't. Celia eyed the murky puddles of rainwater and cold marsh, that started to crop up but thought it best to find water elsewhere. It didn't look, oh what was the word... Patable? No, that wasn't it.

Dusk was coming on quickly. The light was fading, sun setting behind the western mountains.

So naturally, that's when she found the graveyard.

"Ohhh boy." Celia whispered, as she realized that the rows of rocks among the dead trees were actually tombstones. "Yeah, not drinking water here." Her voice was a rasp at this point, but she knew what graveyards meant, and there was no way she was drinking water that was anywhere near dead people.

Threadbare tottered over to one of the tombstones, and saw there were words carved into it. He squinted, but didn't see any that usually appeared when he did things. No, no wait, there was one.

Threadbare pointed at the stone. Celia came over and read it. "Here lies Axey Dent. Like most barbarians he shorted Int."

The little bear pondered, then looked at it again, trying to match up the symbols with the words she'd just said. He was close, he knew, so very very close...

"Okay, somebody's got a weird sense of humor," Celia said, still spooked.

Threadbare moved to the next stone, and checked it for words. Celia followed, reading as she went. "Here lies Sandra Schtupp. Pissed off a vampire, never looked up. Here lies Barry the Bold. Went into my mausoleum to get out of the cold. Here lies Dorothy Gunn. Looted my lair but failed to run."

Words started to repeat, here and there as she went, and Threadbare's mind expanded.

INT +1

Midway through the morbid recitals, Celia stopped, as a spreading look of horror crossed her face. "Oh. Oh no."

And from behind her, from the darkest part of the trees, she heard the slow, steady sound of leather smacking on leather, as someone clapped their gloved hands Trembling like a leaf, she turned...

...to see a girl just a bit shorter than her, leaning against a tree.

She looked about the same age as Celia, but even skinnier, with short brown hair covered by a polka-dotted green and purple bandanna. She had an apron very like Celia's daddy wore, only hers had hammers and chisels and measuring tape sticking out of it. She wore a sturdy pair of work boots on her feet, and had tough leather gloves on each hand. Short, poofy trousers and a simple bloodstained white shirt that was three sizes too big completed the picture.

"Finally, somewahn gets it!" The strange girl said with a nasal accent. "Good on yah! Four stahs! Now scram, kid, befahre I eat yah."

Celia shrieked, ran, tripped over a tombstone, struggled back up, ran back for Threadbare, scooped him back up, and ran.

The girl laughed hard, clutching her belly and doubling over. Then her belly grumbled "Mff. Your bad luck, I guess. Sorry kid, but mama's hangry." She straightened up, giving the tree next to her a pat. "Looks like yah're on the menu tonight-"

An arrow sprouted between her fingers, quivering in the tree trunk. The girl's eyes went wide. Two more arrows appeared in between her fingers.

"Oh. Ah. She's one a yours, then, Mordecah?"

Arrows sheeted down, tocking into the tree with rapid-fire precision, tracing out a word in feathers above her.

"YES"

"Raht. Raht. Message received. I'll play nahse."

Oblivious to what was happening behind her, Celia ran for her life... again. But the day's exertions had taken their toll on her, and she was losing steam rapidly. Also, it was very dark now, and she'd moved from the field of tombstones to the thickets beyond, and she was having trouble seeing her way through. "I... I have to rest. I need water," she told Threadbare, as she leaned against a tree, and panted. "I... need to find a place to sleep. Do you think we're far enough away from... from the... oh gods..."

Threadbare looked around, and saw nothing chasing them, so he nodded.

"Okay. Find a spot, and build a shelter to sleep in. Like Mister Mordecai showed us." She forged back upslope, until she saw the signs of pine trees just past the dead trunks. "Maybe this is the limits of the v.v..v... of her territory? I hope so. I can't take another step." She took another step, then six more, then knelt down and started gathering branches. They were well into twilight now, and the light was going. Threadbare helped as best he could, and aided her as she tied them together.

DEX +1

"Fire. I... undead hate fires, right? It should be safe." She pulled out the knife Mordecai had given her, and the chunks of flint she'd pocketed from his last demonstration. It took about twenty tries, but finally they got a small fire going, out of the wind, and at the mouth of the shelter. Celia curled into it and went out like a light, entirely exhausted.

Threadbare crawled in beside her, but hesitated. She said she'd needed water earlier, right? And she'd probably want more food, too.

But there was that other girl out there who had threatened Celia. No, the little teddy bear decided to stay. Anything could happen out here, and he didn't want something bad hurting Celia while she slept.

WIS +1

So a little while later, when the girl in the apron faded out of the shadows, pale skin gleaming in the firelight, Threadbare hauled out his dagger and put himself between Celia and the stranger.

"Relahx," the girl said, offering a bloodstained goat. "Here. This'll be good breakfast, yah?" She mopped her stained mouth with one free hand.

Threadbare tilted his head, then nodded. He assumed it would be. It was made of meat, after all, like the rabbits and fish had been.

"So she's an animahtah?"

Threadbare nodded again.

"You her pet?"

Threadbare considered the word. Then he walked over and petted Celia's tangled hair.

Your Adorable Skill is now level 10!

The girl laughed, showing really big fangs. "So she's yahr pet? Aw that's cute! Don't suppose I could steal you away from her, yah? Come live with me? Sleep in a really swanky stone cahffin all day, an' carve gravestahns all naht?"

An arrow flew past her ear, tweaking her bandanna just enough to catch her attention.

"Just an ideah, jeeze, keep ya trawsahs on old man."

Threadbare was shaking his head anyway. He looked to her, looked to Celia, and hugged Celia's form. His little girl drooled on him.

"Mm. Awraht. Well, if you go that way, ya'll come to tha big tree. Kind of a central point around here." The girl pointed.

Threadbare looked. Sure enough, there was something against the moon. It could be a really big tree.

"Just past thah's a rahck with a great view. Icewahn river's not fah north. Find tha river, there's roads beyond." She grinned. "I should know. Good huntin' on them. Lots a King's Gahds to eat."

Threadbarc shrugged. He'd never seen Celia eat any gahds so he couldn't say.

"Oh relax, they all have it cahmin. Things the King gets up ta, hells." The girl plopped down, and stared into the darkness. "I'm a monstah, I admit it, but he's got no excuse. I mean, who thinks summoning demons is a good idea?"

Threadbare shrugged.

"Yahr a good listenah, ya know that?"

CHA +1

Threadbare nodded. Idly, he sniffed at her, found her scent to be old blood and cold meat. Strange, and not human at all.

PER +1

Your Scents and Sensibility skill is now level 6!

"Wanna play some Grindluck?" She hauled out a deck of cards. "No stakes, dahn't warry."

Grindluck was a game taught to very young children. It pretty much did what it said, allowing them to get their luck up to the point that they could survive a walk outside without heavy armor, the best buffs available, and a small party of higher level relatives.

She taught him the game, and they played as the fire burned down. It was a fairly simple thing where you tried to match cards, and kept the cards you matched. It did indeed help his anemic luck, giving him four points worth as the hours passed.

The strange girl kept up a chatter as they went, talking about how she used to be a minion in a smaller dungeon, before it got busted up by the King's troops, and her master had gone and gotten splattered. She'd tried to blend into the local town, but it hadn't gone so well.

"Too many scouts. They can look at yah and see yahr status. Just like that. Well, the good ones can anyway. So I found my way out here. Lahts of folks don't look too hahd at strangers who mind their own business. I can even go into Taylah's Delve now and again. It's nahse. Lonely sometimes, but nahse." She sighed, and put her cards away, looking up at the moon. "Thought about making my own dungeon, but what's the point? Used ta be you made one, it was fun fahr the whole region. Brings in adventurers, tourists, falks who spend mahney. But nah the King's running tha show, yah gahtta have permits ta go into dungeons. Yah gahtta hand ovah all ya magic loot when ya get out. And if people staht cheating or if he feels like it he sends in tha troops, and they mine it out and break tha core. Where's tha fun in that?"

Threadbare examined her carefully, and shook his head.

CHA +1

"Raht. Ah'm glad we had this talk, mistah bahr." She ruffled his head, and reclaimed her cards. "Ya little gahl's lucky to have yah. Ya take care of her, aright?"

He nodded, and she faded into the shadows and away, as the first light started to appear on the horizon.

Finally, Celia stirred, as the dawn's light fell on her face. "Mfrafef. Feh? Fah!" She sat bolt upright, put her hand squarely on the bloody dead goat carcass, looked down at it, and screamed.

Five minutes later, after she'd calmed down, she started cleaning and dressing the goat. Well, trying to. Well, she got maybe a few pounds of usable meat off of it. Goats were way harder than rabbits, as it turned out.

"I'm still so thirsty," she croaked, her voice rattling around inside her throat like a stone in a bowl of dust. "Do you think there's any water around here?"

Threadbare wandered off into the trees, looking left and right. "Okay, just... don't go far," Celia croaked, trying to cook the goat without burning herself too badly. "This cook job is really tempting..."

It took about twenty minutes of searching, but eventually Threadbare found a small stream.

Your Forage skill is level 5!

But he didn't have any good way to bring the water back.

He thought about it for a bit, trying to scoop it up in his hands. It seemed an insurmountable problem, right until the point he remembered what happened to him every time he got soaked.

INT +1

The little bear flopped into the water, got himself good and soaked, and waddled back to the campfire, leaking with every step.

"Threadbare! What did you... oh. Oh, that works." Celia smiled. Then she picked up the little bear, put his knife to the side, and wrung out his limbs over her mouth, greedily gulping down the droplets that squirted out.

Being made of cloth had a few advantages, after all.

"Aw, your feet are all muddy. Sorry. Well, the rest of you's a little stained too. Daddy can clean you once we get home." She winced. "Nineteen hours left. I need to get a move on."

But it took half an hour more to cook and eat the goat meat. Then ten minutes for Threadbare to lead her to the little stream, so she could more properly drink her fill.

After that, he seemed pretty insistent on tugging her in one direction. "You're sure?" She measured the cliff ahead of her with her eyes. "We'll have to go around that, there's no way I can climb it."

He was insistent, nodding up and down over and over again.

So she followed him, and after quite a bit of walking, she found her way up to the top of the ridge where he was pointing, and looked to the northwest. "Waitaminute. I know that tree!"

It was indeed the tree that Mister Mordecai had her examine during their hike up. "I'm just seeing it from a different angle, that's all." She considered the rocky escarpment between herself and the tree. "It's a long way, but it's a clear shot. Come on, let's go!"

Three hours later, she sat at the base of the tree, looking up it.

Threadbare looked up it as well, button eyes held by the hypnotic patterns of the bees high up in its branches, hard at work making wildflower honey. And within him instinct stirred again.

"I don't think I can climb that, not as weak as I am," Celia told him. "But if you could climb up there and look—"

Before she could say another word the little bear scrambled up the trunk, fell down, scrambled back up, got twenty feet up, fell down, and got up for a third try.

Two climb skill level ups later, he got up to that tantalizing beehive.

"Threadbare! Just ignore it. Please go to the top and—"

The bees landed on him as he crept closer to it. He heard Celia's words, but he could no more look away than he could sprout wings and fly from the branches. Slowly, carefully, as the bees hummed and settled on him, stinging him with stingers that did absolutely nothing he crawled over to the hive and pushed his paw into the papery structure.

Your Forage skill is level 6!

He pulled free a dollop of angry bees and some sort of brown liquid that smelled divine, it smelled like nothing he had ever scented before, and while bees stung his button eyes he inhaled the scent, and slowly brought the goop to his mouth—

—only to pat against the cloth patch that served him as a tongue.

Nothing.

The teddy bear had the distinct feeling there should definitely be something going on there. He tried again, and the only thing that happened was that the bees got more pissed off.

With a shake of his head at the disappointment, Threadbare resumed his climb up the tree. Honey pulsed from the hole in the hive, dripping down. And Celia, for her part, shrugged and held out her hands, catching it and licking it eagerly off her palms. The bees weren't coming after her, and food was food out here. She'd burned a lot of energy walking this far, and this would keep her going. She checked her status as she ate, sighing as her stamina ticked back up after every slurp.

After a while, Threadbare crawled down. The bees had long ago given up trying to sting the weird little scavenger, and were concentrating on patching their hive, so that was all well and good.

"Did you see the rock? That was the next thing, that boulder you nearly fell from," Celia asked him.

Threadbare nodded, and pointed.

It took most of the rest of the day, but they made it back to the rock, and from there they could see the house, and retrace their path back. As night fell for the second time, Celia staggered into her front yard, hair sticky and stained with honey, pine needles, sweat, and dirt. Threadbare rode with his arms clamped around the back of her neck, sitting on her pack, knife stowed away so he didn't accidentally cut her.

And as Celia lurched up to the door and put her hands on it, words flickered into Threadbare's sight.

Go Home quest complete!

Congratulations! By becoming lost in the wilderness and finding your way home you have unlocked the Scout job!

Would you like to become a Scout at this time? y/n?

Threadbare read it. The long words didn't quite make sense, but he knew what scouts were. Scouts were Mordecai! He wanted to become a scout.

The words vanished, and instantly he felt better. And more words flashed by.

You are now a level 1 Scout!

AGL +3

PER +3

WIS +3

You have learned the Camouflage skill!

Your Camouflage skill is now level 1!

You have learned the Firestarter skill!

Your Firestarter skill is now level 1!

You have learned the Keen Eye skill!

Your Keen Eye skill is now level 1!

You have learned the Sturdy Back skill!

Your Sturdy Back skill is now level 1

You have learned the Wind's Whisper skill!

Your Wind's Whisper skill is now level 1!

And if his eyes could open any wider, they would have.

Celia, her stamina refilled, jumped straight into the air and almost banged her head on the porch. "Yes! Wow, yes yes yes!"

The door opened, and Caradon stood there, smiling. "I am so, so very proud of you."

"I followed Mister Mordecai's instructions!" Celia beamed, dirty as she'd ever been, with some fried goat tendon sticking out between her teeth.

"Yes, you did. That's the quest complete then. Take this, you've earned it."

Do What Mister Mordecai Says Quest Complete!

You have gained 1000 experience

Threadbare looked on in amazement, as everything got more awesome.

You are now a level 7 Toy Golem!

+2 to all attributes

You are now a level 2 Ruler!

CHA +3

LUCK +3

WIS +3

You are now a level 2 Scout!
AGL +3
PER +3
WIS +3

He looked at his paws, flexed the muscles of his stuffing. Yes. Yes, this was good. Quests did this? Quests were good, then!

For his part, Caradon hesitated. "Two thousand experience? What…" He shook his head. "Getting senile. Must have upped it a bit."

"What was that, Daddy?"

"Nothing, nothing. Come on in. Dinner first or… no, bath first, I think. Mordecai's already here, but no dinner for him. He'll be asleep for a day or so."

"What? Why?"

"It's a trick they have at higher levels, to delay sleeping. Here, let's get you clean. Ah, him first."

One quick Clean and Press on Threadbare later, and he was left to his own devices, downstairs. That was fine. He thought that maybe, just maybe, he could try to write something now.

He remembered seeing paper in the study, so he wandered that way. And sure enough there was paper, and there were plenty of ink quills and parchments…

…but more interestingly, one of the books on the desk glowed with a strange, shiny light.

Threadbare opened it. It was the hollow book with the scrolls, and they were glowing. Vaguely remembering something about these, he picked them up, and instantly a chime sounded, in his head.

More words appeared, and FINALLY, he was smart enough to read them all.

Step one of help Anise Layd'I complete!
Take the scrolls to the hidden chest downriver!

Oh right, right, that thing she'd asked Celia to do, before Celia got mad at the lady for some reason.

Well, it was a quest, right? Quests were good.

He shut the book and put it back neatly like Celia had taught him. Then the little bear toddled out the open back door, hopped down from the porch, and set out toward the river.

They found him in the yard after a frantic search four hours later, muddy, quite battered from having to shank another gropevine on the way, and a bit worse for the wear, but he seemed happy.

After all, why shouldn't he be? He was five hundred experience and another bear level richer!

CHAPTER 8: A WILDLING BROOD

The wind stirred the trees, as the hills fell behind in the distance. A squirrel poked its head out of a bole in a large ash tree, peered around. Seeing nothing, it began the descent, ready for another day's foraging.

"That one," someone whispered, and the squirrel froze—

—then promptly ran for its life as a rock smacked into the tree behind it, knocking loose a bit of bark. With a flash it was gone, back into the bole, chattering its head off.

"Aw," Celia whined, lowering her slingshot.

"Ya tried, ya missed. No sense fussin' about it. C'mon then." Mordecai nodded, and ambled off back to the trail. Celia followed, casting glances back at the squirrel-filled bole. Behind them both, Threadbare trotted, his arms full of smooth stones. Not enough to increase his strength, sadly. But he was alright with being Celia's ammo bearer.

Besides, carrying them around seemed to be slowly increasing his newly-gained "Sturdy Back" skill. It almost seemed like they got a little lighter every time the skill ticked up.

"I don't see how this counts as a thrown weapon," Celia eyed the slingshot. Newly crafted from leather and fresh stretchweed on a wooden stock, it had been Mordecai's gift for her for passing his test. "I mean, I guess you make a throwing motion when you use it."

"Actually ya don't. All yer work's in the pullback, after tha it's a clean release. Ya just do a little nudge. Let the straps do the work. Hsst!" He held up his hand. Celia stopped, for about the tenth time since they'd set out that morning, right before dawn. Threadbare stopped too, and barely managed to keep from spilling the stones all over.

DEX +1

"What?" Celia whispered.

"You tell me."

Celia frowned, then muttered **"Keen Eye."** Blinking a few times, she stared in the direction Mordecai was looking. "Is there something behind the blue jay?"

"Nah. Blue Jay's yer target."

"You want me to kill a songbird?" Celia's voice rose.

"Keep it down. Jays ent songbirds. They're jerks what beats up and drives off songbirds. And they sound horrible."

Celia's lips twisted. Finally she nodded, reached down, and grabbed one of the stones from Threadbare's pile. Carefully she drew it back in the slingshot, aimed, and took a breath.

SNAP!

"AWK!"

The bird fell, broken, and Celia whooped! "Yay! Level seven! It IS a thrown weapon!" Then she fell silent, as she watched blue feathers drift down. "Um."

"Good." Mordecai clapped her on the back. "Normally I'd teach yer to prop'ly harvest the feathers, but yer Daddy tells me ya want to wait on learning new crafting jobs."

"I... yes." She rubbed her face, still looking at the bird's corpse, her smile fading. "After we found Threadbare last night we had a talk. He taught me Enchanter and Tailor. That means I only have four adventuring jobs left that I can choose and uh..."

"Two."

"Two crafting jobs left." She swallowed. "One of them will probably have to be smith, if I want to— If I want to follow in Mom and Dad's footsteps."

"Because of Emmet?"

"Yeah. And more like him, someday. So I'll probably need Tinker too, like Mom had. So I don't have a lot of room to learn more stuff."

Mordecai nodded. "Smart. Wise, y'might say." He grinned at her, as he shinnied up the tree the Jay had fallen from, and scooped a nest from where it had been hiding in the crook of a branch.

"Wait, I just killed a mama bird?" Celia looked stricken.

"Yah. And got us lunch." He retrieved the bird's corpse.

"But... but..."

"But what?" Mordecai pointed at the bark. "Still got yer sight up, yah?"

"Yah. I mean yes."

"See 'ere?"

She squinted. "Clawmarks, really small ones... and I just skilled up

Eagle Eye."

Oooh! Threadbare looked at the tree too, and saw nothing. He tried thinking eagle eye as hard as he could, but nothing happened. And with no mouth, he couldn't say it, either. This was a problem he'd have to fix at some point.

"These are ferret clawmarks. Kinder old. Prolly before the nest was here. Unless the ferret's dead, it'd be back and it'd eat the eggs an' prolly the jay too, most likely. If we didn't eat it now, it would later. This is how nature works. Ya want ta eat, ya got ta hunt. We ent got enough time ta harvest veggies on tha way fer this trip. We eat meat an' eggs or we go hungry."

Celia looked down, searching her soul, trying to get over the fact she'd just killed a momma and was about to eat her babies...

...and was betrayed by her treacherous belly, as it grumbled. It had been a long walk through new territory, and she was hungry. "I'm a scout now," she told herself.

Threadbare nodded so hard his ears flapped, and stones spilled to the ground. The pair of humans looked his way and chuckled.

Your Adorable skill is now level 11!

"Come on. Get some practice wi' Firestarter," Mordecai clapped her back.

One small meal later, as Celia tried hard not to think about the bird embryos she'd just eaten, Mordecai explained. "Firestarter does wot it says. Jus' means ya don't have ta mess with flints, so long as ya got wood or tinder or anything burnable. Also costs only five endurance, so ya can do it ennytime more or less no matter how wiped ya are. Keen Eye's for seein' things from a distance, sharpens yer perception up nice. Sturdy Back's why you ain't griping about yer pack. Camouflage blends you in wiff tha surroundings. Costly, eats up a bit o' sanity fer every minute, but ya got that to spare, especially you bein' an animator."

Celia nodded. "And Wind's Whisper?"

"Focus," Mordecai said. "Think Wind's Whisper Mordecai as hard as you can, an' move yer mouth like yer talkin'. Like yer sayin' the words, but don't put air behind them."

Celia tilted her head, then her lips danced as she mimed speech. Her eyes went wide.

"Ya said I'm a jay murderer," Mordecai smirked. "Yah?"

"Yes."

"Well 'ere's what I says to that," Mordecai's mouth twitched, and Celia glared at him.

"What do you mean you're just my accomplice?"

"You 'eard me."

"I did."

"That's 'cause I thought 'Wind's Whisper Celia', and pretended to whisper my words."

Threadbare, watching all this, realized that he'd finally, finally caught a break! He could finally talk to Celia!

Wind's Whisper Celia, the little bear thought, and then he moved...

...nothing, because he didn't have lips. Or a mouth that wasn't a stitched on piece of cloth. Aggravated, he slumped to the ground.

"Does this work anywhere?" Celia asked.

"Ya got a skill up, right?"

"Yeah, it's level two now. **Status**." Celia blinked. "Oh, that cost a little sanity. Not much..."

"The more ya level it, the further out ya can be heard. Too far out beyond yer level, an' ya start getting hard ta hear. Gets garbled, words get lost. Figger yer prolly limited ta a few hundred feet 'till ya hit level ten. Level thirty gets ya up ta a mile or so."

"Wow," Celia blinked. Then her eyes moistened over. "I can whisper to Daddy while I'm away."

"Eh... we're too far out from him, where we're going. Sorry. We usually sends little golem birds back an' forth."

"So THAT'S what they're for!" Celia raised her hands. "I asked him and he wouldn't tell me! He's got a whole hutch of those things, and they come and go and I never found out why." She frowned. "Wait, why would he need a dozen of them to talk with you?"

"Ah..." Mordecai shifted. "I ain't the only one he talks with." His eyes flickered, and his face darkened. "Though I reckon a lot of his friends up north ain't gonner be talkin' much wi' him no more."

"What?"

"Nevermind. Anyway, come on, time ta dig a hole."

"What? Why?"

"Ya always bury the trash an' bones an' bits. Makes ya harder ta track. Keeps random necromancers from animatin' bird skellies."

"Wait, that's really a thing?"

"Eh, ain't likely ta run into many out here, but ya always get oiks poke their noses in where they shouldn't. Best to keep 'em from temptation. But first..." Mordecai scooped up the bird's head, tugging it free from its body. "**Bonestripper,**" he told it, and tossed away a palmful of bloody meat and brains, leaving only a clean white skull, with beak attached.

"Um. Ew." But Celia's curiosity warred with her disgust, and won. "What was that?"

"Tanner trick. Gets stuff off the bones cleanly. Intact if you cares about it, which I dunt right now."

"Why do you need the skull?"

"Let's just call it a present an' leave it at that." He grinned, and tossed it up and down.

Once the remnants of lunch were buried, and Celia had a pocket full of blue and white feathers and mixed feelings about the whole affair, Mordecai led her onward. Threadbare followed close behind, thinking furiously.

The smarter he got, the more he realized that he'd need a way to talk to people. Or just talk in general. There were all these neat things that people could do that he thought he could do too, if he understood jobs and skills and ideas correctly, but a lot of them seemed to require talking. No mouth, no speech. He'd thought writing would work out, but boy howdy, did humans ever seem to be annoyed whenever he tried to write. So he'd given that up, at least for the minute. Maybe he'd find a good opportunity later to sneak some paper and a quill and experiment. Or a charcoal stick or whatever.

But his sulk didn't last through the whole trip. He saw new territory, mostly woods and fields and meadows, sprinkled among the hills. His perception ticked up a few times, and that sturdy back skill did as well, topping out at Level five. The rocks were as light as they'd ever get, he realized, passing his wisdom check. Maybe something heavier would raise it?

Then the trio crested a small bluff, and Celia gasped. "What's that?"

"Tha's Taylor's Delve." Mordecai gestured to the town, sat on a trio of large hills overlooking a pass between two of the largest mountains. "Mining town. Used ta be a trade town too, but the caravans got nowhere ta go since the Oblivion sealed the South."

"I mean, I saw the smoke, but I thought it was a camp or something..." Smoke did pour out of the place, from foundries and houses and other, larger buildings scattered throughout. Celia shivered, as she looked the place over. It had more people than she'd ever imagined! Why, there had to be at least thirty people out and moving around between the sturdy wooden and stone buildings!

"Get a good look, then c'mon. That ent where we're going today."

"Oh." Celia felt a fluttering sense of relief. That was a lot of people, a whole lot for someone who'd seen three other people in her whole life before. Well, four if you counted the vampire, though she rather thought monsters didn't count.

And Threadbare of course, but he was a golem, so technically a monster. She spared him a glance back, and he waved, dropping half his rocks.

"Go ahead an' drop them," Mordecai told the little bear. He did so, scattering them on the slope and dusting his paws. "No more slingshot practice fer now," Mordecai nodded to Celia. "Ya got the way of it, ya can practice on yer own time."

"Okay-dokay. Where to now?" Celia smiled, and tucked the slingshot into her coat.

"Home." Mordecai pulled the jay's cleaned skull out of his pocket, studied it, and replaced it. "Gonna be good times later. Oh, an' carry Threadbare from here. Tell him ta stay still fer now."

The trio headed back down the bluff, and back into the hills across from the pass, following the trail back into a small hollow. They passed shacks and small houses as they went, half of them boarded up and clearly empty, but others had livestock outside, or hard-eyed men and women who turned into smiling, friendly people who waved and called over when they saw it was Mordecai. Mordecai exchanged waves and a how-do-ya-do back now and then, but he didn't stop to talk, and he ignored questions fired his way. Most of which were about Celia.

The girl, for her part, felt out of her depth and shut up, clutching Threadbare tightly and making sure she didn't make eye contact.

"Jus' the neighbors," Mordecai told her. "You'll meet 'em later. We'll come up with a story for who you are."

"I'm Celia. Who else would I be?"

"It's yer last names that could cause trouble. Just, ah, call yerself Celia Hornwood. Tha's a family that's feuding up north, around Outsmouth. People will think yer down here ta get away from that."

"Won't the other Hornwoods be mad that I'm doing that?"

"Nah. Most of'em are dead already."

"That's horrible!"

"Tha's what happens when yer a clan of humans feuding wi' dwarves. Dwarves don't just hold grudges, they juggles them. And Outsmouth folks is a little strange anyways."

"What?"

"Long story." Mordecai paused, where the trail led down into a dark hollow, on the lee side of a hill. "C'mon. Now… you're gonna see some stuff."

"Stuff?"

"Jus' stay out of it. Remember I'm fine wi' it, wouldn't be doin' it if I didn't love 'er. An' stay out of the hut till I gives yer tha all clear."

"I don't understand."

"Good."

At the end of the trail, sat a wooden and straw hut, with a thatched roof of woven sticks. Skulls poked out from it, capping the end of every stick. Big ones, little ones, mostly animal skulls... though Celia hissed, to see a few human skulls mixed in among them. Others were from creatures she'd never seen before, hollow darkness staring from weather-yellowed sockets. Smoke poured from the center of the hut, and a strange odor, spicy and strong, filled her nose and made her sneeze.

At the sound, the three youths on the porch sat up and peered at her with curious eyes. They wore mismatched clothes, half of sturdy cloth and half of leather and hide.

The youngest was about half Celia's size, a little boy with green skin and yellow eyes, and short frizzy black hair that reminded Celia of her own. He hid a turtle behind his back, and stared at her for only a second, before his gaze slid to Threadbare and his jaw dropped open.

The one in the middle was built like a block of stone that someone had put muscles on. Thick and squat and about as tall as Celia, wearing a crudely-stitched suit of leather armor. He had the hilt of a battleaxe hanging from his belt, and though his skin was pink, he had his brother's yellow eyes and two small tusks poking out over his upper lips. The overall effect was if someone had poured a boar into a human skin. Perhaps he was a few years older? He smiled and waved.

The third one was tall, taller than Celia, with wispy hair on his upper lip, seventeen if he was a day. Green-skinned like the youngest, he was all lean muscle, dressed in a bone-beaded leather shirt, a hide cloak, and a pair of trousers. His black hair was drawn back in a ponytail, and he had a bow slung on his back. Unlike the younger two, his eyes were human and gray. Much like Mordecai's, Celia thought. In fact...

"You never told me you had kids!" She burst out. But Mordecai wasn't looking at her anymore. Mordecai was moving up, staring at the beaded curtain that led into the darkness of the hut. Then he drew his knife.

Celia stepped back, fumbled for her own daggers—

—and promptly dropped one, jumping backward in fear, as something inside the hut roared and charged through the curtain, bowling Mordecai over as they rolled across the grass.

It was green and brown and howling, and it battered him with a heavy club, as Mordecai fought for his life, knife flashing. Blood sprayed and for a second she dared hope—

—but then he reeled back as the club hit his face with a CRACK, and Celia gasped as the two separated, staggering back to take stock of each other.

It wore a painted wooden mask, she saw that, and stood like a human did... broad and scarred and green and muscled, taller even than Mordecai, clad in a leather halter top and loincloth. Black, dreadlocked hair flew out from behind the mask as it snarled, and stalked back and forth like a beast, yellow eyes shifting in the holes of the mask as it stalked Mordecai. The skull-topped club shook, as the creature feinted, testing for weakness, testing for hesitation.

Then Celia blinked, as she realized what the curves under that halter top meant.

"That's a woman?" She asked, putting her hand to her face.

The creature spared her a glance, filled with malice that she'd never seen the likes of before and then Mordecai was on the thing, stabbing desperately, and with a great wail and a blur of motion the fight was back on. Celia turned tail and ran, hugging her bear tight, getting way the hell away as fast as possible. She reached the treeline, turned...

...only to see a limp Mordecai being dragged by one leg, hat off, into the hut.

"No!" She shouted, dropping Threadbare, and pulling out her daggers. **"Animus Blade! Animus Blade! Anim—"**

"Hey, s'all right,"

"Huh?" She dropped the last dagger, stared up at the tall, thin youth with the green skin. He'd worked his way around while she'd been distracted. The two blades whirled around, aimless, as she stared at him, nonplussed.

"Yeah, this is what they do," The sturdy boy said, walking up from the side, with the smallest boy in tow. "Dad was away too long without telling Mom first, so first they're gonna fight. Then she'll heal him up and they'll get to the other part."

"That was your... that's his wife?" Celia realized. "Oh my gods." Then her eyes narrowed. "Wait, what's the other part?"

"Uh..." The tall one shot a look at the fat one, who put his hands over the youngest one's ears. Then he told her.

Celia blushed.

"Yeah, we don't stick around for that part. Wanna come fishing with us?" The fat boy smiled.

"Yes. That would... yes." Celia blushed more. Then as she followed them into the woods, a thought struck her, an old fancy, and she glanced back at the now-quiet hut. "Um. I read... there was a book, once. It had a knight on the front, and a lady with her shirt half-off. I think it was Mom's. It was... interesting."

"Yeah?" The fat boy asked.

"Do you think, ah, what, do you think it's like that?" Celia asked, with something like desperation.

There was a pause. The three boys looked at Celia, then simultaneously the four kids, and Threadbare, turned to look at the hut.

With a crash, Mordecai's head and torso rammed through the straw. He shot an arm through, grabbed one of the larger skulls, and threw it back inside. His wife shrieked, and pulled him back in, as he fought desperately for a handhold.

"No," the tallest one said, rubbing his chin thoughtfully, "I rather fink it ent like that."

Feeling entirely out of her depth, Celia retrieved her fallen knife, and followed the trio into the woods.

"So I'm Garon," the fat boy said. He pointed at the tall youth who was walking ahead of them. "That's Jarrik. The small one with the turtle is Bak'shaz."

"I'm Celia. This is Threadbare."

Threadbare waved, and Garon chuckled. "So you're old man Caradon's daughter, then?"

"Um, yes, how did you know?'

"Not too many moving teddy bears out in these parts. Has to be an animator and I don't know any in town. We used to have one as a neighbor but she was kind of crazy."

"Oh yer talkin' about Mimsy?" Jarrik spoke up.

"You know she hated that name."

"Pssh. She wanted ta bake me into a pie."

"That was only ever a rumor."

"Yeah, right, no baker needs an oven that big. And yer can't tell me them cages was all fer animals."

"Whatever. Her thing was animated gingerbread men. And baking. I think she might have been trying to find an unlock."

"Summat mixed with cultist, prolly."

"Hey, that was never proven."

"What happened to her?" Celia asked, curious. She didn't know any other animators than her Daddy. Didn't know many people, really, when you got down to it, but this Mimsy shared a job with her so it made her more intriguing.

Garon shrugged. "Bad business. Someone pushed her into her own oven."

"I still say she crawled in herself," Jarrik grumped.

"Whatever. She's gone. But yeah, animated gingerbread men. Less fun then you'd think, between the bad weather we get out here and the bugs."

"But..." Bak'shaz spoke up for the first time, and the two older boys immediately stopped talking, and looked at him. Celia, her mouth half open to ask a question, managed to shut up. The little boy's voice was high-pitched, and creaky, higher than hers. "But Mimzal's gingerbread men all said 'animi' in their status. His says greater toy golem." He pointed at Threadbare.

"You can read status screens?" Celia burst out. "That's amazing!"

Instantly the little boy smiled widely, showing all his teeth, and stuck his hands in his overall pockets. "Ow!" His smile disappeared, and he pulled out a turtle, that was chewing on his thumb. "Okay yes Shelly it's feeding time. We're almost to the creek. Please be patient." He cranked up his smile again, and the turtle let go.

Threadbare felt strange. That kid suddenly seemed a lot nicer looking. Totally a good guy, the golem could tell, though he couldn't say why.

"It's not as amazing as you think," Jarrik said. "It's not as awesome as scouts, we can use Scouter to start reading people at tenth level."

"Which you haven't got yet, so shut up," Garon said, amicably. "Bak'shaz is a Tamer. He's all about making friends with monsters, and collecting them as companions. So one of his abilities lets him look at monster status screens. And it looks like golems count as monsters."

The woods thinned a bit, and Celia started to hear running water ahead. But she barely paid attention to where she was going, fascinated by the conversation and her new... friends? Hopefully friends. "Oh, uh, yeah, my Daddy made him. Golems are special animations that you don't have to renew every time their spell runs out. They're pretty tough."

Bak'shaz nodded so hard his frizzy hair wobbled, still staring fascinated at Threadbare.

"I didn't know he was a greater golem, though." Celia looked down at Threadbare, and the little bear hugged her. "I thought Daddy was still working on those. I knew he was special, but I guess Daddy wanted me to have him to protect me. You're the first of his successes!"

Threadbare shrugged.

"What's so great about greater golems?" Garon asked.

"Everything. They're smart. Regular golems are as dumb as animi, but greaters are as smart as people."

Threadbare nodded. "See?" Celia grinned. "He agrees."

"Can he fight?"

"Oh yeah. He helped me fight off a gropevine when Mister Mordecai was teaching me to be a scout."

"Wait, Dad taught yer to be a scout?" Jarrik asked, looking unconvinced.

"Um, yes, why?"

"It's just that yer 'bout to walk right inta a big patch of poison ivy."

One hasty scramble, a dropped bear, and a minimal amount of chaos later, they reached the creek, Threadbare toddling along behind them as Bak'shaz kept peeking at the little golem.

"I'm not a very good scout yet, I guess," Celia sat on one of the big rocks near the water.

"Did he take ya out to Oblivion Point?" Jarrik asked.

"Oh. Yes."

"Yeah, thass a good run. If Dad taught you how to be a scout, yer a scout. Good comes wi' practice."

Garron grinned. Wow, his teeth were sharp. "Jarrik is Dad's son, through and through. Wants to be a scout and an archer just like his old man."

The way he said that was weird. "Wait, if he's his Dad's son... You're... not your Father's son?"

"What? Oh no, no. We're all his sons. It's just I don't want to follow in his footsteps, that's all."

"He wants ter be a mercenary," Jarrik explained. "Do ya have a fishing pole?"

"No, sorry. I can watch, it's all right. Wait, mercenary is a job? I just thought most of them were knights or archers or other fighting jobs."

Jarrik hunted around found a stick, started tying some twine to it. "Oh don't get 'im started—"

Too late. Garon grinned widely, and spread his arms. "Let me tell you about my awesome career path!"

Bak'shaz rolled his eyes and started digging in the mud, putting Shelly down to do so. Jarrik sighed, and worked on the makeshift fishing rod. Garon continued, oblivious. "Most of the fighting types come from the four warrior classes, it's true, but sometimes they don't fight for money. Mercenaries, now? We fight, but it's secondary to getting paid. In fact, we've got stuff that lets us fight better so long as we've got money! And we always get paid."

"Yeah that's one of his skills," Jarrik said, in a sing-song voice, clearly copying his brother. "If you give him a quest and stiff him on the reward he can give you a permanent luck and fate debuff."

Garron punched his shoulder, and Jarrik yelped.

"Wow!" Celia leaned in. "That actually sounds pretty good."

"That's not all!" Garon grinned, rummaging around in his pack and pulling out his own fishing rod. "When I'm on a quest I get bonuses to every attribute when I'm doing something to complete that quest."

"So wait," The girl frowned. "If mercenary isn't one of the warrior classes, what is it?"

"It's one a tha wanderer classes," Jarrik said. "Explorer, Mercenary, Merchant, and Scout."

"Yep. We're made to travel. I won't be around here forever." Garon glanced over to Bak'shaz. "How are you coming on those worms?"

"Shelly eats first." Bak'shaz pointed at the turtle.

"Right, right. Don't leave us hanging, I want to eat tonight too."

"He's got you covered." Bak'shaz pointed into the creek.

The three other kids turned, to see Threadbare in the shallows, claws hooked into a fat trout, dragging it ashore. Another forage level and point of dexterity achieved!

"Okay, I like this little guy," Jarrik said. "I see how he got you through the scout test."

"We kind of helped each other," Celia smiled. "But yeah, he's great."

Threadbare toddled up and laid the flopping fish at her feet. Garon leaned down, grabbed it, and casually beat it against a rock until it stopped moving.

Celia jumped a bit, then settled down, but Jarrik caught it. "Woss wrong?"

"I... guess I'm just new to killing. Ah, things."

"Well yer a girl, I spect it's diff'rent fer girls."

"Maybe?" She shrugged. "I don't have any sisters. It's just me and Daddy, most of the time. And Emmet, but he doesn't do much. And Threadbare, now." She smiled down at the little bear. "Thanks for the fish."

He patted her knee, then started to amble back to the creek. "No, no, I remember what happened the last time you got into running water," She scooped him up. Then juggled him to one side, as Jarrik handed her a rod, with a freshly hooked worm writhing on it.

"Ya know how this works?"

"I've... read about it."

They spent a good hour fishing. After a bit of prodding, Bak'shaz made the toy golem a little rod, too, though Threadbare took care of gathering his own worms. It bumped up his forage skill again, so he figured that was worth the effort.

And finally, he caught something—

You have unlocked the generic skill: Fishing!

Your Fishing skill is now level 1!

—and was promptly yanked into the water. Sure, he had the strength of a weedy human at this point, but he still had the mass of a twelve-inch tall teddy bear.

Here we go again, he thought, as the waters closed around his head. Irritated, he flailed around, looking for purchase.

Your Swim skill is now level 2!

He did manage to get his feet to the bottom. Unlike the Icewine river that ran past Celia's house, this little creek was much slower. Threadbare came to a halt, and walked along the bottom, emerging up on shore...

...and staring right into the face of a creature he'd never seen before. It was four times his size, with a grubby snout, two squinty little eyes, and hooves for feet. It had a ridge of hair down its muddy back, and two tusks that positively dwarfed Garon's sticking up from its lower jaw.

The boar, which had been enjoying a peaceful drink up until now, snorted.

It eyed the interloper, trying to figure out whether or not it was time to start the killing.

CHAPTER 9: BRINGING HOME THE BACON

Threadbare considered his options, and waved.

The boar's eyes narrowed.

"Oh boy," came Jarrik's whisper from upriver. The boar shuffled back, glaring between the tall half-orc and the little bear. "He's over here," Jarrik called, as loudly as he dared, then froze. The young boar stared his direction for a while, then looked back to Threadbare. It snuffled him, and Threadbare snuffled back.

Your Scents and Sensibility skill is now level 7!

Then Celia burst through the trees and the boar whipped around to face her, squealing and pawing the ground.

"Hey!" Bak'shaz burst out behind her, a big goofy grin on his face, with a dead fish in each hand, and Shelly clamped on for dear life to his hair. "Let's be friends!"

The boar hesitated.

Behind Bak'shaz, axe out, Garon moved up, step by step, slowly. "You sure you want to try this, Bakky?"

"I always wanted a boar." Bak'shaz never looked away from the pig. He approached, step by step. "Besides, I got my Beast Truce."

Celia froze, a stuffed animal in both hands, and looked over to Jarrik. The thin scout nodded. "Let 'im try. If it dunt work…" Jarrik tapped his bow.

The boar and Threadbare watched Bak'shaz approach, holding the fish, grin up the whole time. Eventually the smell of the fish became too strong, and the boar sniffed once, twice, then paced forward and tore it from the boy's hands, slurping it down in three crunching bites.

"Tame Monster!" Bak'shaz said. Green light flared…

…and the boar instantly shrunk to half its former size.

"What?" Celia said, staring.

Behind her, Jarrik and Garon relaxed. "It means it worked," Garon said. "He's Bak'shaz's pet now."

"Yeah, but it's a manageable size fer him until he gets ta a higher level," Jarrik explained.

"That's... that makes no sense," Celia said.

"And moving teddy bears do?"

Well, they had her there. She watched Bak'shaz laugh delightedly and tackle the boar, winced as they rolled around on the dirt, and the boar bit and shoved at the little half-orc. Red numbers flashed up, low ones, but still... she hissed between her teeth. "Are you sure of this?"

"Relax, this is why Tamers get good con. Besides, I'm not just a mercenary." Garon pointed at his brother. **"Slow Regeneration."**

"Mom taught 'im shaman," Jarrik explained. "Figgered if he was gonna go off ter fight in battles, he should prolly know how to fix himself."

"His name is Porkins," Bak'shaz finally declared after the scuffle was over, and Shelly was returned to his pocket.

"Well, tha's nice. Let's get tha fish and go home before Porkins eats any more of our dinner."

"As for you!" Celia shook her finger at Threadbare, who looked back at her, seated as he wrung water out of his legs.

CHA +1

Your Adorable skill is now level 12!

"Aw, it's not like it was your fault," Celia said. "We'll just... tie you to a rock or to me next time you're fishing. Here, let me try this... **Clean and Press!"**

Mordecai's sons watched, as the water sprayed out of the bear, along with the mud, stains, and random weeds he'd collected during his dunking. "Neat!" Garon declared. "Is that an animator trick?"

"No, just a tailor skill. The only tailor skill I've got right now. I'm still new at it."

"Huh. Well, none of us can do that so that should make Mom happy." The kids and their assorted companions started their walk back home.

"Wait, should we be going back?" Celia asked, a few hundred feet later. "Are you sure they're... done?"

"Yah, yah," Jarrik nodded. "Dad whispered tha all clear twenny minutes ago."

"Oh, right, we can do that." She shook her head, and Jarrik patted her back.

"Dun' worry. We'll teach yer tha ropes, Da' and me."

Garon chuckled. "Just make sure you tell Beryl about Celia before she finds out on her own. She'll jump to entirely the wrong conclusion."

"Who's Beryl?" Celia wondered.

"His girl." Garon grinned, and blocked Jarrik's punch.

"She is not!"

"Totally is."

"It ent like that!"

"Pretty much is."

"You don't know nuffin' about it!"

"See this, Celia? This is probably like that book you read, with the knight and the maiden and the ripping bodices."

"Oh!" Celia brightened up. "How romantic!"

"Not you too..." Jarik groaned, shooting her a betrayed look.

Garon and Bak'shaz laughed, but then they were at the hut, and Celia felt the gnawing of fear coming back to weigh her down. That look the woman... that Mordecai's wife had shot her... that look had been pure wickedness. What if his wife was angry that he brought Celia home? What if she was going to, to... Celia's imagination failed, but she was sure it was something horrible.

What if she was mean?

"Ah, there y'are." Mordecai rocked on the porch, seated comfortably in a fur-covered chair, feet up on the railing, puffing his pipe. "C'mon up an' meet Zuula." He had a weary smile on his face, that she'd never seen before. It was almost smug.

Gathering her courage, reassured by the presence of her new friends at her back, she pushed through the beaded curtain and into the hut.

The scent was different now, she noticed. Not that raw, spicy scent, that hotness that grabbed at the nose that she'd first smelled. In her arms, Threadbare snuffled, turning his head to see.

The walls were lined with beds, and the largest of them had Mordecai's boots next to it. In the center of the hut coals smoldered in a firepit, the smoke from the bubbling pot escaping through a hole in the roof. Idly, Celia wondered what they did when it rained, but she was soon distracted by the decorations on the walls. Broken weapons, a pair of shattered manacles, what looked like half a dozen shriveled up body parts from animals she didn't recognize, tapestries, dried plants of all kinds, and looming above it all like a god's idol before its offerings, was that painted wooden mask. Much too large to fit Celia, too large to fit Mordecai, it loomed with red-painted wood and bone teeth filling its mouth, the eyesockets empty but seeming to dance in the firelight, shifting around as if it was constantly surveying its domain.

"Child..." A deep voice purred, and Celia jumped. What she thought was a wall hanging was a curtain off to another room. While she'd been woolgathering, it had been swept aside. Yellow eyes peered out at Celia from the darkness, and the little girl swallowed.

But this time, the eyes were free of malice.

"Welcome to Zuula's home, child." A somewhat plump woman swept into the room. She had a robe on this time, loose around her enormous bosom, but snug around her wide hips. Her visible skin was green, dusky green in the firelight, and Celia could just make out the traceries of scars starting where her wrists met the robe's sleeves.

But she had a pretty face, and though her teeth were many and sharp, her satisfied smile matched Mordecai's for friendliness. Her dreadlocked hair was pulled back in a braid now, not loose.

It almost seemed like two different women. Celia's eyes flickered from the matronly figure to the mask.

Perhaps it *was* two different women. She gained a wisdom increase then, and didn't know why.

Zuula merely stood there, arms wide, smiling at her.

"Er, hello," Celia said, nervously stepping closer. "I-ah!"

Zuula swept Celia into a bonecrushing hug, squishing Threadbare against her side. The little bear wriggled, and Zuula looked down. "Ha! De little Golem!"

"Er, yes, he's Threadbare. Say hi, Threadbare."

Threadbare waved.

"Dreadbear. Good name."

"Ah, no, Threadbare."

"Is what Zuula said, Dreadbear." The woman released Celia, dropping her to the ground. The little girl staggered madly on the planks of the floor, trying to avoid going into the stone-ringed fire. "Come come, you is welcome. Mordecai be sayin' you feed him, yes?"

"What?"

"On de way here. You hunt him food, yes?"

"Oh, the Blue Jay…" She rummaged in her pockets, and pulled out a handful of crumpled blue feathers. "Yes, I guess I did, though he did most of the—"

"Then Zuula owe you a dinner!"

"She helped with the fishing too, Mom." Garon offered up from the doorway.

"Ha ha! Fish for dinner! Goes well with every 'ting that Zuula growed this morning! Bring it in, put it in de gumbo, Garon."

"Oh, and we've got a pig now."

"Pig can go in de gumbo too." Zuula pulled a massive, curved knife down from a ceiling rack. "Part of it, anyway."

"No, I mean, Bakky tamed it."

"Hm! Den he go in de gumbo eventually, but not now. Pig, not Bakky."

"Almost done cleanin' the fish," Mordecai called in.

"Tch. Waste of good fish heads," Zuula groused, but shrugged. "Feed to de pig, den."

"Already did!" Bak'shaz yelled.

"Not all of dem, Zuula hope." The woman licked her lips.

"Saved you the biggest one, Mom!"

"Good. Good boy."

And so, a little while later, they all had gumbo. All except Threadbare, which was fine with him. The others seemed to enjoy the taste, but it smelled spicy and weird to his bear nose, and he was much more interested in exploring the hut, anyway. He ambled around freely, peering at things. Behind the second beaded curtain he found a small room with a heavy fruitlike scent over the smell of dung. It had a toilet and small sink in it, a thing he'd never seen before because he'd never accompanied Celia to the bathroom or even been in the bathroom of Celia's old house. Curious, he clambered up and peered into the bowl of it, staring at the water, not seeing any fish.

From there, it was easy enough to climb up onto the seat, and stretch up, take hold of the sink to hoist himself up and examine that…

…which worked until his paws slipped, and he tottered backward, feet sliding on the well-worn ceramic of the toilet seat—

—only to be caught at the last minute by a callused hand.

LUCK +1

Mordecai looked down at him. "You keep fallin' at bad times, mister bear. Need ta work on yer footing."

Threadbare nodded, and patted Mordecai's wrist.

"Glad I ran into yer. Summat we needs ta discuss, anyway." He left the bathroom. "Celia, you mind ifn' I have a word with Threadbare?"

"Um, no? He doesn't talk."

"He lissens, though, yah?"

"Yes! He's great at that!"

"Right, then." Mordecai headed out the door, putting the teddy bear to the ground as he did so. "Walk wi' me a bit, Threadbare."

The bear nodded, and followed.

Mordecai headed out towards the setting sun, to where the woods grew thin and the hills started up again. "You're a bit more'n ya seem, me friend."

Threadbare shrugged.

"I knew Caradon was up ta somefing when he asked me ta bring him toys every week. Bunches of 'em. Rose some questions in town, I tell you that. But I did. An' yer the result."

Threadbare considered it, and nodded.

"Smart golems. Tha's part of what we need. Figurin' out a way to make'em work properly, so he can upgrade Emmet. Because we need Emmet, if this fing is gonna work."

Threadbare shrugged.

"Ya know scouts of tha proper level can look at yer status screen, right? I did when I met ya. And for tha longest time I couldn't figure out why Caradon had given yer tha ruler job."

Threadbare shook his head. He hadn't gotten that from Caradon. He'd earned that through regicide, thank you very much. He wasn't sure what regicide was, but it was the word that had popped up, he remembered.

"Two possibilities come to me, then. Both pretty ugly." Mordecai stopped in a field of grass. It was empty out here, with the sun well on its way down, and the wind riffling through the field. Just Mordecai standing there solemn and patient, and Threadbare looking up at the old wanderer.

"First thing that come to me, was that yer tha way for Emmet to get the Ruler class. Emmet pops you, an' then becomes king. But then I think nah, if he's found a way to give it ta golems, then he could just give it ta Emmet, right?"

Threadbare nodded. That wasn't what had happened, but the statement was true. The part that he understood, anyway.

"The second thought, an' the one that makes the most sense ta me, is that yer how he wants to give the Ruler job to Celia. And it ent through marriage or adoption. Which leaves…"

Regicide, the grass seemed to whisper. Threadbare shivered, though he didn't know why. He'd have to figure out that word at some point. It boded.

"Tha's the one job we need for 'er, the hard one ta get. We need 'er ta have that job, an' there ain't many kings around these days. Or queens. Or other kinds of royalty. Balmoran has fallen in th' North, and the Earl's dead, along wi' his son. The engagement's not an option no more. There's just one king left, an' she'll need everyfing she's got against 'im. And so will them what follers her."

Threadbare stood in the grass, staring at Mordecai as the wind swirled and howled across the hills.

Mordecai stared at the little toy for a long time. He'd seen it in action, first against the eagle, then during Celia's test. Watched it every step of the way. He knew what it was capable of. At least, he thought he did.

"I suppose the question I got fer yer, the big one, is simple. Will ya give yer life for Celia when the time comes? Give up everyfing you 'ave for that little girl?"

Threadbare considered it.

For exactly three seconds.

Then he nodded.

Celia had saved him. Saved him from being dust, he thought, saved him from the cat the first time around, though that had worked out okay in the end. She'd definitely saved him from the Eagle, and they'd more or less saved each other from the troubles during that whole scouting run. He couldn't imagine a life without her, and though he didn't know what love was, he knew that he loved her. She was his little girl, and he was her teddy bear, and that was that.

Mordecai sighed. "Can't say I like it, even if I unnerstand it. Hard times. Hard choices. But I respect yer creator, so if yer at peace wi' it, then I'm at peace wi' it, regardless of what comes. Come on Mister Bear, let's go home."

Wondering what all that had been about, Threadbare followed him back to the hut.

The meal was winding up by the time Mordecai and Threadbare got back. Celia helped wash the dishes in the bathroom sink and put them away in the little cupboard niche behind one of the wall hangings.

"Thank you. That was delicious." She scrunched her nose. "Weird, but delicious."

"You be welcome, child," Zuula smiled down. "Also you be red."

Celia mopped her forehead. "I thought it was just hot in here."

"Hot inside you belly, too." Zuula chuckled. "Be hot coming out too. You know how toilet work?"

"Oh, er, uh, yes." Celia turned redder.

"Good. Mistah toilet gon' be your friend come an hour or two."

The boys chuckled, as Celia turned the reddest she'd been so far, and covered her face with her hands. Zuula shot them a glare, and they fell silent. "Why be embarrassed? You alive. Living things eat, people shit. Is nature of world."

Threadbare wondered if that meant he wasn't alive. If he wasn't that, then what was he? The little bear, his mind heavy with his first philosophical crisis, sat down with a bump and tried to work it out.

WIS +1

And thought that if he wasn't alive, it didn't matter, really. He had a friend, two friends if you counted Pulsivar, who treated him as if he were alive. So that was the most important part. The other troublesome parts of that notion could be worked out later.

Celia didn't notice. Her eyes were wide under her hands. Zuula had just said a forbidden word!

Although...

...maybe it wasn't forbidden, here. Not under this roof, anyway.

"Yeah, I guess so," the little girl said, moving her hands away. "So, um, what now? Do we go to sleep?"

"Nah." Mordecai said. "Clear night tanight. Up fer starwotchin'?"

The family nodded, and Celia nodded with them.

Starwatching, as it turned out, involved climbing a ladder in back of the hut and stretching out full on the thatch-and-plank roof. It was slightly sloped, but not so much that they risked falling off. Which was good for Threadbare, since his agility was still a bit under par. He only managed the ladder because he clung onto Celia's skirts for dear life and let her carry him up that way.

Your Ride skill has increased to level 2!

"Oh, that's the rain plug, isn't it?" Celia pointed to a wood-and-leather object lying off-center from the roof, with ropes coiled around it.

"Clever girl," Zuula said. "We move it up top before rain come. Keeps stuff dry. Have to open windows to let smoke out, den."

"But what if it rains before you can get the plug in?"

Zuula snorted. "Unclever girl. This home to a shaman and a scout. Rain DON'T come we don't know about."

"Oh. Right, sorry. Dumb question I guess."

"Not really. You don't know much about shamans, do you?" Garon asked, from where he was sitting, and honing a knife with a whetstone.

"No. They're... nature priests?"

"Pah. Say more like priests are sellouts." Zuula grinned, all sharpened teeth in the moonlight. Her yellow eyes were almost aglow, Celia noticed. "World come first. Gods come later. World remembers, All tings in nature remember. People forget. Shamans remind dem."

Celia frowned. "But the books say that Kolnol created the world."

"Books, pah!" Zuula threw her arms in the air. "What dey know? People wrote them! People not dere when it all start. Mountains? Mountains dere. Oceans? Oceans dere. In different places now, yes, but still dere."

"Oh." Most of Celia's earliest friends had been books. She wasn't sure how to handle the fact that some of them might be wrong.

Mordecai cleared his throat. "Shamans work wif' plants an' beasts an' natural forces. Comes to a pinch, Zuula can call winds."

"Don' do dat too often, dough," Zuula said, relaxing. "Pull winds out of place, dey get cranky elsewhere. Dey take it out on tings dey shouldn't."

"She also does the sweat lodge," Garon said. "You ever tried that, Celia?"

"I— I don't even know what that is."

"Oh you poor girl!" Zuula rolled over to face her. "Tomorrow night, we do sweat lodge." She pointed at a shape in the darkness back from the main hut a bit. Celia had taken it for a storage shed, the first time she'd seen it. "You get nice an' dirty, sweat lodge get you clean. Also..." She tilted her head, looked to Mordecai. "Dream quest, you tink?"

"Too soon," Mordecai said. "Some things she's got ta learn first."

"Things? Like what?" Celia asked. "What's a dream quest?"

Mordecai and Zuula shared a long look. "Summat that'll require yer daddy's permission," Mordecai finally said. "Gets inta prophecy an' hints a tha future."

"Ways it can go, not prophecy." Zuula corrected. "Possibilities...." She stretched the word out, hissing it.

"Oh. Um. Well, okay. I'll ask him when we go back. When is that?"

"Tired of our comp'ny already?" Mordecai said, teeth glinting in the moonlight.

"Oh no, no no, this is fun!" Celia said. "You're all very nice, and I've seen and done things I've never done before. It's probably doing great things for my human levels!"

The family laughed at that, and Bak'shaz made a googly-eyed face at her. Jarrik kicked him in the butt, and the little kid yelped as he almost slipped off the roof. The family laughed more at that, and Celia, hesitating only a bit, joined in.

Threadbare, getting into the spirit of it, pointed at Bak'shaz and held his belly, shaking.

Your Adorable skill is now level 13!

"Right on, little guy," Garon ruffled the teddy bear's head.

Then they settled back and watched the stars glimmer.

"Um," Celia said after a while. "What's it like being half-orcs?"

Zuula didn't answer. The boys rolled onto their sides, looked at her, then looked at each other.

"I'm sorry. Did I say something wrong? I don't... it's... oh dear. I said something wrong, didn't I?"

"No. Is honest question." Zuula decided. "But let Zuula ask first... what is it like being a human?"

"Um... I don't know. I guess. I never thought about it much."

"You don't have to. Most everyone around here human. But we got tink about it. 'cause we not. But Zuula going to keep her tinkin silent because maybe you a bit young to hear her tinks on it."

"Boys, why don't ya field this one?" Mordecai asked.

Garon nodded. "Sure. First off, people who aren't human might get a little angry because they get asked that a lot. By humans. In fact it's only ever humans who ask that question. Ever."

"I wonder why that is?" Celia's face was innocent, and Jarrik and Bak'shaz relaxed. She hadn't meant anything by her question.

"So... the first thing you have to understand is that orcs come from overseas. There's this bunch of idiots, they're down below the Oblivion now, what's their name again—"

"The Cane Confederation," Zuula spat.

"—Right, them. Bunch of little kingdoms and tiny nations, all feuding and only banding together when bigger nations try to invade them. Thanks to constant warring and not enough people to work the fields and do the lousy jobs, they had the bright idea of using slavery to get by. And for a time this worked for them, but it got them a lot of anger from the surrounding neighbors, who didn't like slavers to begin with and liked them less when it was their folks being enslaved. So some genius, he decided hey, let's go enslave some people nobody cares about."

"Orcs," Mordecai said. "Big, big mistake."

"Yeah. After a few decades, there were big rebellions, bloody wars, that are probably still going on today. The orcs escaped into the swamps down there, and the places too wild for humans to survive, and grew. Every few years a new horde forms and sweeps up, and there's a whole lot of death."

"Orcs don't forgive. Orcs don't forget. Cane be enemies. Cane be dead," Zuula hissed. "It take ten generations or a tousand, dey die."

Celia shivered. "But if they imported orcs... humans and orcs fell in love and got married, right, half-orcs are because of that, right? Proof it can happen?"

The boys looked to their mother, shared a long glance. Mordecai coughed. "Sometimes, ya. The local orcs only got a grudge against the Canefolk. Mind ya, the wild tribes will kill you if they fink yer weak. Or if they're hungry. Or if they fink they could prosper from yer death."

"Dey do dat to other orcs too, so is fair. Orcs do dat to everyone. Stronger peoples makes for stronger world. Means demons and worse tings get butts kicked when dey show up." Zuula made a squiggly hand sign. "Evil beware!"

"But do ya know what orc means, in orcish?" Jarrik asked her.

"Um, no." Celia said. She was far, far offshore in very deep waters, and a storm was brewing, but she didn't know how to avoid it. She just knew she had to ride it out.

"Orc means tribe. Thass it. If they accept ya, yer family."

"S'how I met me Zuuly," Mordecai curled his arm around his wife's shoulders. "Got hired ta raid one of the little Confederation kingdoms. Fort we raided had a captured tribe in it."

"What was left of us," Zuula hissed. "Damn dem."

"I sprung 'em and guided 'em out. An' after I fought alongside'em, I was family. They helped me mop up the rest of that kingdom, an' Zuula followed me north. An 'ere we are." Mordecai sighed. "This was all back 'fore the Oblivion, of course."

"When it done, we go back and see tribe," Zuula said. "Might have to kill a few to get back in, it's been a while."

"When what's done?" Celia frowned.

"The Oblivion."

Mordecai sat bolt upright, as did all the boys.

"What?" The old scout choked out. "What are ya talkin' about?"

"Oh. Right." Zuula smacked her head. "It be coming down. Saw it in last dream quest."

"Dream quests are jus' possiblities," Mordecai insisted.

"Yes. And all possibilities here say it coming down. Few year or few decades. But it gone eider way."

Mordecai was shaking now, hands white-knuckled on the roof. Zuula looked at him serenely. "We need to talk about this." Mordecai whispered.

"Come, den." Zuula rose, and headed to the ladder. "Not you," she told her boys, as they stirred as well. "We be back."

The adults left, disappearing into the darkness. The kids looked at each other, wide-eyed.

"Okay, we don't talk about this. Ever," Garon decided. "This is the sort of news that gets you hauled in front of the Royal Inquisitors."

"They prolly know anyway. Won't their own shamans have figgered it out?" Jerrik asked.

"King ain't got no shamans," Bak'shaz pointed out. "Too un-simple-eyed."

"Uncivilized," Garon commented. "Though maybe the clerics and oracles said something. And who knows what his cultists told him. It would explain why everything's so tense in the garrison in town. I thought it was just because of the troubles in the North, but... this could be it."

"What?" Celia asked.

Jarrik looked over at her. "The garrison of guards in town grew four fold in the last two weeks. Something big's going down."

"Word is they're bringing in dragonriders!" Bak'shaz grinned. "I wanna see that!"

"Not up close and personal you don't," Garon told him. "But we don't talk about this. Not till Dad says it's okay. Swear?" He held out his hand. "Put yours on mine and swear," he added, at Celia's look of confusion.

The four kids and Threadbare touched hands, as they swore their first oath of secrecy against the rest of the world. Well, Threadbare thought it, anyway. He got his head ruffled for being cute again.

Afterwards, they were silent for a while, digesting the news in their own way as the stars wheeled overhead.

"Hey," Garon finally said. "You wanted us to tell you what it was like being half-orcs?"

"Oh. Never mind, it was a stupid question anyway."

"No, it's fine. You're tribe now. You're family."

"Oh, uh... thanks!" She gasped. "My charisma just went up!"

They laughed at that. "Ya must've lead a pretty sheltered life," Jarrik jeered.

"You have no idea," the girl muttered.

Garon shrugged. "Alright. So being a half-orc means people are gonna look at you and think to themselves 'wow, that guy's really tough and really violent and really dumb.' It means having to live with that, knowing that people will think you're either a threat or an idiot."

"That's horrible!"

"Well... it can be, if you let it. But here's the thing. The people who are stupid enough to think that's all there is to you, they underestimate you. So if they're your enemy, you can exploit that. They die easier when you pull off something smart. And if they fear you, you can use that to your advantage, too. Me, people look at me and think hm, axe, half-orc, the dude's a berserker, who's going to murder his way through life, go into a rage, and kill indiscriminately."

"That's horrible!"

"Yeah, especially since what I want to do is murder my way through life, go into rages, kill discriminately, and get paid for it."

"But you aren't a berserker, how can you rage?"

"Race skills. We get born with one orcish skill and one human skill. In my case I've got that human drive to achieve, which gives me bonus experience for quests and stuff like that. And I've got twisted rage. It's... pretty horrible. It's a rage that burns me up, eats up hit points."

"Oh. That's... kind of dangerous, right?"

"It would be if I weren't smart." He tapped his forehead. "Shamans get slow regeneration which helps me survive, and mercenaries get Blood is Gold, which lets us trade money for instant healing. I'm gonna be a legendary fury on the battlefield, when I start getting paid enough. And when I'm on a battlefield. Which is going to be soon, if the Oblivion's going down in our lifetime." his eyes gleamed. "It'll make grinding all that charisma totally worth it..."

"We didn't get his rage," Jarrik said. "Just as well. He goes through so much crap keepin' his temper down. We got Darkspawn instead. Lets us see in tha dark, get bonuses to stuff at night or in tunnels and such."

"Oh. That's pretty handy!"

"Yeah, all the best monsters come out at night," Bak'shaz grinned. "Downside is I'm stuck with Orky charisma. But my tamer job helps there."

"Mom put a scorpion into his crib to toughen him up when he was a baby," Garon explained. "No shit, he made friends with it! Didn't sting him, slept with him, kept other bugs away from him."

"Wait, she did what?" Celia's voice rose.

"It's all right. She had the antidote right there, and was ready to heal him up. She did stuff like that to all of us. Orcs are born with lousy luck and no real clerics among most tribes. So children have to get tough fast or improve their luck quickly, or they die because they just didn't have the luck or fate to survive."

"She lost a few children that way, before she started getting tough on us," Bak'shaz said. "Then we lost one more 'cause she got stupid."

"Don't talk about Mastoya that way," Jarrik scowled. "You don't know nuffin' about it."

"What... um..."

Garon glanced Celia's way. "She joined the King's guard. She had twisted rage too, she'd be dead if she couldn't find an outlet for it. Can't blame her. She's off in the North somewhere right now. Still sends letters and money back. Dad keeps the letters and gives away the money. Which is a shame, because I could put it to good use. In fact..." He bit his lip, considered Celia.

"What?"

"You're family now." He glanced around. "Jarrik, are Mom and Dad gone out of earshot?"

"**Keen Eye**," Jarrik whispered, then stood up and looked into the woods. "I think so."

"Good." Garon smiled, and leaned in close to Celia. "How would you like to help us run through a dungeon?"

CHAPTER 10: CATAMOUNTAIN

"I still don't know if this is a good idea," Celia confessed, clutching Threadbare to her as she followed Bak'shaz up the lonely pass. The wind howled alongside the trail, dusting snow off the sheer drop to the valley below. They were alone, one of the others gone ahead, and the other swearing to catch up once his errand was done.

In the distance, through the curtain of snowflakes, the three peaks of their destination loomed like forgotten idols to dead gods.

"It'd be a bad idea if we was going far in," Bak'shaz shrugged. "But the Catamountain don't get nasty unless you cross the first bridge. Long as we stick to Housecat Peak we won't have no trouble."

"I guess." Celia chewed her lip, and shivered in her coat. "I wish we'd come up here with the others. All in a group."

"Won't be any problems until we get in. Guards keep the path up clear. Might be problems with the guards."

"Problems?"

"Yeah. It's why I left Porkins at home. The guards don't like us too much because we're half-breeds. I used to have a Bloodhound, but they kicked it off the mountain, said it was because he was too weak to survive in there, so they were saving it the trouble of a slow death."

"That's horrible!"

"Yeah. I loved that hound." Bak'shaz sighed, and stuck his hands in his overalls. "So I'll find a pet in there an' use it for the run, then let it go 'fore I come out."

"I— you don't think they'll do that to Threadbare, will they?" Celia hugged the little bear tight.

Threadbare didn't like the notion of being kicked off the mountain much. He started fumbling in Celia's pocket for one of her daggers.

"Hey, no. Settle down, I won't let anyone get you," Celia reassured her teddy bear.

Bak'shaz watched them, and chuckled. "No, they won't do that to Threadbare. You look rich. Uh, they might call you some nasty stuff because you're with us. But whatever you do, don't let them see you getting mad. They got cells up there they can stick 'troublemakers' in."

"Why are the guards so awful?"

"Dad says it's 'cause good men don't get assigned here. Just the jerks who can't cut it in the reg'lar military, so they get their kicks picking on people and 'busing their authority. But they're mostly cowards, they know Dad would kill them in their sleep if they killed us or disappeared us. Besides, they need him to train their scouts. He's the best at that."

"There y'are!" An unfamiliar voice came from ahead, and Celia flinched, thinking they'd hit the guards already. But no, it was a strange young woman, Celia's height but three times as broad, wearing jingling chain mail. Her green eyes were barely visible above an oversized shield. "We figured you'd be late. Not as late as I thought, from how Jarrik described you."

"Um, you must be Beryl." This was the first time Celia had ever seen a dwarf that wasn't in a picture book. She had a horned helmet with multicolored braids hanging out of it, purple and black and pink. As Celia got closer she saw the girl's eyes were surrounded by black makeup, that matched her lipstick. The ankh on her steel breastplate gleamed silver, though, and Celia thought it looked familiar.

"Is that a holy symbol of Aeterna?"

"Yeah. Not my choice but you got to keep the fam happy, right? And she's actually pretty cool when you get to know her." Beryl sighed, and rolled her eyes.

From behind her, Jarrik waved. He had black lipstick smeared on his throat and mouth, and Celia's high int let her put two and two together.

She decided not to say a word, and blinked as her wisdom increased.

"Just so you know, girl, if you try to steal my boy I'll rip your tits off," Beryl grinned, showing flat, even teeth. "Do you understand?"

"I, I, I wouldn't, I mean yes. I understand."

"Great. Come on, let's go make some money."

Beryl stomped forward, and Celia watched her go. Jarrik smiled, looking a little out of it.

"You got a hicky, bro," Bak'shaz mopped his own neck and mouth.

"Oh! Shit." Jarrik wiped them away, fell in with Bak'shaz and Celia. "She's the leader, okay?"

"All right." Celia shrugged. "I'm just along for the ride with this one."

Ahead, a gatehouse loomed out of the snow, sealing off the trail. It looked like the construction ran back into the cliff to the side, with arrow slits and parapets above. Two guards stood stock still, wielding halberds, dressed head to toe in black plate with red glowing glyphs on it.

"Magical armor?" Celia sucked in her breath.

"Aye," Beryl had stopped, and heard her question. "Work for the king, you get the good stuff. Just costs your soul."

"What?"

"He consorts with demons. Everyone knows it." Beryl spat off the cliff. "But if you get me going I'll get political and it's too cold for that shit now. Where's your damned brother, Jarry?"

Jarrik pointed a thumb back down the trail.

Celia turned, and saw a fountain of snow rushing off the cliffside, as something brown sped up the trail, moving way faster than she'd seen anyone run before. She took two steps back... and Garon appeared out of the snow cloud, skidding to a stop on the rocky path. "Forced March. So useful." He tossed a package at Celia, and she almost dropped Threadbare as she caught it. "Got your tailoring kit. Wasn't too expensive so we'll just take it out of your share."

"Tailoring kit?" Beryl snorted. "You gonna make us pretty dresses while we're in there, girl? Maybe some pretty bows for our hair?"

Celia frowned at her. No one had ever been this rude to her before, and she didn't know how to handle it. "No. They told you I'm an animator, right?"

"Right. So what?"

"So it takes sanity to heal my toys. This will let me repair them without spending sanity points."

"I do the healing for the group. That's the rules, squirt." Beryl took a step forward, squinting at her.

"Then try it," Celia held out Threadbare. "See what happens."

Threadbare waved.

"You're joking, right?" Beryl squinted harder.

"Uh, Beryl? That bear's got more class levels than you do," Bak'shaz told her.

Instantly Beryl's eyes opened wide. "Get the fuck out!"

"He's a golem," Celia told her, and Beryl's jaw dropped.

"Seriously? They have a pair of big stone ones guarding the gates of Shalekeep. My Da' told me about how they came alive during the troubles, and crushed armies."

"I think I heard of those," Celia said. "My mom's notes mentioned that she helped build—"

"Okey-dokey then!" Garon interrupted, clapping them both on the back. "Let's get sorted. Beryl?"

"Right, what's the little bastard's name then?" Beryl knelt down a bit to smile at Threadbare. "Oooh, he's got a wee knife! How cute!"

Your Adorable Skill is now level 14!

"He's Threadbare, but, uh, it takes a special skill to invite golems into a party. I've tried without it and it doesn't work. The only way to do it takes scrolls I don't have."

"Well what use is he then?" Beryl frowned.

"He's pretty smart and he'll do what I ask him to. Won't you, Mister Bear?"

Threadbare nodded, and patted her arm. Celia put him down. "Let me get a few other toys out to fill out our ranks. And maybe a dagger, I'm thinking."

After a bit of animation and sorting, it ended up being Beryl, Celia, the brothers, a floating dagger, and the little dragon toy.

"That's all seven then," Beryl nodded. "Sorry Bakky, no temporary pets for you."

"S'okay." He hauled out a slingshot that looked quite a bit nicer than Celia's. "I'll just be support, and if her stuff gets wrecked I can tame something."

"Works better this way. Your little golem won't siphon our experience," Beryl grinned. "We'll just have to make sure we make the kills, not him."

"Okay. Time for the next step." Garon sighed. "Let's hope they're in a good mood."

"They can't do anything to us. My family's rich. She looks important, too," Beryl pointed a gauntleted finger at Celia.

"What? Me?"

"You look soft, like you've never had to work much. They'll think you're rich too. I'll pretend you're my friend if they ask or give you a hard time."

"Thanks, I think." Celia frowned.

"If you want to thank me, do well in the dungeon and help make me rich. Then we'll see about being friends for real." Beryl punched her in the arm. Hard.

"Ow!"

But the dwarf had already turned, and was trudging up the path again, with her back and forth gait.

Wondering what the heck she'd gotten into, Celia followed along, Threadbare up on one shoulder, the dagger orbiting her in slow circles, and her dragon at her side. The boys fell in behind her, keeping their empty hands visible and their weapons obviously stowed in their respective sheaths or hangars.

"Scouts'll be checkin' us out from this point on," she heard Jarrik whisper in her ear, and recognized the Wind's Whisper skill. "Don't say nuffin' suspicious or that you don't want'em ta hear."

She nodded back, and shot him a thumbs up.

"Full party to enter Catamountain," Beryl waved at the guards.

The rightmost one called back, his voice deep and echoing in his helm. "The dungeon is closed. Turn back."

"What? Why?"

"I don't have to give you that answer, citizen."

Celia looked back to the boys, but they looked as confused as she was.

"Is this normal?" Celia asked the guards. "Is it being remodeled or something?"

The leftmost guard facepalmed. The rightmost one shook a bit, and there was a little mirth in his voice. "Orders, I'm afraid. It should be only be sealed for a few days. After that, you're free to come back."

"I don't recognize your voice," Garon asked. "Sir, are you new here?"

Instantly the mirth left the guard's tone. "Be on your way."

"All right," Celia said, half feeling relieved. "We'll go. Sorry for the fuss—"

The gatehouse portcullis shuddered, and started to rise. The guards started, then whirled and pointed their halberds at the children. "Drop to your knees! Hands in the air!" The leftmost one yelled, but the rightmost one grabbed him, pulled him back, and said something in a low voice.

The recalcitrant guard immediately straightened up, stepped aside, and banged his fist against his breastplate about where his heart would be. "You may enter. I apologize, miss."

"Oh-kay..." Beryl said, glancing around at the group. "Let's go then."

Silent, they filed by, entirely uncertain of what had just happened, and how they should feel about it.

And only Threadbare, peering over Celia's shoulder, was looking in the right direction to see a face peering out of one of the arrow slits. A face with blue eyes as cold as ice, framed with long, straight black hair. He waved, and Anise smiled, waved back, and faded into the shadows.

LUCK +1

PER +1

What a nice lady! Threadbare turned back to watch his friends struggle up the path.

*****

Anise put her hand on the scout's shoulder, as they peered down at the pass, and the group of children below. "You're sure?"

"Yeah. The bear's got a magic item equipped, the stat boosts are too diversified for any mundane equipment."

"Unregistered, most likely," Anise considered her options, then nodded. "Whisper to the guards. Tell them the kids are on an exemption list."

"Ma'am?"

Anise's cold, cold eyes narrowed. "Did I stutter?"

The Scout, Jericho was his name, paled and nodded, lips moving as he used his magical skill to pass on the message.

Anise threw the lever to open the gate, and hurried over to the arrow slit at the sound of shouting. But it was just the typical problem you ran into with Whispering Wind, and people who were on hair triggers. The guard who hadn't heard overreacted, but fortunately his friend had calmed him down. They were all on-edge, and highly trained, over-trained really, for this situation.

But then, Melos had insisted on bringing only the elites out here. She rather thought it overkill, but it didn't matter in the end. She had what she needed. Everything else was details to be arranged at her pleasure.

Like those details outside. She peered out the window at the children moving up the path, and stifled a giggle as the little golem waved at her. She waved back.

"No," she told Jericho, as he reached toward a clipboard of parchment. "Don't record this one."

"Well, they brought an item in, we don't want any misunderstandings after they come back out—"

Actually, Anise did. "I'll tell the next shift personally. Keep this one off the books."

"Those are Mordecai's kids, miss. I..." Jericho snapped his lips shut. Like many of the King's scouts in this region, the old man had trained him personally. Which was why they were still around, unlike the local garrison. They were the best scouts in the Crown's army, and the King had nobody more elite to replace them with.

"You need to be going on back to town, to the mustering point," Anise told him. "We're moving tonight, and your help will be crucial to the Crown's success, Jericho."

He paled. "Yes ma'am!" Snapping off a salute, pounding his fist against his heart, he rose and departed.

Anise smiled, and pinched out the candle, leaving the observation room in darkness…

*****

"What just happened—" Celia started, but Garon shook his head. "Wait."

They turned the corner in the path—

—and instantly the light falling snow cleared. Celia gasped, as she could suddenly see a rocky slope, filled with boulders and prowling forms. The slope led up to a cave. Further up the peak she could see some sort of scaffolding, ending up in a weave of ropes that stretched from a low peak, up to a trail on a second mountain.

"What just happened there?" Celia asked.

"We entered the dungeon." Beryl replied. "Sweet Aeterna, you are green."

"Dungeons are weird," Garon said. "No one outside can hear or see us, even if they're literally five feet away from us. So it's safe to talk now."

"Okay, what was that back there? Why'd they suddenly let us through?" Celia burst out.

Jarrik raised his hand. "When the rightmost one told 'is buddy to stand down, he said ya were on the azempted list."

"Exempted list?" Celia frowned. "I don't know why I'd be on anything like that. How'd he know?"

"Easy," Garon said. "They have scouts checking out every party on the way up. One sent a Wind's Whisper to the guards, telling them to stand down. They just got one before the other, that's all." Garon frowned, creasing his forehead as he pulled on one tusk. "What I can't figure out is why they were so polite."

"That was polite?" Celia shook her head. "Didn't seem like it."

"You don't know them," Bak'shaz spoke up. "Usually they give Beryl all kinds of shit for being with us, and push us around some."

"Fuckin' cunts," Beryl spat. "They know that's all they can do, but they don't miss a chance to be shits."

Celia shuddered. This dwarven girl cussed worse and more in the few minutes she'd known her than Celia had ever heard before in her whole life.

Beryl mistook the shudder. "Aye, you're all right then." She punched Celia's arm again, lighter than she had before.

"I think it's horrible that they treat you that way. But these guys didn't."

"Yeah. They're new." Garon's frown deepened. "They didn't even try to get a bribe out of us."

"Somefing's going on," Jarrik decided. "But we need ta get our heads in tha game. Came here to sweep this peak and get loot and experience, an' if we worry about problems we can't solve we might screw up. So let's focus on tha dungeon."

"There's my Jarry." Beryl beamed with pride. "I keep tellin' Da' he's wrong about you but he just won't listen."

"Um... I don't know much about this place," Celia said. "And those things look very big. They're cats, right?"

"Right, right, you're green." Beryl tapped her shield with gauntleted fingers. "So dungeons are made up of different sections. Each section has different challenges to get through. Some are monsters, some are traps or puzzles, some are combinations of those, and some are weird."

"The Catamountain's a pretty easy one," Garon said, drawing his battle axe, and strapping a wooden shield to his arm. "Comparatively. For this peak, anyway. We just have to fight our way through the slope ahead, get through the catcave, and climb the catwalk." He gestured to the scaffolding. "That'll take us to the Kittyhawk's bridge."

"Wait, does everything here have a cat theme?" Celia was pretty sure they were kidding her.

"Yes," the brothers and Beryl chorused.

"That seems a bit... silly."

"Well it's how it is," Beryl said. "I don't make the rules of how the world works, I just exploit them for my own gain. And yours, if you follow my lead and don't fuck up."

"I'll do my best." She sat Threadbare down. "You might as well keep that dagger."

Threadbare nodded, and thumped his chest like he'd seen the guard do when he did what Celia asked.

"Don't you start," she told him, and he nodded instead.

They fought their way up the slope cautiously, creeping from boulder to boulder, staying out of sight of the bulk of the mountain lions. The trick here, as Garon explained, was to only draw the attention of one or two at a time. They were hard of hearing from constant exposure to the winds, but had decent eyesight, so noises from fights wouldn't bring more of them down.

The lions were tough and fast, and the tactic they fell back on was using the dragon toy to soak up their initial pounces, then send Garon, Beryl, the Animus dagger, and Threadbare in to wail on the large felines while Celia, Jarrik, and Bak'shaz pelted it with slingshot stones and arrows. Celia mended Threadbare and the dragon when necessary, and Beryl healed everyone else.

It worked pretty well, and Threadbare got some dagger practice out of the deal... along with a few stat boosts.

CON +1

Your Golem Body skill is now level 6!

STR +1

Critical Hit!

LUCK +1

Critical Hit!

LUCK +1

Critical Hit!

LUCK +1

By the end of the slope, his dagger skill was up to level nine, and his Dodge skill had risen to two.

"Okay, we're clear. This shelf is a safe space," Garon said, plunking down on a rock.

"I got some good mending practice out of that," Celia said. "But I'm down about a fifth of my sanity. How is yours doing?" She asked Beryl.

"I'm going to need to rest a bit." Beryl dug out a hip flask, and uncorked it. Instantly alcohol fumes filled the air. Threadbare sniffed, sneezed as the unfamiliar odor teased his nose. "Kff!"

Your Scents and Sensibility skill is now level 8!

"That's not water, is it?" Celia asked.

"Nope. Want some?"

"No thank—" Jarrik's hand landed on her shoulder, as Beryl's eyes went wide in shock. Her face reddened, and her eyebrows wrinkled in anger.

"Drink with her! It's a dwarf thing!" Celia heard Jarrik whisper to her through the wind.

"—On second thought, sure," Celia said, and Beryl's reddening face slowly went pale again.

"Here you go then." Beryl said. "Small sips. You're a weedy one."

Celia took a small sip, trying to ignore the fumes.

Five minutes later after she stopped coughing and Beryl stopped laughing, the dwarf corked her hip flask again. "Humans are so funny. You're all right, kid. I think we're friends now, yeah?"

"Yeah," Celia wheezed. "Hate to see... enemies. Drink made my... con go up."

Beryl hooked a thumb downslope. "Enemies? We left them down there. For now."

"For now?" Celia blinked, clearing her throat. "What... do you mean?"

"Dungeons," Garon said. "It makes monsters much sturdier than they would be outside of here, and it removes their corpses after a few minutes. New mountain lions will show back up soon. We'll have to watch for them on the way out."

"If it gets bad we can just cut an' run," Jarrik said. "They don't leave tha dungeon."

"That's bizarre..." Celia said. "What keeps them here?"

"The master," Beryl said. "Not that we're going anywhere near it. Whatever it is."

"Each dungeon has a boss monster, or master, or whatever," Garon said. "But the garrison put a barrier between the second peak and the third, so no one's ever seen it. That I know of, anyway. Rumor is they're hunting him, to shut down this dungeon for good. So whatever he is, he's either smart enough to set up obstacles to keep the guards off of him, or tough enough they can't kill him."

"Of course, most of the guards are shit and weak, compared to the troops in the north," Beryl said. "So maybe he's not that tough."

They rested there for half an hour, regaining a bit of spent sanity and endurance. Celia touched up Threadbare's hit points by practicing tailoring on him, saving her mending for more dangerous situations. Finally Garon nodded. "Okay, this next part is easy, so long as we keep the torches lit."

"Torches. Ya brought 'em, right?" Jarrik asked Garon.

"No, I only brought the sewing kit, and supplies," Garon said. "That was all you guys asked for."

"I thought you'd know ta get torches too!" Jarrik told him, crossing his arms.

"If you don't ask for things, how do I know to get them!" Garon threw his hands in the air.

"Settle down. Half o' you can see in tha dark, and I can feel nearby monsters so long as they're on stone floors," Beryl said. "They'll be tougher, but we can handle it. Maybe. Just need to stick close and be cautious."

"Um, is it just torches?" Celia asked.

"What?"

"I've got an enchanter level."

"What's that do?"

"Among other things, I can make objects glow."

"How bright?"

"I don't know, I learned it two days ago. Never tried."

"Give it a whirl."

"On what?"

"How about your bear?"

"Okay... **Glow Gleam!**"

And then Threadbare was shiny, shiny enough that they could tell it even in the bright light of midday.

"Wow. Yeah, that'll do," Beryl nodded. "You were smart to bring her," she told Jarrik. "Unlike some!" She glared at Garon, who rolled his eyes.

"Whatever. Let's get going."

"Hang on, let's have some backup, here. Throw it on our shields too, okay?"

"Sure, it's cheap." Celia cast it a few more times, smiling as it skilled up. "I think the effect is boosted by my intelligence."

"So hiring a stupid enchanter is pretty dim, right?" Beryl asked, and Celia laughed way more than the poor joke deserved. But when you're tired from hard work, any laugh is a good one.

The next part was the night hunter's cave. It twisted and turned, with a lot of side passages where glittering eyes watched them go by. Most stayed out of the light, but a few cat-headed scorpions scuttled after them, biting with mandibles and toothy maws, and jabbing with stingers. Fortunately Threadbare and the dragon were immune to poison, though Threadbare's golem body got a workout and two levels out of the business. And Beryl knew something called "Curative" which detoxified the living members of the group.

Midway through the last fight, Threadbare got his dagger knocked out of his paws, and it skittered off into the darkness. The brightly-glowing bear switched to his claws, and the party had a good view of him shredding the Minicore that had trapped him into shreds.

Your Claw Swipes skill is now level 7!
Your Claw Swipes skill is now level 8!
STR +1
Critical Hit!
LUCK +1
CON +1
Your Golem Body skill is now level 9!
Your Brawling Skill is now level 10!

Before the rest of the group could catch up, he punched his claws through the Minicore's face, and ripped it asunder.

You are now a level 5 Bear!
CON +5
STR +5
WIS +5
Armor +3
Endurance +3

Mental Fortitude +3
You have learned the Growl skill!
Your Growl skill is now level 1!
You have learned the Hibernate skill!
Your Hibernate skill is now level 1!
You have learned the Stubborn skill!
Your Stubborn skill is now level 1!

"Damnit, he stole our kill!" Beryl shouted.

"He earned that one, let him have it." Garon bent down, searched in the darkness with his glowing shield. "Here it is. And whoa, this one was guarding a chest!" He handed the dagger back to Threadbare, as Celia inspected the little golem and applied a few mends. In the shadows beyond, the Minicore's brood shifted uneasily, but seemed unwilling to press the attack. It would have been a deadly encounter without the light, but with it, the outcome had been inevitable.

They stared at the chest. Celia reached out a hand, and Jarrik caught it. "Nope."

"Oh. Aren't we going to open it?"

"We? Yes. You? No." Beryl said. "Ready, Gar?"

"Ready. See, we don't have anyone here with any rogue jobs, so... I've got the most hit points. Should be fine though," Garon mused. "Worst I've ever taken from one of these popping a trap in this area is one hundred and twenty."

"One twenty!" Celia shrieked. She grabbed up Threadbare and her dragon and hurried to the rear of the group, who backed up and left Garon by himself.

"Here goes!" Garon yanked open the lid...

...and nothing happened. "Whew. Hey!" He pulled out handfuls that shown silver in the light. "Come back, we've got loot!"

The loot, as it turned out, was a good-sized pile of silver and copper coins, and a staff that shone with blue light.

"Blue is sages and water elementalists, right?" Celia asked.

"Mostly. I guess Bak'shaz could try to use it, Tamer's a sage job...wait, you've got enchanter, don't you?"

"Yes! Does this mean..."

"You get to use it until we're out," Beryl said. "But don't get too attached to it. We'll have to give it to the guards."

"What? Why?"

"It's the King's decree. All magic items looted from dungeons must be turned in to representatives of the crown at the first opportunity."

Celia picked it up. "Well, it'll be fun anyway... wait, I could disenchant it at the end of this run. Ooh, it shoots little static electricity balls!"

"No good, it's been tried. Disenchanting, I mean," Beryl said. "The guards take the components and fine you half your coin."

Celia sighed. "Well, it'll be fun while I've got it I guess."

"That's the spirit." Beryl punched her in the arm. In the same place as before. Celia was getting pretty sure it was bruised under her coat, but was too cold to haul it back and check. "Come on. Let's get to the Catwalk."

The catwalk was an agility challenge. Celia scooped up Threadbare for this part, and left him sticking out of the top of her pack. It involved crossing terrifying rope and plank bridges up the side of the mountain, which actually wasn't as hard as it seemed, so long as you were careful and went slow. But this was broken up by divebombing attacks from winged cats, Flying Tomcats, as Bak'shaz helpfully identified them.

They weren't deadly, but they chose the most inopportune times to attack, and their caterwauls were hard on the group's sanity. But Jarrik reigned supreme here, using his archer skills to harass and drive them back, and finish off the ones that skirmished then tried to flee.

Threadbare, for his part, didn't care. He'd heard worse from Pulsivar.

Though interestingly, it did raise his willpower a few more points and his new Stubborn skill to level four by the time they were through it.

Finally they came to the top of the peak, and a long rope bridge that stretched across a slope filled with tall pine trees, that reached almost to the underside of the bridge. It was shadowed there, down between the pines, and Threadbare's eyes just managed to pick out slender shapes moving through the bristles of the evergreens.

PER +1

But it was what was above the bridge that was of more concern. A thing looking much like a squarish, spindly creature made of wood and cloth and fur and fangs floated in the air currents, glaring down at the party with suspicious eyes.

"That's the Kittyhawk," Garon explained. "And this is where we're done. Fighting that thing on the bridge is suicide. I saw someone get knocked off once. And that was pretty much it for the poor guy."

"Aye," Beryl said, but she was squinting up at the Kittyhawk. "Fighting on the bridge would be suicide. But fighting it here, might just be doable."

"We got some treasure and experience," Celia offered. "I leveled, too. Are you sure we want to push our luck?"

"You got a ranged attack item, and I'm still pretty good on healing," Beryl said. "And we've got Bak'shaz on the slingshot and Jarrik with his bow. As long as we dodge when it comes in for attack runs, we should be fine."

"You just want to see what it drops," Garon said. But he was considering it, Celia could tell.

Maybe this thing wouldn't be too bad, Celia thought. "Okay, come here," she picked up Threadbare again, and put him in her pack, with just his head poking out. "It's a long way down and I'm not losing you."

"How about your dragon?" Bak'shaz asked.

"No, let's leave him out," Celia decided. "I can replace him if I have to."

"All right. I'll get 'is attention. We ready?" Jarrik asked.

The kids chorused their readiness, and prepared for battle.

The first arrow embedded itself deep into a cloth wing, and it zoomed in fast, dodging the static orb from Celia's new staff. Bak'shaz cracked it with a slingstone and it turned on the little half-orc, veering in and spreading claws wide—

—only to be knocked off balance as the little dragon threw itself into its side. But the toy soon fell away as the Kittyhawk flew up again. For all its size, the bizarre creature was very light. It whirled a few times, regained some altitude, and hovered, directing jets of wind down upon the party.

"Grab a boulder or get low!" Beryl called. "It can't keep it up forever!"

Celia, skidding backward, just managed to grab a boulder in time.

The little dragon didn't, and disappeared off the cliff, falling into the pines as it tried to flap non-functional cloth wings.

And Threadbare felt himself start to slip free of the pack. Desperately he grabbed on, using his full strength to hold himself tight to the cords keeping the pack shut—

—the cords that tore, spilling the contents of the pack to the forested slope below, and sending Threadbare sailing down to join them.

"No!" He heard Celia yell, and then he was falling...

CHAPTER 11: CATACOMBS

The world spun as Threadbare fell, broken by the occasional THWACK of a branch, or SNAP when he hit one small enough that he broke it and kept going.

About thirty hit points later he came to a stop, with Golem Body up a level and Toughness increased as well. Snow sprayed around him as he dropped into a bank lightly dusted with pine needles, and he poked his head up warily, certain that the fall had been the least of his problems.

The second he did, the deep shadows in the trees fled. He'd had glowgleam cast upon him back in the tunnels, and it chased away the darkness in the little hollow.

What it revealed was far, far worse.

Tons of tiny minicores filled the shadows under the pines, skittering on the snow, hissing with tiny kitty mouths, and twitching their stingers. But as the light touched them they retreated, turning tail and scampering in fear.

All save for some who were clustered around a twitching green form some distance away. Red zeroes and ones drifted up, lots of them. Threadbare squinted, and recognized Celia's dragon toy, fighting desperately for its existence against a mob of minicores. Well, that would never do! He ran over there, waving his arms and making the shadows dance on the trees. The minicores ripping up the little animated toy glanced up and rain for their venomous lives.

But he'd arrived almost too late. The animated toy was in two pieces, stuffing spilling out of it. The upper part, its torso, wings and head twitched and looked at him with an almost sorrowful expression. Filled with feelings that his little fuzzy form could barely express, Threadbare picked the dragon up in trembling paws. He hugged the toy to him, then turned to glower at the shifting, buglike forms hiding in the trees.

Then he froze. Up above, far up in the pines, bigger Minicores clung to the branches, ignoring the unease of their brood below. They were on par with the one he'd taken out solo back in the tunnel, but there were about six or seven per tree, at least as far as he could tell.

He was glad he'd spotted them before he tried climbing out of this place.

PER +1

So. What now?

"Got it!" He heard Jarrik yell from above, and with a screech and a sound of more snapping branches, the large form of the Kittyhawk crashed down below, a little ways away. "Aw man, now we won't..." the wind picked up, and Threadbare couldn't hear the rest of the scout's words. They were pretty far up there.

Suddenly, the dragon toy twisted, and looked directly at him. Its eyes had shifted, he noticed. They looked almost human now.

"Threadbare! Oh my gods. Where are you? What is this?" He heard Celia say in his ear, and turned to look for Celia, but didn't see her. Then it struck him, she was a scout now. Wind's Whisper was totally a thing she could do, and that was probably it.

The little dragon toy looked around. Then it tapped Threadbare on the arm with its nose, and pointed off in one direction. Threadbare stared at it. It tapped again, tugged harder.

Oh!

INT +1

Threadbare set off that way, following the dragon's pointing head, looking around as he went. The bigger minicores stayed to the trees, thankfully, and the small ones shrunk back from his light. For now, he thought he was safe, as long as he didn't run into anything that wasn't a minicore and stayed a good distance away from the bigger ones.

A few minutes later, he came across Celia's waterskin, the dried jerky that Mordecai's sons had given her for lunch later, and the sewing kit. Also what looked like a spare set of trousers and some of her underwear.

Threadbare vaguely remembered seeing some of that stuff spill out of her pack when the winds had ripped him out of it.

"Good! Listen, Threadbare, I need you to pick up that Tailor's kit. I can't mend..." Her words drifted off into hissing "That's annoying. I can't mend you from this distance, so you'll need to sew yourself..." They faded again. A few seconds passed, and Threadbare picked up the tailoring kit. It wasn't much, just a sturdy wooden box. He opened it to find needles, thread, and scissors inside, as well as several small patches, a few skeins of yarn, and a thimble.

"I'm going to teach you to be a tailor." Celia said. "So you can fix yourself and get out of here."

A pause, then she spoke again. "Gods this is skilling Wind's Whisper up fast. Um, here's what you do..."

It took the little girl a few more Whispers to get the idea across, but Threadbare got the notion. Once he was sure he had the steps down, he tried the first one; threading the needle.

Which, as it turned out, was really hard with padded paws.

DEX +1

DEX +1

Finally, more by chance than anything else he got the thread through the loop.

LUCK +1

From there, the needle went through one of the patches, pulling the thread along. Then the needle went through the little dragon. Three painstaking and crude stitches and one point of Dex later, Threadbare had sewn the patch to the little dragon.

By sewing cloth you have unlocked a crafting job; Tailor!

Do you wish to become a Tailor at this time? y/n?

Yes, yes he did!

You are now a level 1 tailor!

DEX +1

PER +1

You have learned the Tailoring Skill!

Your Tailoring skill is now level 1!

You have learned the Clean and Press Skill!

Your Clean and Press skill is now level 1!

The little dragon followed his movements, and the head nodded. "Okay. Now pick up a patch and start sewing it to yourself. Watch for the..."

She faded again. Threadbare waited a bit, then decided she wasn't going to finish the sentence. He tried doing as she said—

—and stared in amazement as a brown frame of some sort of unknown material appeared right in front of him, just like the words did. This one said "Tailoring" and as he watched it filled in with solid brown color.

He looked down at his side just as the bar finished filling in, and with a flicker of motion so fast he wasn't sure he'd seen it, the patch was now sticking to his side.

Your Tailoring Skill is now level 2!

You have been healed for 10 points!

Threadbare tried it a couple of more times. He found out that all he had to do was get the needle in and start a sewing motion, and so long as he fiddled with the needle, the little bar would fill up and the job would complete itself in about ten seconds.

Which was good, because that patch he'd sewn on the dragon had taken minutes. This was a lot faster. Two more patches and two more tailoring skill uses later, he was feeling much better. He was also running low on patches.

"Listen, Threadbare," Celia said in his ear again, "Can you climb out of here now?"

He pointed up at the trees. The little dragon craned its neck, and studied the clustered large minicores.

"Okay, that's a no. Hold on while I talk with the group."

After a moment, in between the rising winds, Threadbare heard shouting from above. Mostly Beryl's voice, though Celia's was mixed in here and there. It eventually died down.

"Okay, that's settled." Celia's voice was tight and low. "We're going to beat up the Kittyhawk again, and go further in…"

"So just keep moving forward and we should meet up somewhere at someplace Jarrik calls the…"

"There should be a connection between the two paths. He didn't know how to get into that hidden area, but you stumbled into…"

"Oh, and wait a bit. Then see if you can find the Kittyhawk corpses. He says there might be loot…"

Threadbare nodded, patted the dragon on the head, and looked back in the sewing kit. Only four more patches left. And he was going to have to go through a lot of stuff to get back to his little girl. Would it last? Probably not, not at a flat ten hp per patch.

What to do?

He looked around, and then his eyes fell upon the bright, fluffy panties that had spilled out of Celia's pack. And the trousers, larger than he was.

Well, patches were just cloth. And cloth was cloth, wasn't it?

INT +1

He hauled out the scissors and got to work, skilling up tailor as he went. He hit level two at the job, happy enough to have the extra dex and per. It wasn't much, but hey.

A few minutes later, he had rigged the trouser pockets into carrying packs, and the panties got sewn together into a shirtlike tunic. The stuff he couldn't wear got cut into patches that went into the tailoring kit. The wooden box would just barely fit into one of the packs, so that was good. That just left one thing to carry.

You have equipped a Pantunic!

He studied the dragon toy remnant, and it looked sadly back. It was his link to Celia, at least until it deanimated. He couldn't carry it in a pack, because she was looking through its eyes somehow. It needed to see. It needed to be somewhere it could see without tying up his paws, while he was fighting or climbing or whatever.

So where could he put it?

And then he had a wonderful idea!

Reaching down, he grabbed the dragon toy, carefully moved some of the stuffing back inside it, and stuck it on his head. A few stitches to hold it in place, and it was up there peering around, sitting comfortably above his fuzzy ears.

You have equipped a Draco Chapeaux!

And words flashed up, entirely unexpected.

By creating and showing off your own unique clothing style, you have unlocked the Model job!

Do you wish to become a Model at this time? y/n?

Threadbare stood there in his panty-shirt, pockets hanging off of his back, his new hat flapping its wings to stay balanced on his head, considering the new option.

Then a noise from above, and he broke off ruminating to watch a second Kittyhawk come crashing down. He marked where it fell and went back to considering this... model... thing.

He really had no clue what a model was or what he'd done of note, but it was a new job, and those made him more powerful. And judging by the things he'd seen in this dungeon, he could use all the power he could get.

So yes, he guessed he wanted to be a model.

You are now a level 1 Model!

+3 AGL

+3 CHA

+3 PER

You have learned the Dietary Restriction skill!

Your Dietary Restriction skill is now level 1!

You have learned the Fascination skill!

Your Fascination skill is now level 1!

You have learned the Flex skill!

Your Flex skill is now level 1!

You have learned the Self-Esteem skill!

Your Self-Esteem skill is now level 1!

You have learned the Work It Baby skill!

Your Work It Baby skill is now level 1!

Well nuts, it didn't boost anything he used to fight? Oh well. At least agility would help him get around more easily.

Right. Next order of business, the Kittyhawk corpses.

With the dragon's help, his still fairly-bright glowgleam effect, and his newly increased perception the little bear managed to hunt down the Kittyhawks. The newly-fallen corpse was in the process of being stripped by a swarm of minicores when he arrived, and they were reluctant to leave, even with the light. He had to kill a few, but they eventually broke and fled. Sadly, they weren't enough of a challenge to give him any boosts, it looked like.

Rummaging around, he found a rolled up piece of parchment that unrolled to reveal drawings and diagrams for something called a "Wrong Flier." He didn't understand any other words of it, and tucked the paper in his pants pocket pack. There was also a small ball of something he'd last seen when Celia was cutting meat out of the goat. Though he didn't know the word for it, it was a bundle of rolled up intestines, curiously clean even though they'd been recently harvested.

It didn't look like much. He considered throwing it away, but decided against it. So far items that monsters dropped had been good to have around, so maybe it would be useful later?

WIS +1

Oh, well, that settled it. He pocketed it as well, and started hunting for the other corpse. It took a while, and as he went, his thoughts strayed back to home. He was starting to miss the place. This was a fun adventure and all, but when they were done it would be nice to get back where he belonged. Hopefully Daddy was okay without Celia there to keep an eye on him.

*****

By the house at the edge of the hills, in a newly-cleaned workshop, Caradon sat and stared at his enchanting supplies. Golems were resource hogs, and he'd used up every smuggled magic item that Mordecai had brought him this week, disenchanting them and mowing through the entire supply of reagents and crystals. And then he'd disenchanted the last two batches of toy golems that he'd tried, and failed to enhance. That hadn't returned as many reagents as he'd hoped.

Sighing, he sat back and did the equations. He had enough left for one more Toy Golem. Not one more batch, one more Toy Golem. He rubbed his knuckles against his eyes.

First, he needed a toy. The old man rummaged through the bin, found it empty. His daughter had taken all of hers, so that was out, not that he'd touch her toys without her permission anyway. That left one option.

He drummed his fingers against the wood of the table, turning it over and over in his mind.

Caradon didn't want to do it. But he'd been through two batches since Celia had gone, and he felt he was on the cusp of a breakthrough. He could work straight through, without interruptions, without having to spare time to tend to her, or mind the house. One good push might do it.

He had to stop holding back.

Caradon went back to the house, rubbed Pulsiver as the cat purred against his leg as soon as he got through the door, and made his way upstairs to the attic. And once there, with only the cat looking on, he dug out the trunk he'd hidden safely away oh so many years ago. Trembling, he opened it, and snatched up the loose sack inside, feeling the weight of the contents. He started to open it, then stopped. No, no. Not here.

Downstairs, at the broad table, with only Emmet and Pulsivar looking on, he poured himself a glass of wine and felt his sanity refill a bit while he drained it. Then he opened the sack, pulling out two things. A framed portrait of a smiling woman, and an old, ragged teddy bear. Six inches tall, with jet black fur, it stared at him as he held it up. One button eye clattered off as the moth-eaten thread gave way, and Caradon sighed.

"Hello Missus Fluffbear." Caradon put down the toy, and looked at the portrait, feeling a lump swell up in his throat. "Hello Amelia." He took a breath, two, three, until he could speak again. "Ten years gone, and I've never missed you more. No man should outlive..." He cleared his throat. "Anyway. I'm sorry, but I have to borrow Missus Fluffbear. Will you... don't worry. I'll take care of her."

Pulsivar purred like a buzzsaw and rubbed against his calves, and Caradon picked up the fat cat, grunting as he did so. He scratched Pulsivar's neck, and waited until the tears that threatened his eyes had subsided.

"I'll take your silence as a yes. Thank you, Amelia." Caradon put Pulsivar to the side, and picked up Missus Fluffbear. Then he dug out his sewing kit and got to work.

Ten minutes later, in his workshop, he made the final pass of his enchanting wand over the little bear, and the crystals and dust he'd arranged in arcane patterns around her glowed, disappearing as magical patterns flared over her body. The vessel was ready.

Fifteen minutes later, he stumbled out of the workshop, pounding his fist against the door frame, barely holding in his disappointment. Another one! Another stunted little barely-intelligent thing! He'd sacrificed Amelia's childhood toy, her favorite, for what?

In fury, he turned back to look at the failed experiment, his still-running eye for detail showing every pathetic detail of its anemic status screen, screaming in wordless frustration…

…and Missus Fluffbear cowered away from him, putting its paws over its head.

He sighed, feeling his anger ebb. Sure, it was only due to its adorable skill, but…

Wait a minute.

Its charisma… hadn't it been sixteen, when he'd first checked the little toy?

Now it was seventeen.

He blinked, as his eye for detail faded.

Implications crashed in on him, but he shook his head. It hadn't responded to the invite. But it had just gained an attribute point, something lesser golems couldn't do.

On the edge, so close to completing the equation, he unbound the little golem from its place on the shelf, and picked it up, hugging it to him. It was stiff in his arms for a bit.

"Hug," Caradon said, and hugged the bear once more. "Hug means this." He embraced it once more, then held it out.

And Missus Fluffbear looked at him solemnly, then held her arms out for another hug.

Caradon gasped, as her intelligence ticked up from five to six.

"I've been a fool. I've been a damned, stupid old fool." He hugged the tiny teddy bear, and now the tears slid freely down his face. "What have I done?" The empty spaces on the shelves where dozens of test subjects had sat haunted him, and he turned his face away. "It doesn't make supergolems. It makes golems into people."

Noise from outside, a rumbling crash, and that's all the warning he got before the wall of the workshop exploded, and a rock the size of his dining room table rolled towards him. He yelled and jumped back, dropping Missus Fluffbear in the process—

—and the boulder swerved, the damned rock hit some tiny obstacle and swerved, heading straight for the prone form of Missus Fluffbear.

"No! **Animus!**" Caradon shouted at his chair, "Invite, ah, Chairy Mcchairface!" Split seconds to go as the rock tumbled, but now the chair was in his party, and subject to his buffs and will, and it scooped Missus Fluffbear up and fled the workshop at Caradon's heels as the thoroughly random rock took out another wall and rumbled to a stop.

A short distance away, Caradon stared at it, then stared upslope, at an outcropping which now looked decidedly less sturdy than it had this morning. "That stone shelf has been up there for years. That's an odd stroke… of… bad… luck…." A horrible thought filled him, and he looked back at Missus Fluffbear.

Sitting calmly in her chair, she held her arms out for a hug.

And to his horror, he realized that her luck had just gone up. From four to five.

"Oh no. No, no, no."

From behind him, he heard the call of Screaming Eagles on the hunt. Eagles, plural.

He grabbed Fluffbear and ran.

Hours later, after the last monster was dead, the fires were out, and Emmet was stomping around the yard hauling monster carcasses away, a haggard and exhausted Caradon looked at the battered but triumphant Raggedy Men. The wards on the house had been damaged a bit, but that was fine.

"Two greens," he told Missus Fluffbear as he put his hand of cards down, and she considered, and put down two blues.

"Good! You win!" He patted her head, and she wiggled with pleasure, something that Pulsivar might have done. Not that the cat had much opportunity to teach her. He'd taken a look at her and fled, for no reason Caradon could tell. "Keep playing grindluck," he told her, studying her status screen's thirteen luck with his eye for detail. "We're going to be here a while."

A few more hands later, and silence surrounded him for once in... hours? Something like that. He'd kind of lost track after the third avalanche. But now he felt secure enough to send the Raggedy Men back to their patrols.

As to the wards, eh, he could get to those later, when he had more enchanting supplies and sanity. As it was, the only ones that were seriously damaged were the ones against demons, and what the hell were the odds that any of those would show up tonight?

He took another look at Missus Fluffbear's luck. The odds were entirely too high, he decided. So he had Ah Chairy Mcchairface go fetch him one of his toy golem birds. "We'll call Mordecai in, just in case," Caradon said, and blinked as his wisdom went up for the first time in years. "Definitely Mordecai!" he said, scratching out a hasty message and sending the bird on its way.

*****

It took a long time, but Threadbare finally found the second Kittyhawk corpse. And it was hard to tell, but he was pretty sure that the light radius of his glow-gleam was shrinking. He hadn't noticed at first, but now it was down to about two-thirds of what it had been. The minicores had noticed this too, and were pressing in around the edges of the light. Worried, Threadbare rummaged through the completely-picked over corpse, that was nothing but bones and wood and cloth, and pulled out another ball of intestines and a large orange and brown gemstone. Into pockets they went.

Now where?

He tapped the dragon, and waved at it. Seconds crawled by, and finally Celia's voice returned.

"Sorry, we're climbing the second mountain and it's hard... everything's tough. I leveled again. We're taking it slow and it's still risky..."

"Oh my gods, you're not even... go towards the second mountain, look for a cave or something. They have to meet up in the middle, near the racket..."

Threadbare immediately started off towards the second mountain, or where he thought it was. It really was dark down here in the hollow between the peaks, with the sun pretty well blotted out by the high stone cliffs and the trees shadowing what was left.

And eventually, the woods parted to reveal an outcropping from the mountain, and a cave with a sign nailed into the stone above the opening.

THIS WAY TO THE CATACOMBS

"Oh geeze," Celia said, as the dragon's head tracked it. "Be careful. It's going to be undead for certain. Find a club for skel..."

She fizzed out again.

"Listen, Dracosnack is about to deanimate, it's been too long. I can't watch you after that happens, the Dollseye..."

"Just do your best! Don't die!" Her voice was raw. "I love you and you come back to me!"

Resolute, shining brightly from his little girl's spell, his dragon hat twitching with every step he took, Threadbare marched into the catacombs. Then he stopped, turned around, and grabbed a heavy tree branch from the forest. He didn't know why Celia wanted him to bring a club, but he was sure he'd figure it out.

Then he waddled back in.

The first section seemed to be a winding collection of corridors, lined with cat skulls in niches to either side. House-cat skeletons ambled out from holes in the walls, and roamed the corridors, pausing to groom themselves with tongues that no longer existed.

To Threadbare, they reminded him of the skeleton puppet that Celia had animated. They were just something like that, he figured. Oddly enough, he wasn't too far wrong, though it would be years later before he knew that.

The teddy bear started toward one cautiously, and sniffed at it. It smelled of dust, and old death. Much like that girl he'd played the card game with, he remembered.

Your Scents and Sensibility skill is now level 9!

The skeleton sniffed back, and whatever it smelled the undead didn't seem to like it much. The cat hissed and pounced on him—

—and met Threadbare's treebranch straight to its skull as it came in.

WHACK!

Critical Hit!

The thing bounced back and came for him again, and Threadbare punched it whenever it got in close, and used the tree branch when it backed off. It took a rough minute of scuffling, and its claws swiped him a few times, but eventually it was done and his Clubs and Maces skill was two higher. Threadbare looked at the scratches, and the loose fur hanging off him, and shrugged. Not enough to be worth breaking out the sewing kit.

He set off down the wide corridor, trying to avoid the skeletons when he could. It was harder than it looked, though they entered and exited the holes in the wall, there wasn't really any rhyme or reason to it. Twice he got jumped moving through what he thought was an empty patch because a skeleton emerged at the wrong time.

After the third encounter, he sat down, dug out the sewing kit, and used two of his precious patches to fix most of the damage, and skilling up his tailoring again. He looked down the hall, as far as his light would let him see, and yeah, it was definitely shrinking. He was down to half what he'd started with, he thought. But in that radius, he could see at least six more of the skeletons roaming back and forth.

There had to be a better way.

Come to think of it, maybe there was. He studied the hole that the cat skeleton had emerged from. It was just about big enough for him.

Threadbare poked his head inside, leading with the bobbling dragon head in an effort to tease any hiding kitty remnants into attacking him. Nothing, so he pushed the rest of the way in.

It didn't look like much. There was a long passage, winding back to a tiny corridor of its own, and what looked like a ramp going up.

Up was good! Up was where Celia was!

Threadbare toddled back that way, leaving the tree branch behind when it wouldn't fit through the holes.

He started up the ramp...

...and tumbled to the ground, as a cat skeleton pounced on him from above, hissing! Over and over he went, with the creature's claws flashing at him, ripping against his seams, ripping patches free.

He fetched up at the bottom with the bony kitty on top of him, jaws around his throat, worrying him—

—and acting purely on instinct he reached up, wrapped his arms around the cat's ribs, and hugged.

Two things happened, so quickly that he barely had time to comprehend them.

First, golden light flared, and the cat went from hissing to screaming, as black essence boiled out of its eyesockets as a red sixty exploded into the air above it.

You have healed Bonikitty for 30 points!

Your Innocent Embrace skill is now level 3!

The second thing was that he felt way woozier all of a sudden. Though he didn't know what a headache was, he definitely felt uncomfortable in his noggin region for a bit. Threadbare didn't know that this was due to the cost of triggering that skill, and that he'd spent fifteen sanity activating it. He definitely didn't know that standard healing magic interfered with the forces which allowed undead to move and act.

All he knew was that he'd hurt it somehow, and the skeleton wanted no more of this particular bear. It turned and fled, and Threadbare struggled to his feet, and shook his paw after it.

After a second to make sure that it wouldn't come back, and half a minute to dig out his sewing tools and patch himself up, Threadbare turned and continued up the ramp.

As he went, a green mist started to fill the corridor. It smelled sharp, and unpleasant, so he turned off his nose after his Scents and Sensibility skill went up a level.

The further he went into it, the more his Golem Body ticked up, too. He gained about three levels of that skill before it stopped reacting to the green haze.

Eventually the small corridor opened up into a larger room, filled with green, rolling clouds. His golden light made weird patterns on it as he entered, and a shape loomed in the center of the room... some sort of structure or object. He headed that way—

—and the green haze cleared momentarily to reveal a stone table, and the biggest cat skeleton he'd seen yet, easily twice the size of Celia, crouching on it. Breathstealer the Toxic-kitty stared down at him, and roared, green haze pouring from its skull.

A green '6' floated up from Threadbare's noggin, and went unnoticed.

WILL +1

Your Stubborn skill is now level 6!

Threadbare halted, turned around, and ran back towards the hole he'd left, dragon wings flapping in the breeze of his passing, and dragon head flopping on its long neck. But Breathstealer was faster still, leaping in front of him and batting him with a paw, sending him flying across the room as a red '28' tore out of him.

He ended up somewhere in the haze again, looking around as he got to his feet, and heard bony digits pounding the stone floor once more. Annoyed, he waited until it burst out of the mist and charged it right back, making the massive creature skid to a halt in surprise. Threadbare's claw swiped right into the side of its jaw...

Your Brawling skill is now level 11!

Your Claw Swipes skill is now level 9!

...and a '4' floated up into the air.

Threadbare and Breathstealer watched it go. Then they looked at each other.

Threadbare bopped it again.

Your Brawling skill is now level 12!

Your Claw Swipes skill is now level 10!

And a '3' drifted off this time.

Breathstealer didn't look at all hurt. Annoyed at the feeble attacks, the bony behemoth opened its mouth and roared once more!

The skill was called Plague Breath...

...and just like before, when Threadbare had been fighting the Rat King, it had absolutely no effect on the little golem!

Your Golem Body skill is now level 14!

He came sailing out of the cloud, latching onto Breathstealer's neck just above its head—

AGL +1

—And hugged it for all he was worth. He had one trick that worked against these things, and by gods he was going to use it!

Golden light flashed, a red eighty rolled up, and Breathstealer went apeshit as Theadbare's innocent embrace literally killed it with kindness. Innocent Embrace was a costly skill, one with a sanity cost that scaled as its healing rose... but the amount of healing it did rose with each skill level gained.

By the time it was done, three skill ups and a strength bump later, Threadbare was on the ground with a four-alarm headache and nine sanity left, and Breathstealer was a smoldering pile of bones.

He lay there exhausted for a second, until—

You are now a Level 8 Toy Golem!

All Attributes +2!

You are now a Level 6 Bear!

CON +5
STR +5
WIS +5
Armor +3
Endurance +3
Mental Fortitude +3

You are now a Level 2 Model!
AGL +3
CHA +3
PER +3

—Suddenly, Threadbare felt a hell of a lot better. Though he didn't know it, leveling up refilled his pools... all save for his poor, battered hit points. He sat down and patched his wounds, and as he did the green clouds cleared away. He saw a green, dripping dagger with a curved blade lying on the stone table, right next to another ball of cat intestines. Grabbing them both, he looked around. The haze had dissipated a bit, and there seemed to be an exit ramp, a large one, going up from here. There was another door out, but the handle was way too high up for him to reach, so he decided to give the ramp a try instead.

While on it, he got another message from Celia. "Testing? Oh thank heavens, you're alive. I miss you. I miss you so much..."

"We stopped to rest. It's rough, it's so rough, we almost lost Jarrik, but we're coming for you, okay? We won't..."

"This is the last sanity I can spare, then I need to drink up for the next part. You survive, okay? You come back to..."

Threadbare squared his shoulders and jogged up the ramp, throwing caution to the winds. Up and up and up, waving his new dagger, not caring what lay between him and danger...

...until the ramp leveled out, and he burst into a dusty room.

In the half-reduced light of his glow gleam effect, he could see that it was filled with old furniture, covered in sheets. And every sheet, every alcove, every dusty wardrobe and cloaked chair had bonikitties sitting on it.

And all of them were watching him. Watching that dragon's head and wings twitch and bop as he scrambled to a halt.

Watching and rising, slinking forward, butts wiggling as they readied to pounce—

"That's enough now! Let me see who's come, hmmmm?" An old woman's voice cracked the silence, as dusty and faded as the room itself.

Threadbare lowered the dagger. The undead cats settled. For now.

"Come closer, my dears! Let me have a look at you... hoo hoo hoo!"

Threadbare paced into the room, and his light showed him the one section of it that wasn't entirely covered in cats.

There was a table, set with fine, if dusty china, and a half-translucent old human woman sitting at the head of it. Her frizzy hair stuck out from under a glowing, crooked top hat, and she wore a patchwork dress covered with embroidery showing cats playing, cats sleeping, cats doing all sorts of cat things.

She was knitting bones. Threadbare watched as she finished knitting spectral strands to old cat's bones, then once she was done, leaned down to the skull and whispered "Rise..."

The new bonikitty stood up, shook itself, and the old ghostly lady clapped her hands with glee. "Oh my dear! You're good as new! Go play, there's a good boy." She pointed toward a hole in the wall, and the skeletal feline leaped down, and paced through, disappearing from sight.

"Now then, I suppose we should get to our... little... fight..." She squinted down at Threadbare, and her jaw dropped open.

Threadbare waved.

Your Adorable skill is now level 15!

"Hoo hoo hoo! Hooo hoooo hooo..." She pounded the table noiselessly with one spectral hand. "Oh my goodness, you're just the cutest little thing! Well, you'd be cuter if you were a cat. But I suppose nobody's perfect. Except cats."

Beyond her, Threadbare could see a set of stairs. He pointed at them.

CHA +1

"Mmm, you want to go through?"

Threadbare nodded, and she giggled as his dragon hat flopped back and forth.

"Well, now we're in a pickle, then. Normally I'm supposed to fight the people who come here. They all deserve it, since they've hurt my poor dearies so! But look at you, you wouldn't hurt a fly, I bet."

Threadbare nodded. He'd never had to fight any flies, after all. And they seemed really hard to hit, too.

"But... Well, the Master never said anything about fighting toys. And if I know you, you're someone's toy. Got a little girl to go back to, hm?"

Threadbare nodded harder, and mimed hugging the air.

"Well, I tell you what. You do something nice for me, and something nice for my dears, and we'll let you through." She pointed at the thirty-some Bonikitties scattered around the room.

Threadbare nodded, then pointed at the kittens, and shrugged.

"Well, they like meat, do you have any of that?"

He shook his head. If he'd brought the jerky from Celia's pack, maybe, but he hadn't seen a need for it.

"Perhaps a toy?"

He considered, then pulled out a ball of intestines.

Fortunately for him, the old lady didn't know much anatomy. "Oh! Yes, that'll do! Just throw it down the ramp, that'll keep them from being naughty."

He hurled it, and with a meowing, clattering cacophony, the bonikitties rushed after it, following it ALL the way down.

"Well done! Come up here." She patted an adjacent chair. "I won't be so easily appeased, though."

Threadbare stood in it, staring up at her, eyes just slightly higher than the table. He pointed at the old lady and shrugged.

She leaned in and grinned. "To get past ME without a fight, you'll have to play my favorite game. Tea party!"

And if he could have, Threadbare would have smiled.

Twenty minutes later, and three Charisma points higher, he bowed deeply to the very happy old ghost, and started to walk up the stairs. She'd given him her second-favorite cat blanket as thanks, buttoning it around his neck as a cape. It was embroidered with paws all up and down its length, and very, very dusty. But overall he was happy, and it almost seemed to lighten his step as he walked.

But not a second later, words flashed up right before his eyes.

Through repeated peaceful contact with the undead, you have unlocked the Necromancer job!

Do you want to be a Necromancer at this time? y/n?

Wow, another word he didn't know. But job levels made him stronger, so why not?

You are now a level 1 Necromancer!

+3 INT

+3 WILL

+3 WIS

You have learned the skill Assess Corpse!

Your Assess Corpse skill is now level 1!

You have learned the skill Command the Dead!

Your Command the Dead skill is now level 1!

You have learned the skill Soulstone!

Your Soulstone skill is now level 1!

You have learned the skill Speak With Dead!

Your Speak With Dead skill is now level 1!

You have learned the skill Zombies!

Your Zombies skill is now level 1!

The bear shook his head, as ideas burst together, filling and expanding it. Then he ran. As thankfully peaceful as that last room had been, it had eaten up precious time. He needed to find his little girl. He needed to get her out of this place! It was dangerous, he now understood that. Any of those things down below could have seriously hurt her, or worse. What was the upper part of this mountain like, if the secret way was so rough?

The stairs topped out in a long corridor, broken by stony pillars.... Stalagmites, he knew, though he couldn't say how. They thinned to sharp, wicked looking points up top, and they were packed in tightly. He picked his way through them, and the ceiling widened up and up until it disappeared.

"Hey! Something's coming!" He heard Jarrik call, and sped up, overjoyed to hear the half-orc's voice.

"I see it... Threadbare? Is that you?" Celia called. Threadbare stopped and jumped up and down, in joy. They were all right! They were alive!

"So that's how you get down into that chasm. I thought there was a way." Jarrik said. "Hang on, I'm lowering a rope."

Threadbare picked his way through the stalagmite field, to the side of the wall which wasn't a wall at all, but a sheer cliff up to the ledge of a deep chasm, a chasm which he was at the bottom of. He grabbed the rope, gave it a few tugs, and got hauled up.

And then he was in Celia's arms, and everything was okay.

Golden light flared, and she said "Oh!"

You healed Celia 70 points!

Your Innocent Embrace skill is now level 7!

Threadbare rubbed his head, as thirty-five more sanity drained out of him. But what looked to be a bunch of scrapes and bruises and cuts along Celia's arms were now gone, so that was fine.

"Right, that's done then," Deryl said. "Let's... ah... "

"What?" Celia said, turning to look at the dwarven girl.

"What the hell is he wearing?"

Celia put him down, and Threadbare waved to the group, dragon hat flopping on its loose stitches, resplendent in his panty tunic and paws button cape.

Your Work It Baby skill is now level 2!

And then there was nothing but laughter, as the exhausted children sat there giggling, deep in the heart of the dungeon.

CHAPTER 12: CATASTROPHE

Eventually, the laughter faded. Beryl resumed her resting scowlface. "All right, fun time's over. Jarrik, do your thing, okay?"

"On it. **Camouflage**," he whispered, and faded, as his skin took on the colors and patterns of the surrounding rocks and darkness. Threadbare could just make out his outline, as he jogged toward the winding tunnel exit that led into darkness, at the end of the chasm.

There were two more exits out of here, the little bear saw. Both had daylight filtering down into the tunnel. The bigger one had a massive grate set across it, with glowing red runes carved into it. SEALED BY ORDER OF THE CROWN a nearby sign instructed.

"Jarrik's going to go see if the boss we just beat has respawned. Well, bosses, I guess," Celia said, as she brushed dirt and dust from Threadbare.

"Boss," Beryl said. "My Ma told me about the Cataphracts. They think and fight as one. Which is why we can't go back through there again unless—"

Jarrik faded back into view. He did not look happy. "They're back."

"—fuck a duck we waited too long." Beryl rubbed her eyes. "I wish you'd been a little earlier Threadbare."

Threadbare walked over and gave her a hug. Beryl glared down at him suspiciously, then deigned to rub his head. In some ways the dwarf reminded the little bear of Pulsivar. Lots of noise and swagger, but good to have at your back.

"Well. Now what?" Celia asked.

"First things first, get those dumb clothes off of your bear. I can't look at him without laughing. Second, let me think..."

"We could always run past the Cataphracts," Garon suggested.

Jarrik shook his head. "Naw. They're set up in a formation that puts most of 'em between us and tha exit. And they're spread out enough I can't camo past them and go get help. They'd detect me an' well, SHUNK."

Shunk sounded pretty bad to Threadbare.

"And even if we get through, there's tha rest a tha dungeon. Tha other bosses will 'ave respawned. An' most a tha monsters."

The group chewed their lips. The odds were very, very bad.

"How about the chasm Threadbare came out of? We got rope," Bak'shaz pointed down into the pit.

Garon shook his head this time. "We've got rope but nothing to attach it to. That grate will fry anything it touches, and the closest tie-off point is in the Cataphract room. And even if we did, those Stalagmites are set really close together. I don't know about the rest of you, but I haven't been grinding agility. They'd flat out kill me if I fell on them. And if they'd kill me, sorry, but they'd turn any of the rest of you into gibs."

"And there's no telling what Threadbare went through to get here," Celia said, stripping off Threadbare's 'clothes'. "His sewing kit's out of all the patches that came with it, it looks like he had to resort to cutting patches from, uh, from... ahem."

"What?" Garon asked.

"Nevermind," Celia hastily tucked away the frilly remnants of her best set of panties. "Oh hey, he made little packs for himself. How cute!"

"Smart bear." Garon sighed. "Beryl?"

"Coming up empty. It kills me, Clerics get Divine Transit at level ten. That would solve all of our problems! But I'm one level short, just one friggin' level!" She pounded her chainmail skirt, with a jingling clash. "If only we had a couple of decent fights, or maybe one big one, I could get there. But there's no monsters in here. And the Cataphracts are too tough. We burned up all our coins so Garon can't use his twisted rage blood is gold combo, so there's no way we'd get the experience without fatalities. They're just too smart and too tough."

Threadbare walked over and tugged on Garon's leggings, then pointed to the remaining exit.

"What? No. That goes to a puzzle, but I don't think we have the components for it."

Threadbare started ambling that way. "Oh gods! No, hold on!" Celia said, and gave up sorting through his clothing as she hurried to catch up.

"Don't go far!" Beryl yelled.

"Relax, it's just a catapult," Garon said. "Nothing else out there."

The cave opened up onto a high ledge, far up the second mountain. It overlooked the final mountain, about five hundred feet away. On an opposite ledge, some sort of large tarp secured to a matching cave entrance flapped in the wind.

To the side, Threadbare could see a long stone bridge, stretching over to another, larger entrance into the mountain. A pair of Flaming Tygers paced back and forth there, not that they had anything to guard against. Judging by the angle of the bridge, it led to a corridor that ended at the runed grating.

Sitting on the ledge, pointing toward the opposite cave, was a heavy wooden device. It had a bunch of ropes rolled up on a tightly bound crank, and a wooden arm with something like a huge spoon on the end. However the spoon had no back to it, just a bunch of hooks on its inner rim. It was like a ring on a stick.

On its side, burned into the wood, was the word RACKET.

"I've seen pictures of these in books," Celia explained. "Beryl's a tinker, she knows machines, and she thinks it can throw people across, but it's broken." She tapped the ring. "We don't know how to fix it. It's probably a shortcut to the Dungeon's Master, so I don't know if that would help our situation any even if it was."

Threadbare ambled to the edge of the ledge, knocking a pebble with his paw, as he did so. It tumbled off the cliff and fell hundreds of feet, disappearing into fog.

"Yeah, that's probably instant death," Celia said, keeping a careful hold on his arm. "Come on, let's go back inside."

"Oh!" She said as she got in. The rest of the group was huddled around Threadbare's packs, sorting through his loot. "Hey, that's..."

"Keep your knickers on. The few you've got left, anyway. We're looking for something to help us survive this," Beryl snapped.

"Of course, that's fine. What did he pick up, anyway? I didn't look too closely."

"Well, he got a kick-ass dagger for you to animate, so you're getting that for now," Beryl slid it across the ground to her, and Celia picked it up and frowned at it.

"Status. Oh, wow! Yeah, this will be great for an animus blade."

"It improves our chances a bit. Let's see..." Beryl slid open the scroll, and her eyes went wide. Her gauntlets shook, rattling the chain mail sleeves coating her arms as she surveyed the paper. "This is a tinkering recipe! Holy fucking shit he found a tinkering recipe!"

"Really? That's good?"

"Those things are really rare," Garon explained. "Beryl's a tinker, and most of the rest of her family are smiths and tinkers. That recipe, whatever it is, is worth a whole lot of money to them."

Beryl whooped! The dwarven girl shot to her feet and literally jumped for joy. Maybe. It was hard to tell under the chain mail skirt. "It's a flying machine!"

Instantly Jarrik laughed and scooped her into a hug, kissing her passionately. She kissed him back, grabbing his ass as she did so, and still laughing into his mouth.

Celia turned beet red and looked away, clearing her throat.

"Get a room," Bak'shaz whined.

"Bitch, I've got a cave and no reason to keep quiet so don't tempt me," Beryl said, popping her mouth off of Jarrik's. "Okay. If we're really lucky, let's see... here... well, shit."

"What?" Jarrik said, squinting at the paper.

"It's a single seater. And it takes wood and cloth. Lots of wood and cloth."

"Well." Celia said. "We've got our clothes. And the wood from the catapult."

"And it takes a flight skill to manage."

"Um..."

"Yeah, I didn't know that was a thing either."

"I did," Garon said. "Mom can shapeshift. She told me if I stuck with shaman I'd learn that skill eventually."

"Ah-huh. And how many crashes did she say you'd have when you were starting out?"

"Let me put it this way. She said the best way to survive and learn the skill is to cast slow regeneration before I tried."

"Doesn't matter," Beryl sighed, as she read further down. "It also takes a Mark I Fizznocker engine. This is too high end for me to build, guys, even if I had the parts. Hell, it might be too high end for my Da. Which is a pity, because we've been looking for something like this for years."

"Won't the guards just take it like the other magic items?" Celia asked.

"Nope. It's nonmagical. Their wizard's scan won't detect it. Yeah, technically this belongs to Threadbare since he's not in the party. We'll have to do some formal negotiations with you Celia, see if we can buy it from you. This is too valuable to us, no matter how much it'll cost Da."

Celia considered. They'd had a pretty big argument, when she tried to convince the dwarf to help save Threadbare. Technically, Celia's conviction had been the one to land them in this situation. So... "Then it's yours for free when we get out of here, no negotiations necessary." Celia decided.

Beryl's jaw dropped. "What? You... you're just GIVING it to me?"

"Yes."

"But... I..." Beryl stared straight ahead, and for a second Celia thought she'd done something wrong.

Then Beryl lifted up in her strong arms, and hugged the hell out of her. Celia squeaked, and tried to avoid being grated like cheese against the other girl's chainmail.

"Thank you," Beryl choked out. "We owe you a debt. Know now you're a friend to clan Wirebeard."

"Can she do that?" Garon whispered behind her.

"Sssh," Jarrik cautioned.

Finally, Beryl put her down. "Right. Right, ahem." She cleared her throat, mopped away something that she stoicly pretended wasn't a tear, and glanced back to the little pile of loot. "What else do we have?"

Oblivious to the drama, Bak'shaz had kept sorting through the loot. "A tigerseye gem. Worth some money but no help. Unless you can blood is gold it, bro?"

"Nah. Only works on coin," Garon shrugged.

"Um, we got his cape. Which sized to him when he picked it up. I don't think we can wear it."

"His cape does something?" Beryl asked.

"Yeah, bullet time. It's the Paws Time cape because this dungeon is silly."

Jarrik's eyes got wide. He snatched up the little blanket, tried to button it around his wrist. "Nothin'. Damn. Woulda been nice."

"Yeah, he's the only one who can use it, so..." Bak'shaz handed it back to the little bear, who put it back around his neck with a gravitas he hadn't had before the model job.

"Bullet time is really that good?"

"It would let bro here dodge a massive spell," Bak'shaz hooked a thumb back towards Jarrik. "Or let him stop time, fire a dozen arrows, then start time and the arrows would all hit at once."

"Wow." Celia studied Threadbare, who waved back. "What's a bullet, anyway?"

"Beats me," Jarrik shrugged.

"The only other thing he's got in there is these." Bak'shaz held up the two balled up tangles of intestines.

"Ick. Why did you even touch those, Threadbare?" Celia made a face.

Threadbare shrugged. It had seemed like a good idea at the time.

"Wait, hold on," Garon said, leaning in. "I found one of those on that Lion Eyes midboss we took out. I left it there because I thought it was just a tanner component—"

"It is. It's catgut," Bak'shaz interrupted.

"—right, but it looked exactly like these. I think we're looking at a key item, here. Key items, anyway."

"Key items?" Celia blinked.

"They open up new sections of the dungeon, or you need them to solve puzzles," Beryl said. "It's a long shot, but maybe there's a hidden puzzle around here."

Celia stared at her. And behind her eyes, gears turned, and the young animator's eighty-nine intelligence earned its keep. "Beryl?" She asked, very carefully, "this dungeon is big on puns, right?"

"Yeah, it's one of the silly ones. They do stuff like this."

"What if that catapult isn't a racket. What if it's an unstrung racquet?" Celia's grin shone in her moment of triumph.

The rest of the group was silent.

Finally Beryl asked "What's a racquet, then?"

*****

Not far away from the dungeon, the mother sat in a sweltering room and saw the world. Steam filled the room. Steam filled the world, and gusted and eddied, and pooled in Zuula's vision. Herbs smoldered in their pots, mixing with the hot, wet clouds and soaking into her as the sweat left, breathed in, not just by her lungs but her very pores. And as the steam billowed, the walls of the lodge expanded, fell away, became darkness and stars.

And Zuula drifted in the darkness, turning in the sheltering heat of the steam, peering down upon the green and white and blue, seeing the patterns that ran through.

She saw, and she grieved. *Ah, that is how it is*, she thought not with her mind, but with the soul that was all she was now, for she'd left her brain behind in her other body. Where she was, you didn't need fleshy eyes to see. Or a brain to think, for that matter.

Slowly, once she was sure of what she saw, she began the long drift back to her body. Oracles really had it easier, she thought. Gods were oddly small, in the grand scheme of it all. They could throw easy puzzles at their Oracles, symbols and hopes and visions. Dream quests were much more difficult, because the grand sweep of nature not only had no real interest in things that weren't it, it didn't bother to adjust its comprehension so that smaller things could understand it. How could the ant comprehend the elephant, or the pebble comprehend the mountain?

The bottom line was that dream quests did better with natural things, and stuff that disturbed them. Which is why she knew the Oblivion would fall, in five years or twenty-seven. She knew that the wild animals around here would get a population boom soon, and with a sick feeling she thought she knew why that was so.

But the thing of being a shaman, is that to do so you had to put yourself into nature, but keep a foot back in the world of people. You had to stand in the middle, and nature being what nature was, it got into you, grew outward, made you more of a part of it then you would be otherwise.

Which was why Zuula knew for certain the time of her death. And precisely how many worms would eat her corpse after all was said and done.

Nude, she left the sweat lodge, trekked back to the house, and dried herself by the fire. Flipping up the loose board beneath the hut, she withdrew her good club, the one she hadn't turned in to the king's men when they demanded that her family register all their magic items.

Then she stared up at the totem mask. It stared back, purring with restrained power, holding all the primal emotions she'd poured into it through the years. Fear, rage, and lust, mostly. Easy stuff to work with. Powerful stuff, when all was said and done.

Mordecai had thought she was just into rough foreplay. Well she was, but like most things she did, it served a deeper purpose. High wisdom let you do that sort of thing, after all.

With both hands, she took the mask down, feeling it writhe within her hands, the painted wood becoming more than wood, stretching to her face. Put me on, she heard within her mind. Her own voice, but not a part of her that normally bothered speaking, just doing. Put me on, it whined again, and Zuula shook her head.

"No just yet," she sighed, staring out the door of the hut. Her death she'd seen, but others were far, far from decided. "No just yet. Soon..."

Everyone was pebbles, and the ocean was life. One would sink and be gone for none the wiser, but perhaps others would remain ashore. All she could do was hurl herself into the future, and go out fighting.

*****

Twenty minutes later, the children finished stringing the catgut through the hooks around the enormous catapult's ring.

"Wait!" Garon said.

"What?" Celia asked, her throat dry. It had taken about five minutes to explain the concept of badminton racquets and another five to sell them on the notion of, well, this.

"Just so we're clear, we're hurling ourselves across the gap to fight the boss, in hopes that he's less of a lethal fight than the Cataphracts were, in the hopes that he'll provide enough experience to level Beryl up so she can cast her dungeon escapey spell."

"Divine transit," Beryl clarified.

"Right, that."

"Yeah," Celia nodded. "I know. It's really bad odds, but—"

"Okay. Give me a quest and offer the tigerseye as a reward."

"What?"

"I get bonuses when I'm on quests with material rewards."

That was a good idea, so she did it.

"Do the Job!" Garon intoned. Then he smiled. "There we go! Hey, skill up! Mff. Not much. I haven't had much chance to level this yet. But hey, every bit helps. Then once we get in there I'll use fight the battles, that'll help us all more."

"That's the party buff, right?" Celia asked.

"Yeah. Oh, wait... Do you want any of your little pets out for this?"

"Just the dagger. Which leaves... crud, I guess I could stuff a pet in there, otherwise that leaves us with six."

"Nah. There's a little guy here who's earned his place," Beryl said. **"Invite Threadbare."**

"That won't work," Celia said. "You'd need one of Daddy's scrolls to —"

Threadbare has joined the party!

There was a pause. Celia stared at the little bear, mouth open.

"Guess it does work," Beryl grunted. "Okay, **party screen**." She stared at the air in front of her, eyes getting wider and wider as she went. "The fuck?"

"What?"

"Okay, Greater Toy Golem you told me about."

"Yeah."

"Bear makes sense."

"Uh-huh."

"Bak'shaz, you said he had ruler and scout levels, right? And Celia, you taught him tailor?"

"Yes. I'm very glad that worked," Celia said, still trying to wrap her head around the fact that the golem had just done something she'd been repeatedly told he couldn't do.

"So why in the ninety-nine hells does he have model and necromancer levels?"

That brought silence.

They all stared at the little bear.

He shrugged.

Garon broke it. "Models get that thing where they get bonuses or something from wearing clothes, right?"

"I think so. Don't know much about them," Beryl said, eyes unblinking on the teddy bear. She'd poked a molehill and been blindsided by a mountain.

"Well then, give him his clothes back," Garon said. "We need every edge we can get right now."

"But they're made of my—" Celia broke off.

"What?"

"My... I mean..."

"You can get new crotchrags," Beryl told her. "Sew his gear back on him."

Blushing, Celia did so. Then they piled into the catapult.

"Necromancer," Celia said, staring down at the bear, clutched tight in her arms. "So you can cast spells too, now?"

Threadbare shook his head and tapped his mouth.

"Right. We'll do something about that." Visions of teddy-bear led zombie apocalypses filled her mind. "After I talk with Daddy. Most definitely after that. This is... yeah, I think something's gone off the rails here."

"Yeah," Garon said, unslinging his battle-axe, and gripping the side of the racket. "Us."

And he cut the rope holding the arm in place.

"You could have just thrown the levvEEERRRRRRRRRRRR!!!!" Beryl screeched, as the party went flying.

WHUMP! The tarp against the cave entrance on the opposite cliff gave way, billowing inward, as they fell into a pile of thousands of balls of yarn. The tarp flapped, loose, as the youths sorted themselves out.

Celia cast Animus Blade, and sent the magical dagger whirling around her, dancing with grace far beyond her normal blades. Then she checked her static rod, and took a deep breath. "Ready."

Garon pulled out the Cataphract shield he'd earned from the last fight, and hefted his well-used battle axe. "I'm good."

Bak'shaz waved his slingshot and shrugged. But he was wearing the Lion Mane he'd snagged from a Lion Eyes boss earlier in the day.

And Jarrik nocked an arrow, and shared one last kiss with Beryl.

"Right," Beryl said, smacking her lips and clearing away the last remnants of her black lipstick, "Let's go get this fucker."

A flight of stairs later, they came to the Master's Chamber.

Tall, vaulted ceilings filled a Cathedral like-hall, complete with an altar up front, covered with well-thumbed copies of "Cat Fancier." Balls of yarn were strung across and around the candle-sconces, hanging between the pillars and draping down, ends blowing in the draft from the high windows. It had the reek of a thousand thousand litterboxes, and as the group stood coughing, Threadbare took the bump up to his Scents and Sensibility level, and shut his nose off as fast as it could go. To either side of the altar stood large chests, overflowing with coins.

"Hoomins!" A voice boomed from above. "Ceiling Cat is watching you!"

A blur of white above, that shifted away as a door slammed open, next to the altar. Greenish eyes glared out. "And Basement Cat will swallow your souls!" Came a hiss that would have put Pulsivar to shame.

"Oh sweet Aeterna," Beryl gasped. "A two part boss!"

"Um, excuse me?" Celia raised her hand.

"What?" The white blob above in the ceiling poked out through its hatch, silvery eyes shining with a gentle light, extending into a halo that surrounded its head. "What is it, my child?"

"I'm the only human here."

There came a pause.

"Right, sorry," Ceiling Cat apologized. "Hoomin, I am watching meOWWW!" A red '43' drifted up as Jarrik pegged it with an arrow, and then there was no more time for grammar correction.

"Holy Smite!" Shouted Ceiling Cat, dropping from the ceiling, paw glowing as it became surrounded by a silvery outline of a much bigger appendage. It aimed for Jarrik, but the scout dodged, and Garon took it on his shield, grunting as a red '25' drifted up from him. **"Fight the Battles!"** he roared.

Instantly, Threadbare felt... heavier.

You are affected by a temporary party buff!

+7 STR

+7 CON

+7 Armor!

+7 to all weapon skills!

Ceiling Cat flipped off the shield, landed, and darted back in clawing and scratching, just as Bak'shaz screamed. He was on the floor, being dragged backwards. Basement Cat had charged out, nabbed him, and was trying to carry him off into the darkness.

"Oh no you don't! Come on Threadbare!" The dagger zipped out at Basement Cat, and Celia angled for a clear shot, readying her static rod. Threadbare, for his part, simply dashed in and unleashed his ultimate attack! Before Basement cat could react, the little bear hugged him!

You healed Basement Cat 80 points!

Your Innocent Embrace skill is now level 8!

Basement Cat paused. He dropped the squirming Bak'shaz and stared at the little bear. "Thank you?"

Threadbare let go of him, puzzled. That hadn't worked.

"Uh, what the hell are you even wearing?" Basement Cat continued, thoroughly distracted by the bizarre figure's garb.

Your Fascination skill is now level 2!

Then a static orb slammed into the cat, and he howled again, lashing out at Bak'shaz and Threadbare.

Well, Threadbare had claws too, didn't he?

Basement Cat blurred, fading in and out of sight, striking from unexpected angles, aiming for critical points on the little bear.

He found none.

Your Golem Body skill is now level 15!

CON +1

Your Golem Body skill is now level 16!

"Celia! Switch fire to Ceiling Cat!" Beryl called. "Basement's a rogue type, keep the dagger on him!"

"Got it!"

Threadbare didn't care about the long claws sliding into places his organs should have been, and the damage drifting up was a secondary concern. Celia would keep him healed there, if he needed it. So the little teddy bear swiped and clawed back, aided by the magical dagger which whirred by and cut into the boss' side every now and then, and Bak'shaz, who got to safety behind the altar and pelted it with slingstones.

Five more brawling levels, two more strength, a point of luck, and six more Claw Swipes levels later, Basement Cat staggered back. Threadbare spared a glance to the others, found Garon tanking Ceiling Cat next to Beryl, supported by shots from Jarrik and Celia's static orbs.

"Lesser Healing!" The white cat mewed, flying just out of reach for a second.

"Yeah? I got that too, you little pussy!" Beryl yelled. **"Lesser Healing!"**

Garon grinned as his wounds sealed. "Thanks!"

The fight went on for a few more minutes, and gained the little bear another Brawling level, but Threadbare could see how it would end up. Which made him wonder... were these guys supposed to be the strongest monster here? The group was handling this one fine. Why had they worried about it so much?

He got his answer as the two polar opposite cats reached the same conclusion, glanced to each other, then disengaged and bound upwards, to stand on the altar.

"By our paw-ers combined," meowed Ceiling Cat.

"Call the ultimate magus!" finished Basement Cat.

"Come forth, Nekomancer!" The two cats blurred and bended together, mystical energies crackling and flaring, obscuring them from view.

"What the fuck you mean they got a final form!" Beryl bellowed. "Ah shit, uh, uh... **Party Heal!** Get ready, guys!"

"Mend! Mend!" Celia shouted, and Threadbare felt himself pull together. His cape fluttered in the wind, as the flashing light resolved...

Into a girl. Small, thin, wearing a black fur bikini, with white kitty ears. A twisty tail, made of swirling black and white fur, waggled behind her. "Nyaaaa-aaan," she purred, squatting on her haunches, and grinning big...

...showing very large, but cute fangs.

"Awwww," the youths chorused.

Threadbare wouldn't have joined in if he could've.

You have resisted the Adorable effect!

WILL +1

Your Stubborn skill is now level 7!

With a magic-item boosted leap, he hopped up on the altar, and bopped her in the face with a fistful of claws, sending a red '40' skyward.

AGL +1

Your Brawling Skill is now level 19!

Your Claw Swipes Skill is now level 16!

"Me-OWWW!!! That is NOT KAWAII!" She kicked him off the altar, and Celia caught him.

Your Toughness Skill is now level 9!

Max HP +2

"Yeah! You're not cute at all!" Celia shouted. Then she looked down at her bear, and blanched, stared up in shock at the red '65' that drifted its way up above. "Oh no! **Mend! Mend!"**

The Nekomancer leaped into the party, slashing and gouging with unbelievable strength, and slowly but surely, the youths were driven back. Garon went down first, coughing blood, gasping as he hauled himself away from the fight.

"Shit shit shit! **Lesser Healing! Lesser Healing! Lesser—**" Beryl broke off as the Nekomancer caught up to her, ignoring the slingstones and arrows that thunked into her. Beryl raised her shield, and staggered backward as red numbers crashed out from her, glaring against her armor. That was the only thing that saved her, as she scrambled away.

Then Threadbare was there again, and punted away again, for another fifty-seven points of damage.

Jarrik fell next, holding his side and gasping as he bled on the stone floor, and the Nekomancer chuckled. "Hee hee hee! Is that all you've got? You're no match for meee-eeee nyan nyan nyan..." She posed, somehow managing to get her bikini-clad boobs and butt in the same line of sight to the onlookers.

Then a static orb bounced off of her, sending up a red '24' and she turned.

To glare at Celia.

"Oh no!" Celia whispered, bringing the dagger in front of herself. "Stay back, or—"

"Blood Is Gold!" Garon thundered, and the entire group and the boss froze, and whipped around to stare over by the altar—

—and past it, to one of the large, coin-filled chests, that now looked a lot-emptier.

Next to it knelt Garon, glowing with health, one hand buried up to the elbow in the loot. He grinned at the Nekomancer.

"He-ey! My shinies!"

"Oh you're gonna love this, lady." Garon sneered. **"TWISTED RAGE!"** He howled, and as the Nekomancer charged him he scooped up the treasure chest with one arm, muscles bulging and popping open his leather armor as he roared pure hatred at the boss!

Seconds passed, as Celia and Threadbare stared. The half-orc's immense, boosted strength brought his axe crashing down again and again on the head of the Nekomancer, and her claws flashed so quickly that they could barely see them. Red numbers flew up left and right, blending together so much they couldn't tell whose wounds were whose.

"Blood is Gold!" Garon howled again, and the coin level in the chest shrunk again. Then he hit the Nekomancer harder.

"Don't just stand there, help him!" Beryl yelled.

"Right!" Celia tried for an angle where she wouldn't catch Garon in the crossfire, but it was tricky. She sent in the dagger, and waited for her moment.

"Divine Shield!" Beryl yelled, pointing at Garon as energy flared around him. Some of the numbers got smaller, but not by much. "I'm almost dry!" The cleric yelled.

"Analyze Monster!" Bak'shaz took a look, and paled. "She's only down to half!"

"Half?" Celia shrieked. "He's almost out of money! When that happens..."

"We need a distraction," Beryl called back. "So he can switch chests!"

And Threadbear knew what he had to do.

The first major boss battle of his life had been against a housecat, after all. And this girl seemed to be at least part housecat.

He ran toward the fight, pushing himself to the limits, leaped for her, saw he was going to miss—

—and time slowed, as his Paws Button cape sped him up to the point where everyone else was in slow motion.

Hitting the ground, Threadbare marched over, grabbed the Nekomancer's tail with both hands, and hung on. He knew what was coming.

Time renewed—

—and the Nekomancer flipped out.

"AH! Getitoff getiitoff getitofff!" She screeched, breaking off the fight and bouncing from pillar to pillar, flipping around, slamming the little bear against the stone again and again. If he'd had bones they would have been jellied, if he'd had internal organs they would have been ruptured. But as it was...

STR +1

Your Ride Skill is now level 3!

Your Golem Body skill is now Level 17!

Your Ride Skill is now level 4!

"Mend!" shouted Celia

CON +1

Your Ride Skill is now level 5!

Your Toughness skill is now level 10!

+2 Max HP

Your Ride Skill is now level 6!

Your Brawling skill is now level 20!

Your Golem Body skill is now level 18!

Your Ride Skill is now level 7!

"Mend!" Shouted Celia.

All told, it lasted for far less than it seemed it did.

Finally, perhaps a minute into it, Threadbare heard a rip, and went flying. One of his arms was gone, he realized, shortly before he hit a pillar and fell, cloak flapping, dragon hat dangling to one side, the stitches torn.

"My tail! You brute! I'll use your stuffing for my litter box—"

"Ahem," Garon said.

She turned, and her eyes went up three sizes as she shrieked. "Not again!"

"Again!" Garon roared, his arm buried into the coins of the other treasure chest. **"Blood is Gold!"** The treasure chest shuddered as coins evaporated.

"Twisted Rage! RARRWRWRWRWAREAW!!!!"

It took every last bit of stamina they had.

But finally, finally, they brought her down.

You are now a level 9 Toy Golem!

All Attributes +2

You are now a level 3 Ruler!

CHA +3

LUCK +3

WIS +3

You are now a level 3 Scout!

AGL +3

PER +3

WIS +3

Threadbare dusted himself off, went over and picked up his arm, leaking stuffing with every step, then hauled out the sewing kit and started patching himself up.

Your Tailoring skill level is now 10!

You are now a level 3 Tailor!

DEX +1

PER +1

And just as he finished, he noticed that new words had appeared before him.

By defeating a foe using a level 20 or higher weapon skill, you have unlocked the Duelist job!

Do you wish to become a Duelist at this time? y/n?

Well, any job was a good job!

You are now a level 1 Duelist!

+3 AGL

+3 DEX

+3 STR

You have learned the Challenge skill!

Your Challenge skill is now level 1!

You have learned the Dazzling Entrance skill!

Your Dazzling Entrance skill is now level 1!

You have learned the Fancy Flourish skill!

Your Fancy Flourish skill is now level 1!

You have learned the Guard Stance skill!

Your Guard Stance skill is now level 1!

You have learned the Weapon Specialist skill!

Your Weapon Specialist skill is now level 1!

Searching...

Your Weapon Specialist skill is currently set to: Brawling!

That felt weird, but good. Threadbare flexed his paws, feeling separate pressure points rise and fall beneath them. It was like he had claws under there that weren't claws. He picked up the tailoring kit one handed, and marveled at the ability to do so.

"What the fuck?" Beryl said, staring at Threadbare. "The little shitter just leveled into duelist."

"To be fair, that was a pretty swashbuckl-ey move back there," Garon said. "Kinda fits."

"This is definitely not supposed to be happening, I'm pretty sure," Celia said. "Threadbare, just... let me talk to Daddy before we do any more adventuring, okay?"

"Tell me ya got to level ten," Jarrik begged Beryl, who nodded, sweaty-faced, bruised all up and down her side, but with a big grin.

"I did. I can get us out of here."

"Oh, give me that tigerseye, will you?" Garon asked Celia. "Quest's done."

She handed it to him, then hugged the fat youth tightly. "Thank you."

"Eh. Most of our loot's gone. Except some small gems, and a few of magic items we'll have to turn in so there's no point in getting attached." He scooped up an armload of weapons and armor. "Let's go. Experience is its own reward, looks like."

"Divine Transit!" Beryl said, and the world blurred around Threadbare...

...and instantly, they were back at the beginning of the dungeon.

"Oh this is gonna make things so much easier," Beryl grinned. "Thanks, guys. Good party."

"Good party," Celia agreed. Level eleven! In one day she'd gone up four levels! And that wasn't even counting her gains as a scout, and an enchanter. She was so close to her level five skills there she could taste it...

...but it was time to go. Night had fallen while they were up there, a trip that was supposed to take perhaps half the day gone way late, due to Threadbare's unexpected fall.

They walked out of the entrance, and headed back to the gatehouse. It was shut once more, and the guards were on the dungeon side of the gate, now. Atop the gatehouse, a man dressed in blue robes, with a bushy beard, stared down at them.

"Halt and surrender your unregistered magic items," the guards demanded.

"Sure. It's a good haul, the Crown should be happy," Garon said, offering the collection from the chest one by one. "Come on, get his little cape too," he reminded Celia.

Forlorn, she handed over the Paws Button cape, the dagger, and the

Static Rod. "I think that's it."

"We're done here too," Beryl said, after checking with the brothers. Come on—"

"Analyze Magic," The old man in the gatehouse window said. Then his eyes narrowed. "Check the bear."

"What? No!" Celia said. "He's not a magic item, he's a golem, that's all."

"Yes, and there's something in him that's registering," said the wizard.

"Don't—" Then one of the guards tore Threadbare from Celia's arms. He fought back, but the armored man ignored his attacks, squeezing each part of him, compressing the stuffing. Red zeroes flew upward as he swiped at the guard, to no avail.

"Something inside him," The guard said, then Threadbare shuddered as the man casually tore his side open, and a red '120' floated up into the air.

Your Golem Body skill is now level 19!
Your Toughness skill is now level 11!
Max HP +2

"Don't you rip him up—" The other guard moved past Threadbare's field of vision, halberd leveled, and he heard Beryl shouting.

And the guard holding him pulled out the scepter. A tiny golden thing, with a teddy bear's head on it.

The shouting stopped, replaced by stunned disbelief.

"There it is," said the wizard. "Trying to smuggle out items, hm? Trying to cheat the Crown?"

Threadbare feebly grabbed for the scepter, and the guard tossed him aside. Jarrik just managed to catch him, before he went over the edge of the cliff.

LUCK +1

"Mend! Mend! Mend! Mend!" Celia shouted, and Threadbare was mostly whole again. He leaped out of Jarrik's arms and squared himself, glaring at the guards, standing between the one with the halberd and his girl.

"I don't know why you decided to break the law over such a small trinket," said the guard holding the scepter, "but it makes no difference. You are under arrest, for smuggling. Come quietly and be tried for your crime or resist and die here, it's your choice."

CHAPTER 13: WHEN BAD IDEAS COLLIDE

Mordecai approached Caradon's house with caution, caution that turned into concern, as he stepped out of the woods. Half the windows were broken, one wall was covered with holes, and the yard was filled with bloodstains and fur. Mordecai knelt down, looked at it. "Manticore?" he gasped in disbelief. Then the old scout remembered what he'd taught so many others, and stepped back into cover, fading into the trees as he activated his camouflage. Wind's Whisper, he thought, and the skill activated. "Caradon, ya in there? Give me a sign if it's safe ta come in," Mordecai mouthed.

After a pause, a bedsheet waved from one of the upper story windows.

Mordecai walked into the lower room. The table was on the floor, legs shattered, and the chairs were scattered kindling. A glass picture frame lay shattered and spiderwebbed on the table remnants. All the pictures and trinkets on the mantle lay scattered about, and the floor around the fireplace was scorched so badly that he could see the basement through it. Smoke filled the air.

Emmet was nowhere to be seen.

The stairs looked broken, gaping gaps where some steps should be, and jagged nailed boards sticking up from impact craters. Emmet had done that, Mordecai could tell.

"Run Silent," Caradon shouted from upstairs.

"Run Deep!" Mordecai shouted back. "What the hell, Caradon?"

"Get upstairs!"

Mordecai leaped, caught the upper railing, and flipped himself over, hatchet out and ready for trouble. Then he relaxed. Nobody but the old man was up here, his senses told him. And two things moving clumsily, one big and one tiny. Animi or golems, and the big one was Emmet.

"Invite Golem," he heard Caradon mutter, as he entered the old man's room. Books lay strewn all over the place, one of the windows was broken, manticore spines were embedded in the wall across from the window, and Caradon turned to him with a sigh, putting down his cards. "Still not responding to that," Caradon explained, beaming. "Probably intelligence related. She can't read or speak, I bet that's why!" The golem maker said, standing and waving his hands. His clothing was torn, his apron hanging askew.

"What happened?"

"I succeeded." Caradon smiled. "I succeeded." He pointed at a tiny black teddy bear, who waved back and showed him her cards.

"A grindluck deck? What..." Mordecai's eyes went wide.

"She came out with minimal luck. That's what caused all this. Worse than an infant's, worse than a goblin's. But she's up to about twenty-five now. We'll keep working on that, won't we Missus Fluffbear?"

"That's Amelia's old... bear..." Mordecai blinked.

"Yes. And she works. They're people, Mordecai. They can gain stats, and I'm pretty sure they can gain class levels."

"Going by tha last teddy bear you made, yeah, yeah they can."

"Oh, did he pick up something? That's nice," Caradon said. "But it doesn't matter. You're here now, and I need you to stand guard."

"Did he pick up something? What are ya talkin' about? You mean you didn't give him tha rul..." Mordecai froze. "Wait, guard? What are you—"

"It works. And I know what I did wrong. I'm going to give Emmet the upgrade, I've got just enough sanity left for that."

Mordecai froze. "Caradon..."

"He's a superior golem, Toy Golems are at the bottom of the chain. Armor golems will surely have superior luck!"

"Caradon—"

"These are our hopes and dreams, Mordecai! Moreso than we ever planned! It's a chance, it's our only chance, and every minute I delay is a minute that the King's forces draw around us! Balmoran has fallen, Mordecai, and this is our only hope! This is Celia's only hope!" Cardon's fist hit the table.

Missus Fluffbear tried to give him more cards.

"What? No, thank you." Caradon said, momentarily distracted. He turned back to the old scout. "Look, we can handle this."

"This is a bad idear," Mordecai said.

"I'm low on sanity, just enough for the upgrade, but I've got ten years worth of spare scrolls downstairs. You stand guard, I'll chip in if necessary, and Emmet will grind his luck through fighting or cards. We can do this. I just spent the day doing it, and this was a worst-case scenario. Help me, Mordecai. Please, help me."

"It's a bad idear, ya. Didn't say I wasn't gonna do it. We come this far on bad idears, why stop now?" Mordecai sighed, pulling out his bow. "Dark as a witch's asscrack out there, but I should be able to hear most things comin'. Lemme go get them scrolls for ya. Where are they?"

"Downstairs in my study. A book entitled Keep an Ace in the Hole."

"I'll go get them for ya, then set up on the roof. Good luck, old man."

"You too, old man."

Mordecai leaped down to the floor below, as Caradon thundered behind him.

"Greater Golem Upgrade!"

The book was empty. Mordecai stared at the hollow space where a bunch of scrolls had once been.

"Caradon!" he shouted.

Then the first lightning bolt struck the house, as the storm built overhead.

*****

Lightning rumbled, far off, and Celia shivered. There wasn't enough warmth in the cell. The little girl had never been in jail before, and she didn't like it one bit.

Ten feet by ten feet wide, it held a bedroll in one corner, and a chamber pot that smelled like it had been changed a few years ago. Though Celia desperately needed to pee, she couldn't quite bring herself to do that, even if the boys had promised to turn their backs.

The cold stone walls were only a little warmer than the snowy mountains a few feet outside, and the bars set high in the wall looked out over a sheer drop. They'd thought of pushing Threadbare out of them and sending him to get help, but even with his stuffed form and the benefits of Golem Body, there was no way he'd survive the fall.

The guards had shut them in here and left them. Nobody guarded the dark hallway beyond, lit by a single glowstone hanging from a chain. The guards hadn't even bothered taking their equipment, except for Threadbare's confiscated scepter. At first they thought it had been an oversight, but as an hour crawled by and Jarrik wondered for the seventh time why that was so, Garon voiced the truth of the matter;

"The guards don't care. We can't take them on even with our stuff."

"We didn't even try," Jarrik shook his head.

"Yeah, because it'd be suicide. They're knights for sure, and did you see how Threadbare was wailing on that one? He was doing decent damage to the Dungeon Boss. But it was all zeroes on the guard, he had to be double his level if he was a day, or that magical armor was stupid tough, or both. And with a wizard up out of our reach? No, we would've died."

"That one guard hurt poor Threadbare more than the dungeon boss too," Celia added. "In one hit, anyway, and he wasn't even trying."

"Guards ain't usually this buff," Bak'Shaz said.

"Aye," Beryl frowned. "They go off duty in town and get into bar fights, and they're not that hot. They're decent, but not that badass."

"Goes back ta what I was saying before," Jarrik put his arm around Beryl, and leaned back against the cold wall as he considered. "Something's goin' on. High-level guards out here, dragon riders comin' inta the barracks, closed dungeons... I don't like this. This ent good."

"And they planted a magic item on poor Threadbare!" Celia hugged him tightly. "Why?"

The little golem tried to gesture and explain that no, he'd had that to begin with, and he was quite sorry because it had slipped his mind, but Celia just thought he was squirming and put him down.

"We could send him through the bars," Beryl nodded to the darkened corridor. "See what he could find."

"No! You saw how that one guard tore him up like he was... just a... just a thing!" Celia was horrified. "If they catch him out there they won't think twice about killing him!"

"It might be our only option," Garon said. "Besides, he can handle himself. He fell into certain death and walked out of that hidden dungeon area with two new jobs."

"Three if you count tailor," Bak'shaz offered.

"Look, I got this, maybe." Beryl said. "Let me talk with Aeterna. Ask her for advice."

"Oh. Oh!" Jarrik brightened up. "Yeah, good idea."

The little cleric closed her eyes, cupped her hands, and chanted. **"Pray to Aeterna!"**

The children, and Threadbare, leaned in to watch Beryl as her lips moved, silently.

They were hoping for divine intervention. They didn't get that. No, not at all.

*****

Anise's heels clicked as her boots hit the stone floor. The corridor was dark, lit only by a single glowstone. She approached the bars, taking no effort to hide the sound of her approach.

"Someone's coming," She heard one of the half-breeds whisper.

"Shh! Don't interrupt Beryl!" The girl whispered back.

"It's all right, I'm done. She said say yes."

"What?"

"The goddess said say—"

Anise moved into the pool of light just outside the cell. "Oh dear, such a misunderstanding." She looked down at the little golden scepter in her hands, and looked back to Celia. "Would you and your little friends like to go free?"

There was a long pause. The dwarven godlicker slapped her forehead. "Yes!" she said.

"Come along then." Anise took out a slender key and unlocked the cell door, then unlocked the door to the rest of the keep. The children filed out, cautiously, save for Threadbare who marched up and pointed at his scepter. She handed it to him with a closed-mouth smile, and patted his head, before moving further into the keep.

They followed her through empty halls, past abandoned rooms and arrow slits letting in nothing but darkness and the cold night's air. The wind howled down the hallways as they went, playing an odd sort of tune entirely by accident. Anise sneered to herself as she felt the tension build behind her. The glowstones were few and far between here, leaving large pools of darkness between them, and she felt almost at home.

It was one of the half-orcs that broke the tension. "Where are all the guards?" The fat one asked.

"Gone," Anise replied. "Seven of them went to go seal this dungeon for good. The rest are headed to town. There's a small matter to take care of tonight."

"Seal the dungeon? What?" The godlicker gasped, her ridiculous braids swaying as she stomped up to walk alongside Anise. "You can't do that!"

"Me? No. The guards? Yes," Anise said. "King's orders. As is the business with the town."

"Business with the town? What business with the town?" The tall half-breed with the bow moved up to flank Anise on her other side.

Anise halted, and nodded to a thick wooden door. "There's the exit. I trust you can find your way home?" She opened it, letting a sliver of moonlight into the darkness.

"What business with the town?" The tall green one insisted, moving towards her, pushing away the fat one's cautioning hand.

Anise ignored him, walked past him to kneel by Celia. "Thank you so much for trusting me," she said, icy blue eyes staring into the girl's own green orbs. "I won't forget it. We're going to sort matters out with Caradon, and then your long nightmare will be over. We will do what we must, and then I will help you, Cecilia. I will help you become who you were meant to be."

"Nightmare?" Celia blinked, staring uneasily at the pale white arm, almost shining in the moonlight, and the bloody hue of the scarlet nails on her shoulder. "I don't understand what you're talking about."

"You will, soon. Which is good, because we've got so much to talk about," Anise smiled. "But you're going to have to hurry if you want to say goodbye to him." Anise turned and stood, stepping back out of the moonlight into darkness, regarding the children without pity. "That goes for all of you. Say goodbye to everyone you know and love, children. Ladybug ladybug, fly away home..."

Green skin turned pale. The children backed away from her as one, and Celia clutched Threadbare tight as they ran out the door. Anise smiled. "No," she said, grabbing at the air well after they'd left. "Wait," she said, going to the door. "Stop!" she commanded the air, shutting the door.

She gave it another five minutes to make sure they weren't coming back or anything stupid like that, then hauled out a disk of black marble. She kissed it, then knelt, holding it aloft with one hand as she watched a red image blur into existence, standing on the flat disk. A man in heavy armor, his horned helm crowning plate worked with demonic faces and glowing with its own enchantments.

"Master," she whispered. "The children have escaped me. I tried to stop them, but failed."

His anger smote her down, and she fell, gasping as she continued. "Cecilia is returning home, master, home to Caradon! But her friends, I don't think... I think they might go into the town! I fear... I fear we have loose ends."

Her master bowed his head. Seconds passed, and Anise kept her face sorrowful, kept her ambition caged in her heart, hoping against hope that she'd struck the right tone...

"No loose ends," her master said. "We planned for this, if necessary. Once Cecilia is clear, put the town to the sword. Then join me. It's time to end this sordid farce."

"Thy will be done," she said, closing her eyes. "My love..."

*****

Zuula sat on her porch, and listened to the night. She listened to the song of hunting creatures falling silent, listened to trees rustling against the wind, and finally, listened to the sound of running feet moving poorly through her woods.

It was time. She reached for her mask—

—and made her perception check, as she realized that she knew the sounds of those particular approaching feet. She stood bolt upright, and stared out at the woods, possibilities churning in her mind. No, this would not do!

"Mom!" Jarrik shouted, as he burst out of the treeline; first as usual, her little scout. But she pushed down motherly pride, drowning it in a sea of motherly worry.

"What you do? What you do here? You should no be here!"

"Mom, they're going to kill everyone! The soldiers are here to kill everyone!"

"Yes, which is why you must go!" Zuula shouted, green knuckles turning white as she gripped the porch.

"No! We're not leaving you!"

"Child!" Zuula threw up her hands as the others came out of the trees, Garon's forced march faltering as he reached his destination, and the others who had been swept up in it coming down from it, feeling their stamina drain all at once. "Ksh! Inside, quickly!" The shaman commanded, holding the curtain open. "Much to do and you can help, but then you go!"

The children piled in, Celia clutching Threadbare tight, and Zuula punched through the floorboards, pulling rag-wrapped bundles from below and tossing them. "You, Jarrik, take these." She threw a bundle at him. "Put high in trees around clearing."

Jarrik opened the bundle, and looked at its contents with a puzzled expression. "But these are—"

"Do it!" Zuula bellowed, digging out another parcel. "Bak'Shaz, here be food. Elven waybread. Keeps forever, little bit last whole day. Elves not miss it, they be Zuula's gumbo and shit out long ago. Porkins be out back. Get him and get back in here."

"Oh man, Porkins!" Bak'Shaz took the pack and scrambled. "I almost forgot about him!"

"And for you," she turned to Celia, with a large sack and a bundle of papers. "Take these. Animate with scrolls and invite to party. Then invite Zuula in and leave party."

"What? You're..." Celia took the bag and looked at the five items inside. "Okay..."

"Once they animated go put in treeline around clearing. Ask Jarrik if need help. Go!"

Celia scrambled.

Zuula looked up at Garon and sighed. He had his arms folded and his eyes set in a familiar glare. The same glare he always gave her as a child, whenever she tried to get him to eat sprouts.

"I'm not leaving you here," Garon said. "Not alone."

He never did eat those fucking sprouts, Zuula reflected.

"Your father left Zuula here. Trouble coming for him too," Zuula said, thinking fast. "Need him if we gonna win this one."

Garon squinted at her, and his eyes un-narrowed a bit. "You have a plan?"

"Yes," she lied. "He out at Caradon's. You go get him!" Zuula tossed him the last sack.

He opened it, and gasped. "This is… you just made a quest out of it? What the heck, Mom?"

"You get bonuses, right? There reward. Don't spend none until you get you father safe!"

"This is at least…"

"Mordecai maybe not take foolish daughter Mastoya's money when she send it, but Zuula got no problem with pride. Use it if you need to."

"All right…" He frowned. "I don't know if the others have the stamina to get there. I should leave them here—"

Zuula almost howled in frustration. "Unclever child! You be talking to shaman! Get them in here!"

After a few frenzied minutes, the crew was assembled. They'd left Beryl back in town to warn her family, so she was out of the equation, but Celia was looking ragged, Jarrik was wobbling, and even Bak'shaz, her little ball of energy, was drooping a bit.

Zuula sighed. "Gonna use the heavy stuff."

Garon's eyes flew wide open. "Whoa, mom, no, that stuff is—"

"Then make sure they don't never get it again. Not for about five years or so." Zuula reached into the bundle of herbs on the wall, pulled out a bright green and orange one that almost seemed to almost glow with slickness, and threw it in the fire. Smoke billowed up, and the children coughed as it filled their lungs.

When the smoke died down, they were vibrating, literally vibrating as the boards underneath them rattled.

"What is this?" Celia said, staring at her fingers. "I feel so weird… status?"

There was a pause, as the other brothers did so, all save Garon who palmed his face.

"Um…" Celia frowned at the air, blinking five times faster than she normally could. "What is the 'high' condition, please? And why is everything all weird colors?"

"You don't want to know," Garon said. "Come on, let's go before it wears off. **Forced March!"**

Zuula watched them go, then sucked in the smoke with a few deep breaths. The old familiar smell hit her again, peeling a year or two off her lifespan and filling her veins with fire. Being a shaman, with the poison resistance she had, it carried more benefits than the agility and stamina restore and buff it had given the children. It also added to her perception. And right now her heightened ears heard the flap of leathery wings in the distance and the tromp of metal-shod feet.

She stepped outside, seeing the air swirl with smoke, seeing through the darkness as clearly as if it was day. Better, even. Darkspawn was a good trait, about half the time.

"Call Winds," she said, waving her good club in the air, and the distant howling changed, started to grow as they peeled away from the mountains and gathered behind her. In the distance a storm rose, a good ways west. For now.

Then, before she could regret it, Zuula clamped the mask on her face. It bit into her, taking its toll in blood.

"Slow Regeneration," she gasped, casting her buffs before her mind could go to the place the mask sent it to. **"Beastly Skill Borrow, Owl! Call Vines! Call Thorns! Fast...** ah... hah, hahahhaha..." She laughed, as the mask became her, and she became it.

"Come then!" She roared, in three voices at once, raising her club to the air. "Come and die!"

And in time they did come. They came, with the runes on their armor suppressed, without torches, not that they needed them. Behind the unit of soldiers, Taylor's Delve burned, sending smoke and fire far up into the sky. They came with a veteran of the northern wars leading the raid.

Not that it helped them, in the end.

*****

Just one more house, Grant figured, then they'd be done with it. Bad for morale, running down civilians and killing them, but he'd done worse in the North. Besides, they were all traitors. And he had his orders, there, with the King's Declaration of War buffing all his fighting stats. Death to Traitors, it said, and that was their job tonight.

A dragon flew overhead, heavy wings beating. The first pass had shown only darkness, its rider had reported.

"Gonna kill us some piggers," one of the footmen next to Grant said "Gonna roast 'em up and hear 'em squeal. Makin' bacon."

Grant shot him a look. "Shut up."

"Just saying, I bet they smell like ham when they burn."

Grant's fist crashed into the footman's helm, and the idiot fell like a poleaxed cow. Grant didn't even break stride.

"What the shit? What the shit was that about?" The idiot was saying as he got up, and Grant heard Boyle and Kaney restrain him.

"The Grand Knight's a pigger, you idiot," Kaney hissed. "Lucky she ain't here yet! Say that word around her you're dead!"

They made it out into the clearing, and the crude little hut on the hill. Smoke seeped out of it, and for a second, Grant wondered if the family that lived here had saved him the trouble. He was running without scouts this time, for reasons that hadn't been made clear to him, so he was running blind and pissed about it.

"Come out with your hands over your head! By order of the King!" he called.

No answer.

He started forward—

—and the winds whipped up, as thunder roared across the clearing, as the freakish storm that had suddenly sprung up to the west roared in, pounding rain and hail, and instantly visibility went straight to hell.

The fires of the town were rendered down to a shrinking glow, and the night pressed in...

And a voice rang out from everywhere and nowhere.

"Stupid boys..." It hissed, and Grant turned, barking orders, spreading his squad into a perimeter.

"Unclever girls..." the voice growled, and somewhere behind Grant, Kaney screamed.

"Come out and show yourself!" Grant barked.

"You come to kill an orc? You come to kill an *orc* in the *night?*"

Then the drums started all around them, and the rain fell harder as the soldiers screamed in the darkness...

*****

Jericho stared at his hands, as monsters screamed and died in the darkness.

He could only see them due to his enhanced perception, and the Sensate-created illusions they were hiding behind didn't help matters. It was dark out here, Dark as a Witch's asscrack, he remembered his mentor saying, on nights like this.

His mentor, the traitor.

Jericho hadn't wanted to believe it, but there the old man was, up on the roof of the house across the river, dodging lightning bolts and firing at the Spirewolf pack below.

Up the line, past his unit and the next two, the King paced back and forth, his crimson plate cloaked and silenced by yet more illusions.

They'd been waiting for hours. The army had rolled in at the beginning of the night, but the King hadn't given the order yet.

"What are we waiting for?" Yules said in the party whisper. Jericho could just see her blonde crewcut, crouched among the reeds of the riverbank. He'd have to talk to her about that later, she really should have hidden better.

"We're waiting on demons, I hear," Zanzibar replied. His dark skin made him almost invisible, only his white, white eyes giving him away. Top marks.

Jericho wanted to tell them to shut up, to keep the chatter down, but he suppressed it. He was their Captain, and a little pre-op chatter was to be expected. He'd always given them a free hand, more so than the Crown's doctrine was comfortable with, but he found he got better troops out of it. After all, it had worked with him.

Just like Mordecai did with you, back in training, the thought curled around Jericho's brain.

Yules continued. "Demons. Wonder if it'll be imps. Or hellhounds."

"Those are the least kind," Moony said. He'd been a cultist, once upon a time. And not the sanctioned kind, which was why he was working off his crimes in service. "The worst ones are the ones that look human."

"Now why's that?" Zanzibar wondered.

"Demons are from the outside. They have no way to understand this world, unless they're the greatest of lords, or they're bound by a pact, or both. And to seal the pact, you have to give it the head and heart of something. Not the body, just the head and heart. Takes a bird or a bat, to pact an imp. Kill a dog, get a hellhound. So to get one that looks human..."

"You can stop there," Yules said.

But Moony didn't. "They get the memories, some of them, if the brain's intact. They get the senses, and the perspectives, and some people think they get the souls, too. But the ones that look human are the worst. They come back wrong..."

"Enough," Jericho said, looking up the line. "The Inquisitor is here."

And there she was, walking up to the King, dressed simply in her white-furred coat and high traveling boots. She put a hand on his shoulder, and pointed back towards town.

But Moony kept talking. "There's always been talk, you know, of the

181

Fallen Six. Of why they had closed-casket funerals. Why the king had all their portraits destroyed…"

"Stow it, Moony! Look alive!"

The Inquisitor ambled over to them, and nodded.

"I'm with your unit tonight, gentlemen." She brushed back long, straight black hair with one red-nailed hand. "You have your orders. Let's go do this."

Jericho nodded, and the horns blew, as the legion started forward. Scouts in the vanguard, and Jericho and the rest of the ninth were among them, leaping over the rocks in the river's ford, and charging up the hill. He saw Mordecai's head snap toward them, as lightning flared, but then they were in the treeline and charging past the first Raggedy Man. It raked out at Zanzibar and the scout cried out, twisted aside, and nocked an arrow.

"Leave it and keep moving!" Jericho bellowed. The Raggedy Man pursued, but stopped as the first wave of infantry hit it, heavy shields dripping from the ford, swords rising and falling as they clustered around the wood golem. It turned and lashed out with thorny hands, sending troopers flying, but more closed in, and around the perimeter Jericho knew the other units were doing the same.

Then he was out and into the clearing, as the first of the three dragon knights they'd brought flew overhead, breath flaring to illuminate the area. Mordecai was gone from the roof, and Jericho's eyes tightened. **"Camouflage!"** he snapped, and the scouts faded from view one by one.

Unconcerned, the Inquisitor sauntered across the bloody lawn… up until she reached the door, then blue sparks flew from the handle as she tried to turn it.

Sneering, she pulled out a scroll. **"Dispel Enchantment,"** she told it, and magic flared, and dissipated.

Shouts from the left, and arrows flew out of the trees, into the unit following. **"Rapid Fire!"** Jericho heard Mordecai yell, and he held his breath and ducked low as a spray of arrows flew from the trees, into the infantry unit following behind. Men screamed and fell back. Casting a glance backward, the Inquisitor moved through the doorway, and Jericho followed. "Give me a perimeter!" he hissed over the Party Whisper.

"On it, Captain!" Yules said, and the rest acknowledged, but by then Jericho was in the wrecked front room of the house, moving from doorway to doorway, securing the area. "People moving upstairs," he sent a Wind's Whisper to the Inquisitor.

But the woman was stopped, by the ruin of a table. Crouched low, she held a picture frame in both hands, staring at a portrait through shattered glass.

"Miss, we need to move, you're in danger," Jericho tried again.

"No, Mr. Scout," Anise said, rising up, still holding the twisted frame, staring at the distorted image through shattered glass. "I'm as safe as if I was in my own house."

CRIK... CRAKK... CRUNCH. With inexorable strength, the woman broke the frame, ripping it and the portrait below into pieces. She tossed them into the smoldering coals of the blocked fireplace.

"What? Who's there! Mordecai!" Came a bellow from upstairs, and the Inquistior waved a hand in Jericho's direction.

She can see me? A chill ran down his spine.

"Go play with the old fool outside. I'll handle the one in here," she told him, leaping up to the second story.

Jericho nodded, and got outside just in time to see one of the dragons bellow, and fall from the sky, wings torn off by glowing arrows.

Jericho closed his eyes, and drew his bow tight. "All right, boys and girls," he told his squad. "I want him taken alive."

CHAPTER 14: THE END OF INNOCENCE

"This is as far as I'm going," Garon shouted, ending the forced march.

"What? No!" Celia shouted, staring in horror.

Ahead of them, a half-mile upriver, the forest burned. Two dragons wheeled overhead, one rider gone and the other slumped in his saddle. They were visible due to the fires that roared and billowed among the pines, glinting off of corpses in armor, and showing figures rushing back and forth through the trees.

"Yes!" Garon said. "Go and save Dad! Your Dad too!" Garon turned, and started back. "I'm going to get Mom. We can meet back at Oblivion Point, now go! **Forced March!**"

"But..." Celia gave up, as he sped off down the river. Already enhanced by his movement buff, the weird smoke he'd inhaled supercharged his agility. There was no stopping him, and no catching up to him.

"Come on! Follow me an' be quiet!" Jarrik commanded, and they waded through the trees and the chaos.

Amazingly, somehow, they managed to navigate the chaos and get to the side of the house. Crouched down, hidden by the remaining bushes, they were secure for the minute. Celia froze, as she saw the remaining windows shake, as a great, hollow bellow of reverberating metal came pouring out from the structure. Flames licked at the other side of the house where a dragon had sprayed it with its breath during a pass.

"I hear Dad!" Jarrik said, pointing off in the woods.

"You!" Caradon shouted from upstairs. "What is this? What the hell is this?" The old man's voice held a pain Celia had never heard, and she panicked, her somewhat herb-jumbled mind dropping to the worst conclusions.

"We have to save Daddy!" She insisted. The boys shot her a look, looked at each other...

...then looked at the black armored guards, walking out of the burning building's front door. They saluted in unison, as a huge man in red armor, glowing with almost its own malevolence, walked up the hill. Great horns rose from his helm, his featureless visor turning from side to side as he strode forward, sword out and shield leering, showing a moving, demonic face. Hellish images glowed in the firelight as he strode forward, not bothering to step over the bodies in his path, grinding the corpses of the fallen under his heel as he went.

"Oh my gods," Celia hissed.

"We can't take him," Jarrik said. He pointed at the back porch. "Get to the second story from the overhang, get your Daddy out! We'll need Dad to get us out of here. We'll go get him. Use Wind's Whisper when you've got him and we'll figure out a way to escape. Go!"

Celia nodded dumbly. She threw Threadbare up to the porch overhang, then grabbed a few chairs and piled them together. "Go make sure it's clear!" She hissed at Threadbare.

Threadbare nodded, and slipped through the broken window. He ran down the hall, just as Emmet burst out of one of the rooms the little bear had never entered. For a second, the toy golem and the armor golem stared at each other, kindred soul to kindred soul.

"**Command Gol—**," Threadbare heard Caradon croak from back in the room, before the sound of flesh hitting flesh interrupted him.

"Oh do shut up, old man," came a familiar voice. "Let's see..." Paper crinkled. "**Command Golem. Go out of this building with your hands up and do nothing once you're out.**"

Emmet stomped toward the stairs and fell off the railing, with an enormous crash. A lot of yelling came from downstairs, and Threadbare realized that hey, there were guards inside the house too.

"Is it clear?" Celia whispered from the end of the hallway.

Threadbare toddled back and shook his head no. No, the direct approach seemed to be pretty much suicide.

WIS +1

"Ohhhh... Fump it!" Celia swore. She glanced up. "The attic window's broken. Come on, let's move."

It took some careful balancing and scrambling to get up into the attic. Half of the house was burning, and the heat sweltered down on them as they scrambled through the boxes and crates, until they heard voices. Celia lay down, and squinted through the cracks. Threadbare did too.

They saw Caradon, in his bedroom, laying against the wall. He was bruised and battered and bloody, with his apron torn and tools spilling around him. Next to the old man, squatting on her haunches, with one red-nailed hand wrapped around his throat, was a familiar figure.

"You!" Celia gasped, then covered her mouth.

Anise Layd'i looked up. She squinted, as Celia pulled away from the crack, covering her mouth…

Metal-shod boots clanked, boards creaking below, as the crimson-armored behemoth stomped into view. Celia looked back, sighed silently in relief as she saw Anise standing, looking away from the ceiling… a sigh that turned to a gasp as she saw the armored man wasn't alone. Five twisted black blades orbited him, the demonic faces on them gibbering and looking around with glowing green eyes as they circled and looped.

She knew that spell. Sort of… It was Animus Blade, but what kind of blades were those?

"You…" Caradon hissed with a venom Celia had never heard before. "You son of a bitch." The old man stood, and Anise stood with him.

"Are we alone?" The demon knight said, his voice deep and unearthly.

"No," Anise said, and pointed upward. "The girl."

Horns tilted as the man glanced upward and that was all the warning they had.

Celia shrieked as five blades punched a hole in the ceiling around her, then shifted clockwise, cutting through the floor. Before she or Threadbare could do anything, the girl fell through the floor, into the room below.

No! Celia!

Threadbare threw himself through the hole, going after her—

—and one of the demon blades twisted, blurred into position under him, and shot upward.

SHUNK!

CON +1

Your Golem Body Skill is now level 20!

Your Toughness Skill is now level 12!

Max HP +2

The sword pinned Threadbare to the roof of the attic. The blade sunk in easily and kept on going, until the hilt slammed against him, stuffing spilling out, spraying to either side of him as he felt the blade rip through.

He hung there, suspended, as a red '159' filled his vision, and floated up through the ceiling.

"You leave Daddy alone!" Celia yelled, shouting, going red in the face as she ran to Caradon and hugged him.

The old man, staggered, clasped Celia to his apron. He stared at the demon knight, and the womanlike thing that smiled serenely next to the intruder.

"Please, just let us go!" Celia howled.

"I can't do that, Cecelia," The demon knight rumbled. He waved his hand, and his whirring blades fell silent one by one, landing in a clatter on the floor. The one holding Threadbare blackened as he stared at it, green eyes fading out and fiendish face twitching before it fell still. But it was still stuck in him, holding him suspended above the people below.

"It's time to go," the demon knight continued. "Here. **Invite Cecelia.** I'll explain everything."

"I'm not going anywhere with you!"

"Yes you are. It's time to go home."

"This is my home!"

"Judging by those flames, not for very much longer," Anise said, smiling serenely. A smile that turned to a gasp of pain, as the Demon Knight glared at her, and a green '84' floated out from her head as she recoiled.

"Now is not the time for your brand of twisted humor, dear."

"Sorry love," Anise caressed his visor, pretending to forgive the moxie damage he'd just dealt her. "I'll behave for now."

"What did you do to her," Caradon rumbled, finding his courage in outrage. "Why is that thing wearing Amelia's face!"

"Wait, what?" Celia whipped her tear-stained face away from his apron. "You're... my mother?"

Anise winked at Celia.

"No, it's... run, Celia! Run!" Caradon shoved her toward a window—

—and the armored figure shook his head. **"Distant Animus, invite sheets,"** he said before the little girl could react. The sheets peeled off of the wrecked bed and wrapped Celia before she could escape.

Caradon grimaced. **"Ani—"**

Anise punched him, and he fell, with a bloody nose.

"This is pathetic, old man," The demon knight said. "Especially against your own family."

"You're no blood of mine!" Caradon growled, hand over his nose.

"No. But I'm blood of hers," The figure said, pointing to Celia. "And you've kept her from me long enough."

"I... I don't understand." Celia said, from her binding among the sheets.

"He never told you, did he?"

"Told me what?"

"Don't listen!" Caradon shouted, then Anise was hauling him up, and wrapping her hand around his mouth.

The demon knight bowed his head. Then he reached back behind his helm. "Hello Cecelia…"

And as clasps fell away, the big man lifted away the horned helm, revealing a stern face, almost luminescent green eyes, and a manelike spray of red, frizzy hair.

The same kind of hair that Celia combed every morning, and had wrestled with all her life.

"…I'm your father," said King Melos Ragandor the First.

"What?" Celia said, shocked beyond belief. "That makes no sense! I… no."

"Tell her, Caradon," Melos said, sitting heavily on one of the room's few remaining intact chairs. "Tell her how you've been lying to her all these years."

Celia looked up to Caradon—

—and saw the old man bow his head. Tears leaked from the corners of his eyes.

"Daddy?" She whispered, feeling hope sink in her chest. Feeling the first sting of betrayal.

Sighing, Melos gestured, and the sheets holding Celia fell away. She took a few hesitant steps, then ran to stand before Caradon. She stared up at him, eyes wide and uncomprehending.

"Celia…" Caradon started, then choked. He cleared his throat, opened his eyes, and the pain within them made her flinch back. "I'm your grandfather. Amelia was my daughter, not my wife."

"You raised Amelia well, Caradon. But you never did like me much." Melos shrugged. "Not that it mattered. She loved me."

"And you killed her!" Caradon found his anger once more, his hands whipping out, grabbing fast to Celia's shoulders.

"Ouch! Dad—" Celia bit her tongue. She couldn't call him that anymore, could she? Then what he'd said sunk in and her face twisted into hatred as she stared at her father. "You! Did you kill her?"

"No!" Melos looked shocked. "No, no no no no. I swear to you, I swear!" The armored figure fell to his knees, stretching out a gauntleted hand. Celia flinched back, and pain flashed across the demon knight's face. Then his visage hardened, and he glared up at Caradon. "Was that what you told her, you old fool?"

"I told her nothing of her father." Caradon said, his own face harder than stone. "And please, I can read between the lines. Six heroes go down into the dungeon, and the dark knight alone returns alive. Then the King 'mysteriously' passes away. And who takes the throne, but the lone survivor?"

"You have no idea what went on down there, old man. You have no idea how I lost my wife!" Melos roared, climbing to his feet, glaring down at Caradon's stooped frame. "How I lost the few people in this world who trusted me!"

Celia tore from Caradon's grasp, and ran to the corner, huddling, her hands over her head. "Stop it stop it stop it! Please stop fighting! Please just... stop..."

Above them, Threadbare stirred.

He didn't quite understand the situation, not in its entirety, but Celia needed him.

Slowly, carefully, he tried to work the blade loose. But he had no leverage. He put his paws against the ceiling and pushed, trying to get it to come out of the wood...

Rriiiippp...

A red '3' floated up, and he stopped. He was too soft, and the cut was too wide. He couldn't wiggle free of the blade without damaging himself. He bent over as best he could, staring at the hilt. How? How could he get off this without literally tearing himself apart?

Below him, Melos was talking again. "I'm... sorry, Celia. But the truth hurts, and there are things we must set straight now. I don't want..." He palmed his face. "I never wanted this." He said, waving a hand at the house, the destruction, Caradon's battered form... and the creature beside him, who was currently filing her nails. She looked up, put the nail file away, and smiled cheerfully at him.

"You're doing fine, my love. It'll work out."

"I seem to recall ordering you to never lie to me."

"And I've kept that pact. Master." She'd never said who it would work out for, after all.

"She wears her face!" Caradon roared, his face blotching red. "She speaks in Amelia's voice! What did you do, you blasphemous..." The old man's anger faded, burned through him like a wildfire. "What did you do?" he whispered.

"What I had to, Caradon. I've always ever done what I had to and only that. Which is why my friends trusted me, they knew I only did what I had to. You never saw that, in your self-righteousness. In your arrogance."

"Please just stop," Celia whispered again.

Threadbare tried another wiggle, and tore another seam. Stuffing spilled out, and a fleck drifted past Caradon's head, just as Melos shifted to look at Celia.

Caradon looked up.

Hope filled his eyes, and he spoke under his breath, barely a whisper. And words flashed in front of Threadbare.

Caradon Gearhart has Invited you to join his party! Do you wish to accept? y/n?

The old man's eyes filled with hope, as Threadbare thought *yes*. Hope and pride, for his wayward creation, for the first time ever.

Melos spoke again. "Do you know that I was the one who sent her to you, Caradon?"

"What? Impossible! Amelia..."

"Amelia was dead. I put her ashes in an urn, and entrusted her and Cecelia to Emmet. It took the last command golem scroll she'd left behind, but I sent him on to you. I knew you wouldn't trust me if I showed up with her, but you'd trust Emmet when he showed up with your infant granddaughter crying in his arms. You'd helped make him, after all, you and my wife, working together."

"You were the one? Why?" Caradon paled. "I wondered, but I figured... some sort of failsafe..."

Meanwhile, above him, Threadbare found his form charged with power he could barely imagine! The old man had two skills that applied, one from animator that charged his personal creations in his party with power proportionate to his will, and one from golemist that buffed up any golems in his party.

But though they raised all of Threadbare's attributes and his maximum HP, they did nothing for his wounds.

Threadbare tried to tug the sword free again, but even with his strength, he had no leverage. And as he turned to put his paws on the ceiling again, his buffed intelligence told him that he'd literally rip himself in two if he wasn't careful, so very careful with this.

Fortunately, his agility had just gotten the biggest buff it had ever had. He started to squirm again...

"I sent her to you as soon as I knew I had to take the throne. I knew I had enemies, and would have more, who would strike at me through her. And I knew you would raise her right." Melos sighed. "And I wanted you to have some time with your granddaughter, old man. I'm not the monster you think I am. I just use monsters." He gestured, the demonic faces in his armor leering and gnashing their teeth. "But as hideous as demons are, they pale next to the evil that men do. When I found out that you'd turned traitor, started helping the resistance, I gritted my teeth and let it be. You were old, senile, but I'm used to spite. I kept a watch on you and let you be. But then I beat Balmoran, and captured the Earl. He talked before he died, Caradon. He told me of the betrothal. Of how you'd planned to marry my daughter to the son of my most treacherous enemy!"

Celia lowered her hands. Face puffy from tears, her body shaking like a leaf, she stared at Caradon. "What?"

The house groaned and shook, and Melos shot a glance back. **"Party screen,"** Caradon muttered, then he paled. He shot a look up at Threadbare, and shook his head. "Stop," he mouthed. He'd seen Threadbare's hit points. He knew what would happen if the teddy dropped now.

Unnoticed, Anise followed his gaze, glanced up to Threadbare as well. She smiled, then turned her eyes to Celia, drinking in the girl's shifting expression.

"Betrothal?" Celia asked.

Caradon flinched. "We had to... we had to keep you safe. We thought he would win..."

"He promised Balmoran an army of golems, with you commanding them. And your bloodline to theirs, so they had a legitimate heir to the throne." Melos said. "But that's neither here nor there. Now I have Emmet, upgraded to its full potential. And I have you, and with Balmoran gone, we are finally, finally safe."

"I don't feel safe at all," Celia said, shivering. "I'll never feel safe again."

And Threadbare writhed, to hear the pain in her voice. He reached out again, as another seam gave, and a red '5' spilled past his head. But he couldn't get past the hilt that trapped him in place.

"Come. Anise, take her home. I'll get Caradon into custody."

Celia stepped back into the corner. "I don't... I don't know... Who to trust..."

"It's a moot point," Melos said. "You have to come with me now, and you don't have the power to stop me. That's how the world works. It hurts me too. I have to do what I must and I hate it. That's what growing up's all about, Cecelia. That's what Caradon has been sheltering you from. But we have far too much to do. We have responsibilities, and— oh just go with her Anise, that fucking fire is going to drop the wall in a few minutes."

Celia shook, as Anise approached, offering one red-nailed hand. Her head twisted back and forth between Melos and Caradon. "You won't hurt him? Please? If I go with you willingly you won't hurt him?"

"I won't hurt him. But he must answer for his crimes. You won't see him again for a very long time, I'm afraid."

"You promise?"

"I promise."

She gave Anise her hand. Anise handed the scrolls off to Melos, pulled out a crystal, and threw it to the floor. **"Teleport Castle Cylvania,"** she declared.

And in a flash, both of them were gone.

Threadbare sagged.

Here he was, filled with the most strength and resilience he'd ever had, and he was powerless to stop it. Any of it.

The fire raged on, snapping and popping, filling the room with smoke as Melos stared at Caradon.

"I'm not going into custody, am I—" Caradon's speech cut off as Melos crossed the room in two fast strides, grabbed him, and shoved something in his mouth. Caradon gagged and coughed, but the demon knight forced him to swallow.

"What... wha..." Caradon twitched.

"Numbing powder. I won't hurt you because you won't feel a thing." Melos pulled out a curvy dagger, and put Caradon on the bed, just out of Threadbare's sight. "The perks of being a cultist, you learn to say things very, very carefully. I promised Cecelia I wouldn't hurt you, and that she wouldn't see you again for a very long time. She won't, she'll have a long life ahead of her. You'll have plenty of time to reminisce with her in the afterlife."

"So you're killing me... for... vengeance?" Caradon gasped out.

"No. You leave me in a hard spot, old man. I have to do something horrible, because of you. You see, you're the only Golemist left in the kingdom. The only one who's cracked the unlock for that. You had the right idea with an army of golems, after all. Golems don't betray you. Golems don't lie. I could use an army of loyal, tireless, honest monsters. And I don't think you're going to teach me golemist, are you? Not even if I ask nicely."

Silence for a bit. Melos barked joyless laughter. "I figured. And I'll need it to teach Cecelia, for her to follow in her mother's footsteps, since you held her back too long. I can't trust you near her, Caradon. You spoiled her for too long. You made her weak. I'll make her strong, so strong, and I'll hand her a kingdom all of her own. But first, I need golemist from you. Fortunately before I became a ruler, I was a cultist. And we have a ritual, just for this."

"You... bas...trrrrd...." Caradon slurred.

"It works a bit easier if I'm in your party, but you'll never invite me so oh well. Still, it should do. You're all alone here, Caradon. Golems can't learn, Amelia taught me that, so it's just you and me. The rite will benefit the closest person if you're not in a party, and well, here we are. Any last words?"

"Go to Hell...."

"Every night, Caradon. Every night. **Rite of Reclamation!**"

Words popped up in next to Threadbare's head.

CARADON GEARHART HAS OFFERED YOU A PRIVATE QUEST

DETAILS: SAVE CELIA. I KNOW YOU CAN DO IT. I AM PROUD OF YOU, MY SON.

REWARD: NINE THOUSAND FOUR HUNDRED AND SIXTY TWO EXPERIENCE POINTS

COMPLETION: WHEN CELIA IS SAFE

DO YOU WANT TO ACCEPT THIS QUEST? Y/N

Yes. Yes he would. He didn't know how, but he would.

Threadbare shuddered, as he heard wet noises below him, and Caradon fell silent for the last time.

But the King was not silent. The King was bellowing in rage.

More words flashed all around Threadbare, filling up his sight.

Through blasphemous ritual you have unlocked the Animator job!

Would you like to become an Animator at this time? y/n?

Through blasphemous ritual you have unlocked the Enchanter job!

Would you like to become an Enchanter at this time? y/n?

Through blasphemous ritual you have unlocked the Golemist job!

Would you like to become a Golemist at this time? y/n?

Through blasphemous ritual you have unlocked the Wizard job!

Would you like to become a Wizard at this time? y/n?

Through blasphemous ritual you have unlocked the Smith job!

Would you like to become a Smith at this time? y/n?

Yes! Yes to all of those! Those jobs would give him the strength he needed to save Celia!

You are now a level 1 Animator!

+3 DEX

+3 INT

+3 WILL

You have learned the Animus skill!

Your Animus skill is now level 1!

You have learned the Command Animus skill!

Your Command Animus skill is now level 1!

You have learned the Creator's Guardians skill!

Your Creator's Guardians skill is now level 1!
You have learned the Eye for Detail skill!
Your Eye for Detail skill is now level 1!
You have learned the Mend skill!
Your Mend skill is now level 1!

You are now a level 1 Enchanter!
+3 DEX
+3 INT
+3 WILL
You have learned the Appraise skill!
Your Appraise skill is now level 1!
You have learned the Glowgleam skill!
Your Glowgleam skill is now level 1!
You have learned the Harden skill!
Your Harden skill is now level 1!
You have learned the Soften skill!
Your Soften skill is now level 1!
You have learned the Spellstore I skill!
Your Spellstore I skill is now level 1!

You are now a level 1 Golemist!
+5 INT
+5 WILL
You have learned the Command Golem skill!
Your Command Golem skill is now level 1!
You have learned the Golem Animus skill!
Your Golem Animus skill is now level 1!
You have learned the Invite Golem skill!
Your Invite Golem skill is now level 1!
You have learned the Toy Golem skill!
Your Toy Golem skill is now level 1!

You are now a level 1 Smith!
STR +1
CON +1
You have learned the "Refine Ore" skill!

But the last one came up with words he'd never seen before.

You cannot learn the wizard job at this time, all adventuring slots are full!

Seek out your guild to forget an existing job!

Nothing to help his strength or constitution! He wasn't in much of a better situation Threadbare realized, mind churning with the enhanced power from his buffs. He had to think fast, figure a way off of this stupid sword before—

Your party has been disbanded.

—and there went his stat boosts.

Below him, Melos put two and two together and got fifty-seven.

"The Scout!" he hissed. He rushed from the room. "Take the scout alive! I want him alive!"

Grimly, Threadbare considered his chances. He could probably do it, he thought. One last good lunge, hope it didn't rip him completely open, and he could be off the blade. Then he'd find his way outside, go to find help, and try to communicate matters to Celia's friends. It would be hard, but they could find a way to save her. He would find a way to save his little girl!

All it would take was one good push, and a little luck…

…a flash of black fur caught his sight. Movement below? Threadbare stared down, as a teddy bear half his size toddled out from where she'd been hiding, and looked around.

Then she looked up at him.

And the house collapsed, as red numbers flashed by Threadbare's vision and everything went dark…

*****

Mordecai sagged in the tree. Out of arrows, out of stamina, out of sanity. His quivers were empty. Through hit and run tactics he'd dragged them off into the trees and the hills, combing wide for him. They'd find him, soon. He'd trained their scouts well.

He'd had to put down his own students, this night. Every corpse who wasn't armored was a face he recognized, and he hated it. What had it been for? What had it all been for?

Three jobs he'd pulled up from the unlocked jobs section of his status screen and added, strictly for the benefit of getting their level up pool refills. Three times he had refilled his stamina and sanity and fortune. Three times he'd gone back in, using One Last Arrow to pull ammunition out of nothing, and channeling his stamina into his other archer skills. He'd harried the troops, worn them down through hit and run tactics, and used Arrows of Light to take down the second dragon.

But it had taken everything he had, those four times, and now here he was, hiding in a tree, with men spreading out his way and one more goddamned dragon above.

"**Status**," he whispered, and the old scout glared at the jobs he'd grabbed, for no other reason than to buy Caradon time. Assassin, Bandit, and Bard, the first three on the list of options.

Beyond, the house groaned and shivered, and Mordecai closed his eyes as it fell into fiery ruin. His last hope was gone. He'd been buying time for nothing. The king's voice rung out, ordering him to take the old scout alive. Mordecai wasn't the brightest man, but he figured he knew who that was.

"Fuck it," he growled, and below him the King's scouts twitched at the noise and started toward his section of the forest. "Damned if I'll give 'im tha pleasure! **Status**."

If you're going to go out, go out in style. He went down to the job, and found the next one in the list… and chortled at the appropriateness.

"Yeah…" he drawled.

And then Mordecai was a Berserker.

"**Rage!**" he bellowed, and leaped from treetop to treetop as the dragon came in. His agility, already off the charts was boosted as his vision turned crimson, and he leaped up to meet the big beastie, grabbing ahold of its harness and swinging up to meet its very surprised rider. Unfeeling of his wounds, with stamina full to bursting, Mordecai yelled "**Headbutt!**" and slammed his skull into the rider's helm.

But no matter how good Mordecai's attributes were, the Rider wasn't too far a level from him, and the newly-trained Berserker's skill was only at level one.

The rider dropped his spear to draw his sword—

—and Mordecai caught it, broke the heavy spear into two, and wailed on the rider with the two improvised clubs, rattling his armor, knocking him free of the dragon. With a wordless howl Mordecai leaped on him and rode him down, watching red numbers fly out of him, riding him onto the mountain and into a tree, clubs flashing as he hammered him to death and beyond.

And as the all-too-short rage faded, and the crimson washed away from his view, he realized that there were words there now.

By attaining level 25 as both a scout and an archer, and killing a foe using two weapon style while in the wilderness, you have unlocked the Ranger job!

Would you like to become a ranger at this time? y/n?

Mordecai stood, stunned, staring at the air. "Yeah," he whispered.

The ranger skills and stat boosts scrolled by, but he closed his eyes.

Decades he'd sought that job, that job that nobody knew how to get anymore, that job that had evaded him for so long. And now, here at his last stand, he'd unlocked it. His jobs were full now, he knew. That was fine.

But seriously, what the hell kind of weird unlock WAS that? What did two weapons even have to *do* with being a ranger?

"Here! He's here!"

Grinning, Mordecai whirled. **"One Last Arrow!"** He snapped, pulling an arrow from what had been an empty quiver a second ago…

….and realized he'd dropped his bow during his berserk rampage. "Shit."

The scouts dogpiled him, punching and kicking, and he fought, but he was already wounded and tired, so tired, burned through so much stamina in one last mad rush.

Jericho, his own student, looked at him sadly, watching on with his bow down. He had one arrow nocked, just to make sure. Mordecai fought anyway, glaring at him…

…then a rustle in the bushes, and Jericho glared to the left. Mordecai, struggling to get free of the beatings, managed to shoot a look left—

—to see Bak'Shaz looking on with horror. "Run, boy! Run!" Mordecai whispered to him through the wind, and Bak'Shaz withdrew into the underbrush.

Mordecai sagged with relief, which fled as he saw Jericho's eyes. He saw too!

But Jericho lowered his bow, and nodded once to the old scout. Mordecai bowed his head. He'd taught the lad well, after all.

Five minutes later, bound, he was unceremoniously thrown at the King's feet. The barc-visaged demonic helm glared down at him, crimson metal gleaming in the light of the burning house.

"You were his last companion, weren't you? You've got that vital job, the one nobody else in this kingdom has. And let me guess, you've no intention of teaching it to me."

Mordecai looked at him. "Yeah," he said, "Thass right. And the secret dies wi' me." He had no clue why the King cared about the ranger job, but he wasn't about to hand it over to this son of a bitch.

"No lies detected," one of the armored troops to the King's left said. The tyrant shook his head.

"Nothing's ever easy. All right, bring him. We're done here."

*****

Zuula struck from the storm, on spirit wings, gliding silently as an owl. She killed, then swept back into the rain-filled night. She'd borrowed owl skills, using her spell, and they came in useful when one wanted to kill quickly and quietly.

Every time she struck another soldier down, she'd call in the thorny vines she'd summoned to rip at another group of soldiers, keep them panicked and shouting. The totem mask boosted her strength to obscene levels and let her strike down the soldiers with a quick flurry of blows, shattering armor and spilling blood to the ground.

One of the drums in the distance fell silent. "It's a toy!" She heard one of them shout. "Just an animated toy!" Zuula grinned. The girl had done her job well. She commanded the four remaining drums in her party to pound louder, and dove down to snatch another soldier up. He cried in her arms, turning to look at her, and she jammed the pointy end of her warclub through his visor. He died, choking and she dropped him.

"Burn the trees!" She heard the officer call, and she grinned with wicked glee as she soared back past the treeline, knowing what was about to happen.

The dragon overhead beat massive wings, burst through the rain, and its rider gave a sharp command. Flames billowed forth, coating the trees, coating the hut, coating a few of the screaming soldiers who didn't get out of the way in time.

And every firework that she'd had Jarrik tie into the treeline went off at once, sending up flares and bursting lights and smoke trails in a hissing, brilliant roar of pyrotechnics.

"Unclever fools!" Zuula boomed, as she flew up, flew up to the dragon, reeling as it threw its rider, reeling as she caught it around the neck, hung on like a monkey, and clamped her club against its windpipe. "You come to kill an *orc* at *night?*"

Zuula choked the dragon out, shooting glances back as it died, doing her best to keep an eye on things as it tumbled through the sky, trying to shake her. But it was a lesser dragon, barely a drake, and her arms were iron. The totem mask burned through emotion, fueling her strength.

It was a good time to get out of the clearing, honestly. The rain was dying down as the winds let up, and more than that, the hut was on fire. The fireworks had been one of the little traps she'd laid.

The hut itself was another, Or rather, the piles and bundles of dried herbs that lined the walls of the hut had been a trap.

By the time Zuula had killed the dragon and flown back to the clearing, billowing greenish fog filled the air. The pattering rain had dispersed it a bit, but without her Poison Resistance, Zuula couldn't have safely gone back in.

The men who had been stuck breathing the smoke hadn't been

shamans. They didn't have poison resistance. Zuula found them stumbling around the clearing, hacking at trees and each other, frothing through the visors, and she killed them, one by one. It was hard work and tiring work, and by the time she was done, her buffs were about half gone. So was the smoke, but that was fine, it had done its job.

The middle-aged woman sagged, leaning on her club, feeling sweat pour off her mostly-naked form. Tiring, this. Four children and a lot of days tending the hut had softened her, made her fat. But this wouldn't be a thing, soon. Soon she could rest.

And more armored forms moving through the woods meant her job wasn't done yet. Zuula took to the trees again, flying up, silhouetted against the burning hut—

"Dispel magic!" A woman's voice snapped.

Zuula tumbled to the ground, shorn of her flight in the space of two words. But she pushed it aside, for she had bigger problems.

She knew that voice.

"Mastoya…" she hissed. "Traitor girl! Unclever daughter!"

"Hello mother," A woman, clad in form-fitting white armor, enameled plates assembled into a spiky mass of metal. She wore no helm, and her face was as green as Zuula's. But all-too-human eyes found her mother's, seeing even through the glow of the totem mask, and Zuula felt her stomach roll.

"Stand down, mother."

"No!"

"I have the authority to take you alive. You and my brothers."

Zuula sneered. There was only one way this night would end. "You been lied to, or you lying."

"So that's it, huh? You're going to kill me like you did the rest? I knew some of them. Some of them were worth a damn, mother. They didn't deserve you. Nobody deserves you." Mastoya drew her sword, blade shining with blue runes, crackling with ice as she pointed it around the clearing.

Zuula hefted the club, and hesitated. She'd built things into the totem mask, yes. She'd built them in there to protect her mate. Protect her tribe. Protect her… family…

The mask's strength faltered, and Zuula closed her eyes. So this was how it was to be.

"Orc means tribe," she said to Mastoya, her biggest failure and strongest child. "Orc means family."

"Well," Mastoya said, reaching up to run her gauntleted finger along the scars her mother had given her years ago. "You're half right."

They fought in the rain, gentle now, too gentle to help. Between the remnants of the fire and the glowing runes of Mastoya's armor, there was too much light for Zuula's darkspawn skill to help her. And every time she cast a buff, her daughter would dispel it.

"**Corps a Corps!** You taught me how to fight you," Mastoya hissed, as they struggled, blade to club, and the freezing glow sapped Zuula's stamina. "I'm a cleric now, a priestess of Ritaxis. The Goddess of War!" Mastoya shoved her back, and Zuula staggered, off balance.

"And a knight, too! **Pommel Strike!**" Mastoya yelled, striking her mask with her heavy hilt. Wood cracked, and Zuula fell back again, trying to regain her footing. But Mastoya would not give her the space, and her blade flashed, getting past Zuula's guard, carving through her armor and skin and chilling her blood.

Finally, Zuula had enough. **"Beast Shape Five! Bear!"** The shaman roared, throwing her club to the side and spreading her arms.

"**Dispel Mag-** shit!" Mastoya yelled, finally out of sanity. In front of her, her mother grew larger. The newly-transformed black bear lashed back at the armored knight, and Mastoya hissed as she fell backward, slipping in the mud.

"You drove me to this!" She yelled, after the third claw swipe ripped along her side, buckling the plates and cracking a rib. **"Twisted Rage!"** Mastoya screamed...

Zuula fought, but was no match for the raging half-orc. Her daughter's blade clove into her again and again, and the black bear staggered, slumped to the side, and fell.

Roaring in triumph, Mastoya closed in for the kill, sword raised high, any sense of mercy gone to the fury.

And to her horror, Zuula saw a figure racing through the mud, a familiar figure running, axe out, rage shining in his own eyes. Garon, her second son, come too late, far too late and at the worst time. She had failed! Her child would die!

"Run, unclever boy! Run!" Zuula croaked.

And then all was bloody darkness.

*****

The cat sat in darkness, grooming his fur.

Well, that had been a mess. Pulsivar had marked that new little bear for trouble, and fled at the first opportunity, retreating far back into the woods. Then there had been shouting, and fighting, and a whole lot of stuff he was quite sure was absolutely not anything to do with him. The rain had been unpleasant, too, while it lasted.

Those big scaly burny things in the sky had been right fucking out, though. Pulsivar drew the line at those things. He'd fled further, up into the hills, to his favorite sunning spot where he could overlook his domain and pee upon it freely. There he crouched, grooming himself sternly as a rebuke to the silly hoomins below.

It took quite a while to get done, so he took a nap. Tiring, climbing up this high. Took a lot of work. He hoped his hoomin appreciated all the trouble Pulsivar had gone through.

He woke hungry when daylight came and killed a songbird on his way down, to whet his appetite until he got to his bowl of cream. He did hope his hoomin was prompt with it, sure, there had been some trouble last night but whatever. One had to have priorities, after all, and Pulsivar was sure that the old man had learned that by now.

The house wasn't a house anymore.

The house was now a smoldering wreck.

Pulsivar stared at it, tail twitching.

Oh no!

His cream was going to be late!

*****

LUCK +1

The stat increase rolled across his view, in total darkness. Threadbare had no way of knowing that he'd been just lucky enough, that the house had collapsed in just the right way to drop him into the basement without killing him.

Cautiously, he felt around. His life was literally hanging by a thread, he knew.

Then another paw tapped his. Smaller, hesitant, it tapped him then felt up his body. He felt something smaller hug him, and he hugged it back.

Golden light flared.

You have healed Missus Fluffbear 90 points!

In the brief flash of light, he saw the little black teddy bear, now good as new, studying him. Then the light faded. Missus Fluffbear. That was a good name.

Two little black paws found him in the darkness again, and started to tug—

—and Threadbare remembered, with a flash of horror, how he'd accidentally killed the stuffed skunk when he was trying to free it.

A red '1' floated up and he twitched, feeling something give way inside him.

It would be a just death. An ironic death.

He was so very hurt. So very tired. For a minute he thought about giving up, and letting the little toy kill him.

But then he remembered Celia, and he found his conviction again.

The skunk had been as weak, if not weaker then him, but Threadbare had a week of life and many class levels over the juvenile toy golem. He shoved her away.

She came back and tapped him with a paw, and he hugged her.

She tried to tug him free and he shoved her away again.

It took a while to get the message across, but eventually she stopped.

After a time, light came filtering through the cracks above. They were in a hollow spot, Threadbare could see. Most of his lower half was below the remnants of the roof, with the blade hilt twisted, jutting out at an angle. Threadbare's stuffing lay coated in ash and grime, strewn about him.

Across the hollow, Caradon's apron poked out of the rubble, the old golem-maker's body below, laid to rest in the ruins of his house.

Missus Fluffbear waved at Threadbare, once she saw him, and he waved back.

She wasn't trapped, he saw.

He also saw what looked like a small tunnel, formed by the hollow of a crumpled shelf. And beyond it, daylight.He considered it for a long while, considered the strange bear.

And then, inspiration struck.

INT +1

He rummaged around at his side, and found his scepter. It had come through unscathed… he'd been holding it under his arm the whole time. Threadbare took it, and scraped along the floor, digging up grime and dirt and flipping it around. Levering it under fallen trash, and prying at it until the trash moved.

Then he pointed at the shelf.

Over and over Threadbare did this, with the patience of the inanimate. And eventually, he thought she got the message.

CHA +1

He handed her the scepter, and she toddled over to the shelf, and started trying to work it back and forth, using the little magical rod as a pry bar, scraping away at the floor and the trash.

More words appeared.

You are now a Level 4 Ruler!

CHA +3

LUCK +3

WIS +3

Well, that was nice. Still didn't help him much.

No worries, though. Miss Fluffbear could take care of the way out.

Now he just had to get off the hilt without dying. Somehow.

Days passed, with only the sound of the little black bear scraping away at the obstacle in front of her. The embers above finally went out, and it grew cold, cold in the basement...

...and one of Threadbare's hitherto unused skills kicked in.

Animalistic impulses surged, as his body saw that it was damaged, and he was in a good place.

And so, Threadbare hibernated for the first time ever.

He woke much later, to the continued sound of Missus Fluffbear's scraping, and two messages flickering up past his view.

You have healed yourself up to ERROR

You cannot heal to full, due to foreign objects in your wounds.

Your Hibernate Skill is now level 2!

Your Dietary Restriction skill is now level 2!

Due to keeping a flawless diet, all attribute pool maximums are buffed by 4!

The light was different now, outside. The black bear had dug a pretty good hole, he saw, but nowhere near what they needed to get through the tiny space.

However, his wounds were indeed healed... up to a point.

Well.

More hit points meant more room to try to get free, didn't it?

Threadbare twisted and tugged, and worked more of his stuffing around the hilt, slowly getting free, one rip at a time. But he only made it another inch or so.

Missus Fluffbear dropped what she was doing and came over to try to help, and again he had to convince her not to. It was harder to shove her away this time.

He realized that scraping and digging had been increasing her strength, most likely. Though... just how long had she been at it, to get this strong?

Eventually he damaged himself to the point where he couldn't pull free any further.

At which point his body took another look around, realized that he was still hurt and still in a cool, dark place underground, and it knew just what to do.

Threadbare lost count of how many times he blacked out and regained consciousness, but the time came when he awoke to a racket. He looked around, saw that the basement was empty.

The hole under the shelf, however, was big enough for a teddy bear to fit through.

Threadbare angled, just managed to get a view—

—and stared right into Missus Fluffbear's face as she crawled back up the hole, toward him. She stretched out her arms, offering him the scepter, trying to plead, he didn't quite know.

And in the next second she was yanked backward, and at the very end of the hole, Threadbare got a glimpse of a black furry hand. And a wooden mask with the word 'BUNY' scratched on it. In a heartbeat she was gone, taking his scepter with her.

He could do nothing about it, and in time drifted back to his hibernation.

It took several more times and even a couple of bear levels to work more of himself free, hibernate, and repeat the process. Finally he got clear of the now-rusted sword hilt. It left brown stains on him as he went, and he searched around the basement until he found what he was looking for. Caradon's apron…

…and the tailoring tools inside it.

Once he had the tools he crawled through the tunnel, pausing at the exit. Nothing. Birds singing. Tree branches rattling in the wind.

Gathering his courage, Threadbare pushed through and out, grimy and battered, smeared with rust, smeared with grime.

The house was ruined, and creeping vines grew over it now. Birds called, and not a single soul was in sight.

Threadbare patched himself up, raising his tailor skill, leveling as he went. Plenty of cloth to work with, though at one point he went in and snipped off the parts of the apron he could reach, getting as much material as possible.

And then the little bear sat and considered.

He had to save Celia. He had no idea how much time had passed, or where she was.

He should probably save Missus Fluffbear, or find her at least. Maybe she didn't need saving? He didn't know. But she was young, he knew, and he remembered how hard, how very very hard it had been when he was young. So he would find her and help her.

He would save his little girl, and everyone else he could. For them, he would never stop trying.

But none of this would be possible unless he did something first. Something very important.

Threadbare toddled down the path, walking faster as he went, past the overgrown remnants of a raggedy man, past the neat row of graves dug on the hill, unmarked with stones only saying "they fell in the line of duty," and he kept on walking until he reached the river. There he stared into his reflection.

It took him a long time, more tailoring levels, and an unlocked tailoring skill to figure out how to do it. The sun was at the other end of the sky by the time he was done, but finally he had a small hollow in the right place in his head, and some twisty, waxed threads right where the air could push through them, when his stuffing muscles drew it just right.

For too long he'd been silent and dumb. Well he wasn't dumb now, and he knew just what to do.

Threadbare took his first breath.

"Status," the little bear said, in a quiet little soft voice that was completely lost in the burbling of the rushing river.

And a whole new world opened up for him.

EPILOGUE

Once upon a time, there was a teddy bear who made himself a mouth and a voice of strings and things, and said **"Status."** And this is what he saw.

Name: Threadbare

Age: 5

Jobs:

Greater Toy Golem Level 9

Bear Level 8

Ruler Level 4

Scout Level 3

Tailor Level 8

Model Level 2

Necromancer Level 1

Duelist Level 1

Animator Level 1

Enchanter Level 1

Golemist Level 1

Smith Level 1

Attributes		**Pools**	**Defenses**
Strength: 79	Constitution: 83	Hit Points: 216(236)	Armor: 34
Intelligence: 58	Wisdom: 89	Sanity: 147(167)	Mental Fortitude: 24
Dexterity: 41	Agility: 51	Stamina: 102(122)	Endurance: 44
Charisma: 56	Willpower: 47	Moxie: 103(123)	Cool: 20
Perception: 57	Luck: 53	Fortune: 110(130)	Fate: 9

Generic Skills

Brawling - Level 20 (21)

Climb - Level 6

Clubs and Maces - Level 9

Dagger - Level 9

Dodge - Level 2

Fishing - Level 1

Ride - Level 7

Stealth - Level 3

Swim - Level 2

Greater Toy Golem Skills

Adorable - Level 15

Gift of Sapience - Level NA

Golem Body - Level 20

Innocent Embrace - Level 8

Magic Resistance -Level 4

Bear Skills

Animalistic Interface - NA

Claw Swipes - 16

Forage - 7

Growl - 1

Hibernate - 37

Scents and Sensibility - 10

Stubborn - 7

Toughness - 12

Ruler Skills

Emboldening Speech - Level 1

Identify Subject - Level 1

Noblesse Oblige - Level 1

Royal Request - Level 1

Simple Decree - Level 1

Scout Skills

Camouflage - Level 1

Firestarter - Level 1

Keen Eye - Level 1

Sturdy Back - Level 5

Wind's Whisper - Level 1

Tailor Skills

Talioring - Level 36

Clean and Press - Level 1

Adjust Outfit - Level 1

Model Skills

Dietary Restriction - Level 10 (+20 to all pools)

Fascination - Level 2

Flex - Level 1

Self-Esteem - Level 1

Work it Baby - Level 2

Necromancer Skills

Assess Corpse - Level 1

Command the Dead - Level 1

Soulstone - Level 1

Speak With Dead -Level 1

Zombies - Level 1

Duelist Skills

Challenge - Level 1

Dazzling Entrance - Level 1

Fancy Flourish - Level 1

Guard Stance - Level 1

Weapon Specialist - Level 1 (Brawling +1)

Animator Skills

Animus - Level 1

Command Animus - Level 1

Creator's Guardians - Level 1

Eye for Detail - Level 1

Mend - Level 1

Enchanter Skills

Appraise - Level 1

Glowgleam - Level 1

Harden - Level 1

Soften - Level 1

Spellstore - Level 1

Golemist Skills

Command Golem - Level 1

Golem Animus - Level 1

Invite Golem - Level 1

Toy Golem - Level 1

Smith Skills

Refine Ore - Level 1

Equipment

Inventory

Tailoring supplies

Quests

Save Celia

APPENDIX I:

THREADBARE'S JOBS AND SKILLS

BEAR

Bears are large beasts, tough and strong and stubborn. They eat pretty much anything organic and live in a variety of terrains and climates worldwide. Bears gain experience by eating bear-associated foods, roaming their territory, and defeating foes with their natural weapons. You have discovered one or more rank up options. You may choose one of the following unlocked options at level 10 or any point beyond; Black Bear, Cave Bear, and Grizzly Bear.

ANIMALISTIC INTERFACE

Level 1, Cost N/A, Duration: Passive Constant

Allows the beast to use their racial skills without requiring vocalization. All skills that are not passive constants may be turned on and off as the situation and instinct require.

CLAW SWIPES

Level 1, Cost 5 Sta, Duration: 5 attacks

Enhances the damage caused by your hands and feet, and adds the sharp quality for the next five strikes. Currently activated through Animalistic Interface, and will activate whenever you brawl with intent to injure.

FORAGE

Level 1, Cost 10 Sta, Duration: 10 minutes

Greatly enhances your perception for the purposes of finding food, water, or other natural resources in the wilderness. At higher levels, may be used to locate specific naturally occuring resources. Currently activated through Animalistic Interface, will activate whenever you hunt for natural resources.

GROWL

Level 5, Cost 10 Mox, Duration: Instant

Growl at a target to damage their sanity.

HIBERNATE

Level 5, Cost N/A, Duration: 1-3 months

Go into a torpid sleep. Requires a cool, dark place and you cannot be affected by the Starving condition. Restores all pools to full, as per a normal rest.

SCENTS AND SENSIBILITY

Level 1, Cost 5 San, Duration: 5 minutes

Activates heightened smell, greatly increasing perception for that sense and allowing you to catalogue and remember specific odors. Currently activated through Animalistic Interface, and will activate whenever you encounter an interesting scent.

STUBBORN

Level 5, Cost N/A, Duration: Passive Constant

Increases your resistance to sanity damaging effects.

TOUGHNESS

Level 1, Cost N/A, Duration: Passive Constant

Has a chance of increasing whenever you take serious damage. Raises your maximum HP by two whenever it increases.

GREATER TOY GOLEM

Toy golems are the protectors of children everywhere! And also good, reasonably cheap guardians for any fledgling golemist. They aren't the toughest of golems, but they possess a few costly powers good for helping their charges survive. Like all golems, they're sturdy, resistant to magic, and immune to a lot of things that would kill living beings. Greater golems possess sapience, and attribute ranks that lesser golems simply do not have. They can even learn jobs! Limited in that aspect only by the intelligence of their creator, greater golems have theoretically astronomical potential. Greater Toy Golems gain experience by doing adorable things, surviving conflict by toughing it out, and defeating foes using their natural weapons.

ADORABLE

Level 1, Cost N/A, Duration: Passive Constant

Adorable has a chance of activating when you do something cute in front of an audience, or onlookers blame you for something that isn't your fault. It improves the attitude of anyone who fails to resist your charms.

GIFT OF SAPIENCE

Level 1, Cost N/A, Duration: Passive Constant

Congratulations, you now have all the attributes and can think and learn. Good luck with that. You also have 8 adventuring job slots, and 4 crafting job slots.

GOLEM BODY

Level 1, Cost N/A, Duration: Passive Constant

Your body has no organs, and is made from inorganic or once-organic material infused with a magical force. By being exposed to effects that would kill or cripple living beings and surviving them, this skill will level up. As it levels up, you will gain immunity and resistance to a wider range of lethal effects.

INNOCENT EMBRACE

Level 5, Cost: Sanity equal to half the amount healed, Duration: Instant

Heals an embraced target 10 X the level of this skill. Will affect on other golems, is standard healing otherwise. Currently activated through Animalistic Interface, and will affect any legal target embraced. Does not affect uninjured targets.

MAGIC RESISTANCE

Level 1, Cost: N/A, Duration: Passive Constant

Has a chance of negating any non-beneficial magic cast upon you. The chance of success is dependant upon the spellcaster's level.

ANIMATOR

Animators give life to inanimate objects, awakening them to serve and defend the animator. Animators gain experience by casting animator spells and defeating foes with their animi.

ANIMUS

Level 1, Cost 10+ San, Duration: 10 min/level

Turns an object into an animi, capable of movement, combat, and simple tasks as ordered by its creator. Must be in its creator's party to do anything beyond defend itself. The greater the size and mass of the object, the more it costs to animate, and the more hit points, strength, and constitution it begins with. The type of material also factors in, and determines the starting armor rating of the animi.

COMMAND ANIMUS

Level 1, Cost 5 San, Duration: Instant

Allows the caster to issue one command to an animi that isn't currently in its creator's party. If successfully cast, the animi will follow the command to the best of its ability until it is impossible to do so.

CREATOR'S GUARDIANS

Level 1, Cost N/A, Duration: Passive Constant

Enhances animi in the creator's party, boosting all attributes. The amount buffed is influenced by the animator's will and this skill's level. Has a chance of increasing every time a new animi first joins the animator's party.

EYE FOR DETAIL

Level 1, Cost 5 San, Duration: 1 minute

Allows the animator to examine the status of any animi, golem, or other construct he looks upon. Also analyzes any object for animation potential and sanity cost. Can be resisted.

MEND

Level 1, Cost 5 San, Duration: Instant

Instantly repairs the target construct or object, restoring a small amount of HP, influenced by the level of this skill and the animator's will.

DUELIST

Duelists fight with their chosen weapon and swashbuckle around, using mobility and attitude to win their fights. Duelists gain experience through fighting with their specialized weapon, defeating foes with panache and style, and doing risky, flashy things in dangerous situations. Note: Specialized weapons can be changed. Practice hard, your specialized weapon will shift to your highest weapon skill.

CHALLENGE

Level 1, Cost 5 Mox, Duration: Instant

Calls out a target to fight you. They suffer combat penalties based on your charisma unless they are actively trying to attack you. Resistible, because some foes are just too cool for you.

DAZZLING ENTRANCE

Level 1, Cost 10 Mox, Duration: Instant

Used before revealing yourself to foes, the more dramatic your appearance the better. Boosts your charisma and cool for a short time.

FANCY FLOURISH

Level 1, Cost 5 Sta, Duration: Instant

Unleash a fancy set of moves that don't hurt your foe but look really cool. Attacks their moxie.

GUARD STANCE

Level 1, Cost 10 Sta, Duration: Until dropped, or the end of the fight

Assume a guard stance, and gain a bonus to your dodge skill and armor, at the cost of lowering your strength and dexterity

WEAPON SPECIALIST

Level 1, Cost N/A, Duration: Passive Constant

Enhances your weapon skill. Automatically assigned to your highest weapon skill. If you have two or more equal highest weapon skills, you may freely choose which to specialize in at any time.

ENCHANTER

Enchanters are one of the oddest adventuring professions. They do most of their work beforehand, and use their items to devastating effect. Enchanters gain experience by creating magical items, casting enchanter spells, and using their created items to defeat foes.

APPRAISE

Level 1, Cost 5 San, Duration: 5 minutes

Allows you to see all relevant information about a mundane or magical item.

GLOWGLEAM

Level 1, Cost 5 San, Duration: 1 hour per level

Infuses any object with a simple light spell. The luminescence is based upon the caster's intelligence.

HARDEN

Level 1, Cost 10 San, Duration: 10 minutes

Increases the toughness of any object or construct temporarily, adding to its armor and/or damage potential.

SOFTEN

Level 1, Cost 10 San, Duration: 10 minutes

Decreases the toughness of any object or construct temporarily, reducing its armor and/or damage potential.

SPELLSTORE I

Level 1, Cost 10 San, Duration: Permanent

Prepares an object that stores a spell or skill inside of it. Anyone can then read, break, drink, or otherwise use the object in an appropriate manner to activate the spell. Requires and consumes one dose of RED Reagents. The enchanter does not have to be the person storing the spell inside the Spellstore.

GOLEMIST

Congratulations! Through blending Animator and Enchanter, you are now a Golemist! Golemists craft unique magical constructs, and use them to fight their battles. Golemists gain experience by casting golemist spells, creating golems, and using their golems to defeat their foes.

COMMAND GOLEM

Level 1, Cost 20 San, Duration: 1 minute per level

Allows the caster to issue one command to a golem that isn't currently in a party. If unresisted, the golem will follow the command to the best of its ability until it is impossible to do so, or until the command wears off.

GOLEM ANIMUS

Level 1, Cost 50 San, Duration: Permanent

Turns a prepared golem shell into a functional lesser golem, that will obey its creator's commands to the best of its ability.

INVITE GOLEM

Level 1, Cost 10 San, Duration: Instant

Used to invite golems into your party. Automatically affects golems created by the golemist, can be resisted by other golems. Will not affect golems in their creator's party.

TOY GOLEM

Level 1, Cost 100 San, Duration: Permanent

Allows the golemist to construct a toy golem shell. Requires a toy, one dose of YELLOW reagents, and a level 1 Crystal.

MODEL

Models improve their bodies and attitudes, displaying their glory for all to see and controlling how others look upon them. Models gain experience by using model skills, succesfully controlling first impressions, and defeating their foes through social manuvering.

DIETARY RESTRICTIONS

Level 1, Cost N/A, Duration: Until broken

So long as you have spent the last week without eating anything with the UNHEALTHY identifier you gain a small buff to all pools. This bonus is cumulative, up to twice your rank of this skill. Eating UNHEALTHY designated food immediately removes all versions of the buff.

FASCINATION

Level 1, Cost N/A, Duration: Dependant upon skill

Heal, aid, or otherwise be nice to an enemy in combat. If unresisted by mental fortitude, the foe will become temporarily fascinated with you, for a duration proportionate to this skill's level.

FLEX

Level 1, Cost 10 Sta, Duration: 1 minute per level

Buff your endurance and cool by the level of this skill.

SELF-ESTEEM

Level 1, Cost 10 Mox, Duration: 1 minute per level

Buff your mental fortitude and cool by the level of this skill.

WORK IT BABY

Level 1, Cost NA, Duration: Passive Constant

Whenever one of your worn or wielded items creates a favorable impression in at least one onlooker, then this skill has a chance of increasing. All worn and wielded items that confer bonuses have their bonuses increased by a small percentage for each level of this skill. Note that the difference is harder to see with lower level gear and lower levels of the skill.

NECROMANCER

Necromancers raise the dead to do their bidding, and can negotiate with powerful spirits and undead entities. Necromancers gain experience by interacting positively with the dead, casting necromancer spells, and using the undead to defeat their foes.

ASSESS CORPSE

Level 1, Cost 5 San, Duration: 1 minute

Allows the animator to examine the status of any undead creature he looks upon. Also analyzes any corpse for animation potential and sanity cost. Can be resisted.

COMMAND THE DEAD

Level 1, Cost 5 San, Duration: 1 minute per level

Allows the caster to issue a command to a single undead creature. If unresisted, the creature most follow its orders to the best of its ability. Can also be used to invite unintelligent undead into a party, at which point they can be verbally commanded indefinitely by the caster.

SOULSTONE

Level 1, Cost: 20 San, Duration: Permanent

Creates a soulstone crystal, which can house a newly-deceased spirit or an existing incorporeal undead. A spirit in a soulstone may be conversed with, used to create a new undead, or simply unleashed upon the world at a time of the caster's choosing.

SPEAK WITH DEAD

Level 1, Cost: 5 San, Duration: 1 minute per level

Allows the necromancer to converse with corpses, spirits, or normally incoherent undead. In places with particularly strong spirits, the caster may be notified of the presence of conversable spirits.

ZOMBIES

Level 1, Cost: 10 San, Duration: Permanent

Turns a corpse into a zombie. Requires a spirit present in the area.

RULER

Rulers entice people to work for them, and organize them through decrees and rewards to do their bidding. Rulers gain experience by having their subjects do their bidding, organizing others to a common goal, and looking out for the interests of those in their charge.

EMBOLDENING SPEECH

Level 1, Cost: 10 Mox, Duration: Instant

Buffs all allies moxie and sanity by an amount related to the ruler's charisma. Only affects allies within earshot.

IDENTIFY SUBJECT

Level 1, Cost: 5 Mox, Duration: 5 minutes

Allows the ruler to examine a sworn subject's status screen. May also be used on people within your party, giving more information than the party status screen.

NOBLESSE OBLIGE

Level 1, Cost: N/A, Duration: Passive Constant

Buffs all sworn subjects and party members a small amount. The stat buffed is dependant upon your highest attribute.

ROYAL AUDIENCE

Level 1, Cost 10 Mox, Duration: 1 Minute per level

Buffs your charisma, but only when dealing with sworn subjects.

SIMPLE DECREE

Level 1, Cost 10 Mox, Duration: Permanent until changed

Declare a simple command in twelve words or less. All sworn subjects are notified of the decree. Any who do not comply with this decree take moxie damage influenced by your charisma and wisdom, resisted by cool. Only one simple decree may be in place at a time. Simple commands may not be used to inflict suicidal or self-harmful activities.

SCOUT

Scouts roam the wilderness, spying upon foes and using stealth and survival to accomplish their goals. Remember, be prepared! Scouts gain experience by using scout skills, exploring new wilderness areas, and remaining undetected by foes.

CAMOUFLAGE

Level 1, Cost 5 San/Min, Duration: Until dismissed or exhausted

Blends the Scout in with his surroundings, buffing their stealth skill. More effective in the wilderness, scales according to skill level.

FIRESTARTER

Level 1, Cost 5 San, Duration: Instant

Creates a fire, burning any flammable material it's used upon. Intensity of the starting flames depends on the skill level.

KEEN EYE

Level 1, Cost 5 Sta, Duration: A minute per scout level

Buffs a scout's perception, effects dependent upon skill level

STURDY BACK

Level 1, Cost NA, Duration: Passive Constant

Lightens the burdens of any heavy load carried, making items literally weigh less. Does not apply to weapons and armor equipped. Higher skill level means more weight reduction

WIND'S WHISPER

Level 1, Cost 5 San, Duration: 1 message

May be activated silently. Sends a message on the wind to any named target within range. Range and length of vocalization per message increase with skill level.

SMITH

Smiths work with metal, crafting objects with the help of a forge, anvil, and hammer.

REFINE ORE

Level 1, Cost 10 Sta, Duration: Instant

Separates any usable crafting materials in a container or dirt, ore, or stone into neat piles of material.

TAILOR

Tailors work with cloth and occasionally other flexible materials, crafting objects with the help of scissors, needle, and thread.

ADJUST OUTFIT

Level 5, Cost 20 Sta, Duration: Instant

Resizes any cloth outfit to fit the chosen wearer, and also allows minor alterations.

CLEAN AND PRESS

Level 1, Cost 10 Sta, Duration: Instant

Instantly cleans the selected item, and removes any wrinkles, stains, or other blemishes. Only works on items that are primarily textiles.

TAILORING

Level 1, Cost NA, Duration: 30 seconds

Instantly crafts one cloth item that is within your current skill.

NOTE: General skills are self-explanatory, and do not have activation costs or require explanation..